AN INTRIGUING COMPLICATION

"Don't worry about what I am. I'm woman enough—"

She stopped herself so fast she almost choked.

"I am certain that you are," Cord said. "In our brief time together, you've given me no reason to doubt it."

She grabbed the gun, and he wondered if this time she might pull the trigger.

"Do not touch me ever again, Mr. Hardin."

"If that is truly your wish, Miss Kate, then do not look as if my touch is what you want."

They stood staring at one another. She was the first to look away. Whoever she was in the life of T. J. Calloway, she was a complication, and much too brave for her own good. That they would meet again was a certainty. When he was ready to strike, she must not get in his way.

TEXAS EMPIRES:

Lone Star

EVELYN ROGERS

LEISURE BOOKS   NEW YORK CITY

This book is dedicated to two special friends,
Elda K. Bradberry and Jobyana Isbel.
They made the world a better place. They left us too soon.

A LEISURE BOOK®

June 1999

Published by

Dorchester Publishing Co., Inc.
276 Fifth Avenue
New York, NY 10001

ISBN 0-8439-4533-8

The name "Leisure Books" and the stylized "L" with design are trademarks of Dorchester Publishing Co., Inc.

Printed in the United States of America.

Lone Star

Chapter One

Cordoba Hardin centered the man in the gunsight and balanced himself against the trunk of a live oak. Only a few hours riding through the county, scouting, harboring little hope, and here the bastard was, moving slowly on horseback, within easy range.

He took a long look at the man as he rode across the valley below him, watched his face as he looked around, studied the way he held himself. He had put on a few pounds and his beard was now streaked with gray, but it was him, all right.

At last some good luck was coming Cord's way. Perhaps it was too good, but he was not about to question it, not after eleven long years.

The cool slickness of the trigger against his finger was grimly satisfying. The trigger and

the man were all that mattered right now—
and, too, the deliverance of justice. If the justice came from the end of a Smith-Jennings
repeating rifle, so be it. Sometimes life took a
man down unexpected paths.

He tugged his hat low over his forehead,
blocking out the afternoon sun. His target was
no more than fifty yards from the hilltop where
he stood. One shot, that was all it would take.
One. He had taught himself never to miss.

Do it.

What was he waiting for? The man deserved to die, slowly maybe, publicly, but
Cord had never supposed he would find perfect retribution.

In the moment of hesitation, his mind pulled
him back to a darker time, to inky water, to
black pain. He heard the blows of metal strik-
ing flesh and he heard the cries that had caught
in his throat, caught and stayed for far too
long.

The images came upon him fast and without
warning, as they always did. The expected
trembling started, too, mostly in his hands, and
he lost his aim. Worse, the trembling cleared
his mind, made him realize the gravity of what
he was contemplating.

With a curse, he lowered the rifle and eased
the pressure on the trigger, all trace of satisfaction gone. He had come close to killing a man,
and it did not matter who the man was. He was
not a killer. And this was not the way he had
planned to lighten the darkness, to make the
images vanish once and for all time.

The chance at a shot had come too quickly,

too easily. Whatever honor there was in revenge, it could not be gained from ambush on the top of a hill. Another time, in another way, justice would be served, when he was facing his enemy, when the enemy would recognize himself as the cause of his own destruction.

Cord pulled himself upright, prepared to leave.

"Drop the gun."

He froze.

The voice was a woman's, unusually deep and husky, and it was enforced by the click of a hammer and the press of cold metal against his neck.

His initial shock turned to anger for not hearing her approach.

"Now."

The order was spat out, harsh, insistent. Cord slowly lowered his rifle. He sensed footsteps backing away and he turned, expecting to see a large, hard woman to match the voice, a woman as grizzled as any man.

For the second time, she surprised him. She was young, not much past twenty, and she stood only a couple of inches over five feet, the top of her shapeless leather hat coming no higher than his chest. Her lack of stature was scarcely reassuring. She gripped her shotgun like a practiced gunman.

She had thumbed back the hat, which rested on a thick twist of red-gold hair. Wisps of curls framed her fine-featured face. Her eyes were blue, a softer shade than his, and freckles dotted her nose.

Her figure was slim, almost boyish, except

for the hint of breasts thrusting against her yellow shirt. The shirt was tucked into a buckskin split-skirt, her booted feet firmly planted on the grassy hilltop.

With one quick glance, he took it all in, gazing at her from under the brim of his hat. Though lean, he was strong, his six-foot frame clad all in black, and he knew he made a forbidding appearance. He would have scorned the sight of her, except for the fire in her eyes and, of course, the shotgun in her grip.

"Raise those hands," she said, "and start talking. You better have a good story or you're a dead man."

A Texas woman. He had not dealt with one in a long time, but he recognized the gumption in her eyes. He would be a fool to question the threat.

Doing her bidding, he bowed slightly from the waist, an old habit hard to break. "I believe you, señorita. I mean you no harm."

He spoke with both solemnity and formality, another habit that went back to childhood.

She eyed him curiously; then something beyond curiosity flickered in her eyes. She glanced away, but only for a moment. Cord understood. As much as he was aware of her as a woman, she was aware of him as a man.

He started to move in on her; she aimed the shotgun at a spot between his eyes. "Who are you? What are you doing here tracking T. J.?"

He hesitated a moment. "Is that the man on the horse?"

To his own ears he sounded stupid. Thomas

12

Jefferson Calloway, he could have said, and added more.

She nodded. "Everyone around here knows T. J."

"But I am not from around here. If I planned to kill him, I would have done so long before you arrived."

"You were thinking about it."

You are very smart, señorita.

"I was surveying the area," he said instead. "He rode into my path. I am by nature a cautious man."

"I'm thinking by nature you're a liar. This is Calloway land. It doesn't need any surveying."

"You know it well?"

"I run the ranch."

She spoke with a hint of defensiveness, as if she'd had to prove herself more than once. He felt a moment's regret. He had already learned that Calloway viewed his ranch with great pride and was planning to expand the acreage over the next few months. Running the place put her on his enemy's side. It also made her another enemy.

A breeze fluttered the collar of her shirt and the wisps of hair around her face.

"You still haven't told me who you are," she said, little knowing how fragile she looked.

Again he bowed and would have tipped his hat, but a shot through his hand right now would be an inconvenience. Too well he knew how deceptive appearances could be.

"My name is Cordoba Hardin. When I was a young man, Texas was my home. I have returned, hoping to buy land. Today I rode into Medina County and knew this was where I wanted to settle."

He spoke nothing but the truth; the lies lay in what he did not say.

Doubt clouded her eyes.

An unwelcome thought struck him. Perhaps his captor was married to Calloway. The man liked his women young, as Cord knew only too bitterly. Young and spirited.

"Perhaps you could give me advice, Mrs.—"

"Miss Kate. That's what I'm called." She emphasized the *Miss*, and Cord felt a momentary relief. "And the only advice I can give you is to move on."

If only he could do just that, returning to his brother's ranch a hundred and fifty miles to the east, finding the peace he had known there as he grew to manhood. Eventually he would. But not yet.

Weariness overtook him, and he lowered his hands. Let her shoot if she must, wherever she chose. Death held no terror for him.

He glanced around at the land spreading away from his high observation point, at the shrubs and scrubby trees, the rocky bluffs, more hills and valleys sliced by the fast-moving Hondo Creek, running high up its banks after the recent September rains. On this clear day in early autumn, it seemed he could see for miles, almost to San Antonio, a half day's ride east of the Hondo.

The view was deceptively beautiful, for the land held danger as well as splendor—from the venom of a thousand snakes not yet in hibernation to the equally venomous Indians still fighting the encroachment of the white man; to the white men themselves, outlaws and outcasts, as dangerous as the Comanches; and to the Mexican bandits who rode up from the Rio Grande with their killing, stealing ways.

Then, of course, there were the more sophisticated villains such as Thomas Jefferson Calloway.

Slowly Cord shifted his regard to the foolishly courageous Miss Kate. She had no idea how little he cared for his safety, nor how much he disdained those who would stop him from completing his mission.

This time his study of her was open and deliberate. The leafy tree cast shadows over her fine, stubborn face. He spent extra time looking at the way her shirt clung to her breasts.

"I look forward to the challenge Texas offers," he said.

If she read multiple meanings in his words, she gave no sign.

"You're a fool," she said.

"Perhaps. Otherwise, why would I risk this?"

As he spoke, he stepped forward and jerked the gun from her hands, his movements swift and sure, robbing her of defense. He tossed her gun to the ground beside his rifle, and when she raised her hands to strike, he grasped her wrists and pulled her solidly against him.

For all the hardness in her voice, her body was disturbingly soft. Her head dropped back and the shapeless hat fell to the ground. He caught the glory of her red-gold sunset hair as it tumbled about her shoulders.

Despite the restraint he had long ago put on his emotions, he felt the jolt of a man touched by a woman. He found it far too pleasurable.

He moved his lips close to hers.

"No," she said, and again, "no," her voice strong as ever, but he saw fear at last darken her eyes.

He expected her to struggle, but when she held still, he wondered if the fear was directed at him or at herself.

His blood coursed hot and thick, and he felt a rush of the natural urges he had not experienced with such intensity since his youth.

He wanted to take her here on the ground. Was she not Calloway's woman? He told himself she had to be. The man he remembered would not let a woman like this escape his bed. Taking her would be a fitting way to start the retribution, and he knew it would be highly satisfying.

But only for the moment. Disgust rose in him, and he tasted bile. First he had considered ambush, and now rape. In his short time back in Texas, he had become a man he did not know, and very much a man he could not like.

Dropping his hold on her, he picked up her shotgun and held it out for her. The surprise showed in her wide-set eyes, and the thought occurred that she would never make a poker player. To anyone regarding her with care, her emotions were far too visible.

He found the trait irritating. He wanted his enemies strong, else where was the challenge in defeating them? If she wasn't his enemy,

16

she was at least an obstacle that might get in his way.

"For protection against the Indians," he explained when she did not immediately take the gun.

"I'm not afraid of them," she said, and he saw she spoke the truth.

"Then you are more foolhardy than I believed."

"As you said, you're not from around here. You don't understand."

"I know what Comanches do to their women captives."

"They wouldn't do it to me."

He studied the way her hair rested against the gentle slope of her shoulders, the smoothness of the skin at the open throat of her shirt, the rise and fall of her breasts as she drew in uneven breaths.

"Then you are less woman than you appear."

"Don't worry about what I am. I'm woman enough—"

She stopped herself so fast she almost choked.

"I am certain that you are," Cord said. "In our brief time together, you've given me no reason to doubt it."

She grabbed the gun, and he wondered if this time she might pull the trigger.

"Do not touch me ever again, Mr. Hardin."

"If that is truly your wish, Miss Kate, then do not look as if my touch is what you want."

They stood staring at one another. She was the first to look away. Whoever she was in the life of T. J. Calloway, she was a complication, and much too brave for her own good. That they would meet again was a certainty. When he was ready to strike, she must not get in his way.

Grabbing up his rifle, he walked past her toward the downhill patch of thick green grass where he had staked his horse. He made an easy target, but instinct told him she would not shoot him in the back. She could not do it anymore than he could kill a man from ambush.

It gave them another trait in common, this point of honor; the first was that she had wanted his kiss as much as he had wanted to kiss her.

Chapter Two

Kate wanted to shoot the stranger in the back. Her finger itched to pull the trigger. Maybe not the back, but in the leg, or maybe she would put her shot through his fancy tooled-leather boots. The least she could do was hit one of the fancy silver spurs that jangled as he walked. She seldom missed what she was aiming at.

True, she'd never aimed at a man, but she didn't see how it could be much different from bringing down any creature that threatened those she loved.

When she'd first spied him, dressed all in black, standing at the top of the rise, he had looked more shadow than substance. But then he had turned, and she saw the silver buckle at his narrow waist, his face as lean as his body, his shoulder-length hair as black as his clothes. He'd stared at her with black-lashed eyes that

19

were a probing shade of blue, the likes of which she had never seen before.

He was real, all right, as real as her pounding heart. He might as well have DANGER carved on the taut copper skin across his cheekbones. No matter what he said, he was a threat to T. J. It was a good thing she'd seen the glint of the sun on his rifle and sneaked up on him.

A fist tightened in her chest. Cordoba Hardin could also be a menace to women, all women, including a scrawny, freckle-faced redhead with no interest in men. Her view of the gender was not without prejudice, but in his case prejudice had nothing to do with it. She had caught the gleam of arrogance in his eye, and that other, darker attitude, the one that said he wanted things she wasn't prepared to give.

She was proud that she'd held her ground, aimed the gun at him, and taken control, forcing him to drop his weapon. For her, the moment had been fine.

Until her guard had slipped and he'd disarmed her in turn. Worse, he had dared to touch her, to hold her close. For all his fancy talk and bowing, he hadn't been above grabbing her like any ignorant stable hand.

Well, maybe not like just any stable hand, but he definitely had grabbed.

Kate had reached the age of twenty-four having received, and given, a few experimental kisses, all of them unsatisfactory. That had been a long time ago, but she harbored no desire for more. Men were no better than bees, dipping into every flower they came to. It was always the woman who got stung.

The trouble was, even with his I'm-taking-what-I-want approach to gathering honey, Cordoba Hardin promised an experience far different from anything the young men of her acquaintance had shown her.

The thought of what could have happened between them, out here on an isolated hilltop, sent a shiver down her spine. She definitely should have winged him, especially at the moment she saw him aiming at T. J. There was nothing like the crease of buckshot to take the vinegar out of a man.

Kate sighed in irritation. Hardin had more vinegar than most. The nerve of him lecturing her on the Comanches. Hadn't she taken great care to protect herself and those close to her from attack? The great chief Soaring Hawk would never harm her. Of that she was sure.

And that talk of buying land. That was all it was, just talk. Farming and ranching took hard work. Hardin wouldn't like digging his hands into the hard Medina County earth.

Scooping up her hat, she twisted her hair back on the top of her head, slapped the hat in place, and went for her horse, Moonstar, tethered out of sight and scent on the far side of the hill from Hardin's mount. It was time to get back to work. Much as she loved him, T. J. had distracted her long enough. He was far enough on the trail back to his fancy home in San Antonio to be safe.

He'd come to the ranch to check up on things, as he did from time to time, to let her know he was in control, as if she hadn't figured that out a long time ago. He was proud of owning the land, proud of the crops, the stock—so proud that he talked more and more about wanting to expand his holdings.

As if he did any of the work, she thought with an edge of disloyalty. She didn't love him so much that she couldn't see his faults.

"All this isn't enough," he'd said on this recent visit, repeating a theme she hated to hear. "Double the acreage and then I'll feel like a real Texan."

"Who's to work all those acres?" had been her rejoinder, and then, "What you've got ought to be enough."

That included the only daughter he had left, his plain and plainspoken first-born child, but she hadn't put the latter thought into words. Too well she knew what he would say.

"No more of that talk, Kathleen Calloway, about being my one and only daughter. I'll not be reminded of my loss, by you or anyone."

Her father was a master at putting distance between them, even as they stood face to face. Long ago, after some hard times, she had learned not to use the word *daughter* to him.

But enough maundering. Slipping the shotgun into its scabbard, she mounted Moonstar and reined her to the downslope of the hill. She made quick time on the ride back to the ranch house. The foreman, Tug Rafferty, was standing by the corral, looking over a pair of cow ponies she'd bought last week. He caught her as she was unsaddling the mare in the barn.

Tug was a few years older than Kate, of medium height and excessive muscle, his shoulders sloping to arms the size of good-sized tree limbs, his disproportionately short legs as big as tree trunks. He had thick brown brows over round brown eyes, a broad nose in the middle of a broad face, and thinning hair he liked to keep covered with a wide-brimmed hat. She'd seldom seen him out of chaps and spurs, and never when he wasn't covered in trail dust.

He could be brusque at times, but he pretty much did as she said. She doubted he liked taking orders from a woman. Whenever she could, she made the orders sound like they were his idea.

"T. J. get on his way all right?" he asked. Tug thought the way she shadowed her father an unnecessary precaution.

She was about to slip the saddle from Moonstar's back when he took over, lifting it with one hand and setting it down on a wide beam that ran the length of the horse stall. She'd once seen him pick up a horse that had sprained a leg in a rabbit hole, with little more effort than he was showing today.

The injured horse had needed lifting. With the saddle, she suspected he was showing off his strength.

"He's on his way," she said, then hung the tack in place and led Moonstar out to the water trough. "He should be halfway to San Antonio by now."

Tug followed in her footsteps. "You'll be going into town, too, right?"

The question irritated her. It was a childish

reaction on her part, far too defensive. He had a right to know. Still, she was irritated. Probably because she didn't want to go.

She nodded.

"Going to one of those fancy parties?"

More irritation. He had to know her father had commanded her to make an appearance at one of the social gatherings he'd been giving lately. The arguments over her presence had been neither brief nor discreet.

"I'll be going in a few days." She didn't try to make herself sound happy.

Having drunk her fill, Moonstar lifted her proud white head. Kate slapped the mare on the rump and sent her running out to the pasture beyond the corral.

A thought struck, and she glanced at Tug. "Have you seen any strangers lately? Anyone riding around the ranch?"

Tug shook his head. "Why?"

"No reason."

"Something going on I need to know about?"

She avoided his eye. "I was just being cautious."

Holding back information about the stranger didn't make much sense. Outsiders roaming around were definitely Tug's concern. But then she would have to tell him about the rifle and maybe some of the things that had happened out on that hilltop, and she figured they were nobody's business but her own.

Looking beyond the cow ponies, to the pasture where Moonstar was grazing and on to the far hills, she felt a sense of satisfaction. Loneliness hit her sometimes, but it wasn't a desperate kind of feeling, the kind that made a woman want things she couldn't have.

The only thing she really wanted was a change in her father, a softening, a show of affection that would let her talk about some things with him, and maybe change some things, too. She was as likely to get that by working for him out here as she was to get it anywhere.

She would go to town as he wanted, but she wouldn't stay there for long. Out here was where she belonged, not sitting around in a closed-in parlor growing bored.

Town living was lazy living. For Kate, hard work was a balm for both the body and the soul. If only she could have convinced her sister of that fact, things might have turned out differently.

But that was a subject for another day, when her thoughts weren't already in a tumble. With a wave of good-bye to Tug, she went inside the house. Right now she'd best get to mending her good black dress for the journey she didn't want to take.

The thought of black reminded her of Cordoba Hardin and then of how the dress was getting a little tight in the bosom, although why the man should summon thoughts of her bosom, she did not know.

Still, the dress was getting too small, at least in places. She had plenty of money. Maybe she ought to follow T. J.'s advice and order herself a new one from a San Antonio store.

She smiled to herself, but there was no humor in the act. Her father wouldn't care how much she spent. He wanted her to look good before his friends and political allies. But there was nothing she could do about the calluses on her hands and the freckles the sun brought out on her nose.

Worse, she couldn't seem to curb her sharp tongue, or be the meek, obedient daughter T. J. wanted her to be.

But then, why should she? Meekness would have kept her from confronting Cordoba Hardin. Surveying the land, was he? The liar. He was up to something. She felt it in her bones.

And she felt other things, too—a strange distress she had not experienced in all her twenty-four years, a stirring that was not completely unwelcome. She'd felt it sharpest when he held her close, and the feeling had not completely gone away.

That they would meet again was something she understood. That she would be the one to catch him by surprise was not such a sure thing. As tough and wary as she was, she didn't always carry a gun.

Chapter Three

Kate would rather have jumped from the second-floor window than walk down the winding stairs.

There was nothing wrong with the stairs themselves. They were the fanciest stairs in San Antonio, better than anything to be found even in the capital of Austin. A person would have to go all the way to Houston to find the like.

No, the problem didn't lie with the stairs, or with the curved mahogany bannister T. J. had imported from Europe, or the oil portraits of strangers he'd hung on the wall "because they give class to the place," although Kate believed the pictures to be foolish.

The problem wasn't with any of the trappings her father so enjoyed. The problem lay with the men and women assembled downstairs.

There was no way around it. Kate found no comfort in the company of T. J.'s friends. Many were professional men, lawyers like her father, a couple of doctors, with a few store owners thrown in, a judge or two, and more politicians than any single household ought to contain.

Including Governor Elisha Pease.

If she had her way, she would have slid down that curved bannister, catapulted across the hallway, and shot out the front door away from them all.

The problem was they could talk and talk and talk without really saying anything.

Personally, Kate liked the governor. He had a no-nonsense way about him she could appreciate, and he stood for issues she agreed with. Only a few weeks ago he had been elected to his second term, proving his general popularity.

But he was still a politician. Like the rest of them, especially in social situations such as the party downstairs, he put on a public face.

T. J. was developing that same habit. She suspected he wanted to run for the office in 1857, when Pease's two-year term was done. He would probably get elected, too. Few men outside San Antonio knew about the trouble two years ago, and of those who remembered, no one seemed to care. If anything, they viewed T. J. as a hero instead of a killer, though he'd come close to being thrown in jail.

But the almost-arrest had not been generally known. T. J. himself never spoke of it. Sometimes she thought he had completely forgotten, leaving her the only one to mourn their mutual loss.

A governor's mansion was being built in Austin. If T. J. were elected, he would probably want her there for show, if nothing else. She shuddered to think what living in a mansion would be like.

And she had other fears, like what political party her father would join. Surely he would be a Democrat, but there were times she feared he was aligning himself with those rascally Know Nothings in the American Party.

All of which kept her at the top of the stairs.

"Miss Kate, you'd best be getting on down. Your daddy don't want you fooling around up here."

Kate sighed. Caprice was right.

She tried to smile. Caprice was the only slave T. J. owned, but Kate didn't view her as property. The woman served as her father's housekeeper, but to Kate she was more of a friend.

Caprice couldn't remember the year of her birth, but she figured her age around forty. T. J. had bought her from a former professor of English, a childless widower who had come West with his small household seeking adventure. After one Comanche attack at the edge of town, the professor had decided adventure was not what he wanted, especially if danger to his scalp was involved. He had sold all he owned, including his housekeeper, saying he needed to travel unencumbered on his flight to the East.

Slavery was an abomination to Kate's way of thinking, and she refused to have slaves at the ranch, hiring field laborers and ranch hands instead. It was the one indulgence T. J. allowed her.

Caprice fiddled with Kate's thick topknot of hair and ruffled the curls around her face.

"You look fine, Miss Kate. Nothing I can do about that pitiful dress, but what's in it is prime."

She was right about the dress, if not its contents. Not only was its once velvety blackness beginning to fade, it was even tighter across her breasts than she remembered, and, strangely, looser in the waist. At her age, she was too old to be gaining and losing weight in such places, but that's the way things were.

She had done what she could to alter it, but skill with needle and thread was not high on her list of accomplishments. When God passed out talents like that, her sister had got them all.

The housekeeper tugged at the bodice, bringing the scooped front a couple of inches lower on Kate's bosom.

Kate yelped.

"How you ever going to catch you a man," Caprice said, "if you don't show a little of what he'll be getting?"

Kate thought of Cordoba Hardin and the way he had stared at her middle range. Her cheeks flushed.

"I wouldn't want a man who liked a woman simply for the way she was put together."

"You don't know much about men. They're foolish creatures. Got to look at the outside before they can discover what's underneath."

Kate wanted to ask Caprice what made her such an expert on the male species, but there was so much in the world the woman understood, things about people and how they felt toward one another, that she kept the question to herself.

Sometimes the housekeeper understood too much, like a daughter's feelings for a father who was not given to uncritical love.

And that same daughter's grief for a sister who had not understood—

"Kate!"

T. J.'s voice boomed from the bottom of the stairs, and she jumped.

"Come on down here," he ordered. "I've got folks I want you to meet. Can't have a party without a hostess, now can we?"

He spoke in his public manner, the one that despite its loudness approved everything she did.

Everything, that is, but refusing to join his soirée, as he was calling it. Taking a deep breath, she pasted on her own barely adequate public smile and hurried down to her waiting father.

At fifty, T. J. was still a physically powerful man, tall, with a full head of hair and a full beard, both hair and beard dark brown streaked with gray. His straight carriage gave him a distinguished appearance, and so did the black frock coat and ruffled shirt that he wore for such occasions. The only thing Kate would have changed about him were the full lips that turned pink when he pursed them in disapproval.

He was pursing right now, while she was walking down to him, in a way no one else could see. She would also have put a glint of approval in the small brown eyes that watched her approach.

Swallowing the pain she always felt at his disappointment in her, she took his extended hands. Hers were small and callused, not at all the hands of a lady; his were large, but a life spent mostly behind a desk was making them soft.

She gave him a quick squeeze. His response was to let go of her, but then he began to smile and she could see he was in a good mood, despite his disapproval of her gown. Looking past him, she saw a familiar and welcome face in the front hallway.

"Governor Pease," she said, and hurried to greet him. "What brings you to town?"

"I'd like to say it's this fine gathering, but the truth is, family matters draw me from Austin. You understand how family can make its demands."

"Yes, I do," Kate said with more feeling than he had probably anticipated.

With his thinning hair, scraggly white moustache and small white beard, and his long, gaunt face, the governor could not be called a handsome man, but he knew how to grin and to wink, and he had a direct way of catching a person's eye that said he would put up with no nonsense and no lies. If women had the vote, hers would have been cast for him.

"T. J. was telling me you rode in yesterday just to see me. Now is that the truth?"

"My father said you would be here, and so I started packing. What else can I say?"

The governor chuckled. "That doesn't mean one brought on the other, now does it? Cause and effect, m'dear, cause and effect." He looked beyond her to her father. "If you're thinking about going into politics, T. J., you might take lessons from your daughter. Evading questions is one of the primary tactics of a Texas office holder."

"I'm a simple farmer and rancher who practices a little law on the side," T. J. said. "Nothing more. I find my pleasure in running some cattle and raising pigs."

Kate bit the inside of her cheek. Much as she loved her father, she knew that at times he was loaded with cow manure.

"If you're thinking to get a commitment one way or the other concerning any other plans," he added, "I might indeed be wise to evade your questions. No man in his right mind would consider indulging in election talk when a wily veteran such as yourself is around."

Kate wanted to roll her eyes. Political chitchat, especially the kind seasoned with manure, was her least favorite way to spend the time, and that included rounding up strays under a blistering summer sun.

With her public smile frozen in place, she looked past the governor to the crowded parlor. Hesitant steps took her inside. The smile cooled another couple of degrees when she spied Joseph Wharton, her father's closest friend. Thinner than T. J. and clean-shaven, he was another lawyer who dealt mostly in land titles. To Kate, that meant mostly foreclosures. T. J. claimed neither he nor Wharton had ever impoverished a man responsible for a wife and children, but sometimes she wasn't too sure.

Anyway, was it any more commendable to

break a poor unfortunate who was all alone in the world than one with responsibilities?

Wharton looked her way and gave signs he was ready to stroll over and talk a spell. Her heart sank. His attentions made her nervous, and she found it hard to talk to him, especially when his favorite topic was himself. Worse, she had heard he was a supporter of the American Party, which had recently found success in the San Antonio municipal election. This might be one of the rare occasions when he let his politics show, and she would be forced to give him a few of her own opinions about Catholics and immigrants and states' rights.

Under the circumstances, such an argument would not do at all.

He'd taken a step in her direction when one of the county commissioners moved in front of him and engaged him in conversation. With a sigh of relief, Kate attempted to circulate through the parlor. The furniture had been pushed to the sides of the large room, but still the floor was crowded. Most of the men were dressed like her father, and the women wore brightly colored gowns. They might spend their days in simple frocks—San Antonio was still a frontier town—but at night, when they came to one of T. J.'s gatherings, they shone like jewels.

Surrounded by them, Kate felt like a lump of coal.

But she was a lump who knew her duty. She spent the next half hour nodding and smiling, greeting her father's guests without saying much of anything. Then she caught sight of Wharton looking for her again.

With a smile to no one in particular—no one except Wharton had paid any real attention to her anyway—Kate eased from the room, then dashed through the front hallway and out the door to the street.

The air was chilled by a hint of fall, but she found it wonderfully restorative. Tonight was one of those nights when she felt a cry coming on. Must be that time of the month. Her body was so irregular when it came to the inconvenience, she never was sure.

With tears blurring her eyes, she started to pace along the low stone wall separating the Calloway property from the dusty street. The line of carriages and wagons tied out front got in her path, and she just kept walking, wending her way past other houses, toward the river, grateful for the cloud cover over the full moon. She liked darkness; at times like this it was her friend far more than the sun.

The men at the ranch would not believe it if they could see her now. Tears were a woman's curse as much as the monthly cycle.

During the last years of her life, her mother used to cry sometimes. T. J. hadn't liked it; more often than not, when a bout of tears came on, he would take himself from the small house where they were living, on the edge of San Antonio, and not come home for a day or two.

It had been a dangerous thing for him to do to his family, what with the Comanche raids always a threat, but that hadn't stopped him. Her mother had excused him, saying sometimes men just had to get away.

Kate had tried to understand. Jessica hadn't bothered, pouting instead for a while, then going about her lighthearted way.

When Kate was twelve, just before T. J. moved her and Jess to the country, she'd dared to cry over something she couldn't remember now, an injured kitten as best she could recall, and her father had yelled at her.

"You're just like your mother. I always said I should have had a boy as my first-born. He wouldn't be sniveling like a baby when things go a little wrong."

At the time, Jessica Calloway was not yet six months in her grave, her body worn out by a series of stillbirths that failed to give her husband his much desired son. T. J. was drunk—he drank in those days—and Kate had forgiven him. But she had not forgotten. Never, in all the years since, had he again seen her tears.

And he wouldn't see them tonight. No one would.

She brushed at her cheek.

"What has you so upset, Miss Kate? Did you shoot at someone and miss?"

Recognizing the voice, hearing every mocking nuance in its tone, Kate held herself very, very still. T. J. hadn't been the one to see her cry. Instead, it had been someone almost as bad.

Just as she feared, Cordoba Hardin had crossed her path again. And this time, she didn't have a gun.

Chapter Four

Kate forced herself to turn, to look directly at the tall, lean figure standing just behind her. She hadn't heard approaching footsteps, a mistake she rarely made.

The clouds took that moment to part, and in the moonlight she got a good look at the man. Too good a look. He was unlike anyone she had ever seen, and without thinking she edged away from him.

Cordoba Hardin was again dressed in black, this time in a black coat and trousers and a black shirt with a silver clasp at his throat. Without the hat pulled low on his forehead, she could get a better look at his lean, hard face, at the fine lines around his eyes and the firm, mocking set of his mouth.

His whole appearance, including hair worn longer than that of other men, gave him a feral look, as if he were a wild mustang caught in the trappings of a man. It took her a moment before she could speak.

"Mr. Hardin," she said with a trill that was totally unlike her. Embarrassed, she cleared her throat. "You should know I always hit what I aim for."

"I won't forget." Unfortunately, he did not sound in the least impressed. Nor did his gentlemanly bow fool her. She wasn't taken in by fine manners; she'd been around politicians too long.

"You have not told me the cause of your distress," he said. "Surely your friend T. J. has not upset you in any way."

"He's not exactly a friend."

"So I presumed."

He was getting at something, but she didn't want to give him the satisfaction of asking what it was. Clearly he did not understand exactly who she was, and she was in no mood to tell him.

"I don't like people getting together and smiling when they don't feel like it, and telling lies when the truth would be just as good. And I don't like men who ogle. I especially don't like that."

"Were you being ogled? But of course you were. It was rude of me to ask."

He was giving her a look of such intensity that it might be called ogling. But he did it differently, not at all like Joseph Wharton. With Cordoba Hardin, she couldn't bring herself to object.

Self-consciously she smoothed the bodice of

her gown, wishing the skirt had pockets so she could do something with her hands.

"What brings you to town?" she asked. "I figured you were still riding around the county trying to decide whether to shoot any riders you might come across."

"It's a comfort to know you've been thinking about me."

"Why do you always turn everything I say back on me? It's an irritating habit you have, Mr. Hardin. You ought to work on it if you plan to settle around here."

He nodded in apology. "I will most certainly do that. You can help by pointing out when and where I go wrong."

"You're mocking me, Mr. Hardin."

"Then I'm more foolish than either of us thought. You are, after all, a woman who hits where she aims. I shouldn't raise your ire."

Kate gritted her teeth. "You're still doing it."

He stepped close. "I can't ogle you and I can't mock you." His voice lowered and grew thick. "Tell me, what is it I am allowed to do to you?"

She inhaled his scent, which was unfortunately not the least bit unpleasant, and she felt a power throbbing within him that made him different from other men.

Suddenly she had a hard time breathing. She gave up on trying to control the pounding of her heart. Cordoba Hardin had taken control of the night, and for all her tough words she wasn't sure she cared.

"You're too forward, sir."

The words sounded silly. She would have to come up with something stronger than that if she were to stop him from doing whatever he wanted to do.

Despite the cool breeze whirling around her, she felt a distinct flush of warmth.

He dared to ruffle the curls around her face, much the way Caprice had done, but the effect was entirely different. Caprice's touch hadn't buckled her knees.

"We have unfinished business from our meeting on the hill," he said.

"Not anything I can recall."

She lied. Too well she remembered how close they had stood, and how he had made her feel. Tonight was turning into a repeat of three days ago. Only worse. Or maybe it was better. She truly didn't know.

She took a step backward but he followed, keeping the distance between them practically nonexistent. Looming over her, he blocked out the night and pretty much every beam of light from the moon. The throbbing she sensed within him became her throbbing, too. She felt as if she were falling into a bottomless pit. When she finally landed, something was bound to break.

Goodness, he was tall. Her neck ached from the attempt to look up at him, and she concentrated on the silver clasp at his throat. It was the one thing in her fast-narrowing world, outside of his eyes, that glinted in the dark.

"I have neither invited nor do I welcome such advances, Mr. Hardin."

Propriety demanded the declaration, but to her own ears it came out flat and unconvincing.

"You understand a man's touch, Miss Kate. Perhaps it is I who do not please you. If that's the case, you'll have to tell me. And make me believe you."

Kate was having trouble thinking. Somehow he had just insulted them both. She shoved against him, but he did not move. She might as well have tried to move a tree.

His head bent to hers and sent her spinning. She needed to grab hold of something, but everything within reach was attached to him.

His breath warmed her cheek. She wanted to touch his skin. Even in the night, she knew it would be as hot as the sun.

"Open your lips to me, Kate." His voice was as insistent as his presence. "You know what I mean."

But she didn't. And that was the problem. He had the wrong idea about her, especially about her and men. It was a supposition as far from the truth as it could possibly be.

Suddenly he frightened her as much as he enthralled her.

"T. J. will kill you for this."

"Let him try."

There was satisfaction in his voice and a hardness that made her blood run cold. His lips were practically on hers, but the spell he had cast was broken by his last brief words.

"A father has a right," she said in desperation.

The change in him was instant, the withdrawal obvious, though he had not moved away. How she had stopped him, she did not know. He seemed unlike a man who would be discouraged by an enraged parent. On the contrary, more than one must have comforted a broken-hearted daughter and cursed Cordoba Hardin through the night.

Slowly he lifted his head. "Calloway is your father?"

"Of course. Who did you think he was?"

And then she understood. Her cheeks burned with shame. When she stepped away from him, out of reach, he did not follow.

"You thought he was my . . . and I was his . . ."

Normally Kate was blunt-spoken, but these were words she could not say aloud.

He bowed. "I offer my apologies, Miss Calloway. I was hasty in my judgment."

"You were stupid."

"It was not the first time, nor, I fear, will it be the last."

Kate was not moved by his show of humility. He was stupid, all right, but then so was she, not to have realized his misconception. He thought she was one of the easy women that men liked to consort with. In her situation, the notion was particularly cruel.

With sudden clarity she understood a man's need for physical force. More than anything in the world, she wanted to sock Cordoba Hardin in the jaw.

First lust, and now violence. The man was bringing out the worst in her.

In the moonlight she tried to read the expression in his eyes, but whatever he felt was shuttered from her view.

"Please leave," she said.

"I should escort you to your home. The hour grows late and the streets are not safe."

"Of course they're not. You're on them, aren't you?"

His bow was small and brief. "It is a point well taken."

"I'll protect myself, Mr. Hardin, whenever it's necessary. I have for a long while."

She spoke the truth, being uncertain as to whether T. J. actually would have fought to avenge the loss of her virtue. Defending a daughter's good name was something he probably did only once in his life. Jess had used up that once.

"Of course you guard yourself," Hardin said. "It has been your necessity, has it not? In that we are not unalike."

Before she could ask what he meant, he hurried on.

"I should tell you that yesterday I filed claim to land that borders the Calloway Ranch."

Kate stared at him for a moment, unable to speak. "What land? To the south?"

"And to the east and west. It's a sizable claim."

"But that has our place virtually surrounded!"

"Yes."

Kate was as stunned as she had been when his breath warmed her cheek. But this time she felt chilled, and she hugged herself.

"You'll be settling there?" she asked, knowing she didn't sound quite bright. No one, not even the mysterious Cordoba Hardin, laid claim to such vast stretches of land all at once. The Indians made settling risky, along with the poor markets for goods, and the rugged land itself that only the demented thought could be tamed.

T. J. was the possible exception, but then, he had her to handle the difficulties.

Maybe Hardin also planned to be an absentee landlord. If that was the case, he was in for a surprise or two.

"I have submitted the required papers to the land office in Castroville," he said. "And yes, I will be settling there."

"Why?" The question came out a whisper. "You don't look like someone who'd know anything about cows and pigs and dirt."

"What I do not know, I will learn."

The thought of his being so close for who knew how long was more than Kate could deal with. Besides, the acreage he spoke of was part of her father's dream. She couldn't imagine T. J. letting a stranger have it without a fight.

When men fought, strong-willed men like these two, people got hurt. Innocent bystanders, like daughters. She couldn't go through such a fight again. Hardin had to be stopped.

With another nod and a bow—the man was unfailingly polite no matter the circumstance—he turned and disappeared into the night.

Kate watched him leave, and the silly notion struck that at least he had ended her tears. The one thing that brought her comfort was that although he might learn the demands of working the land, he didn't look like the kind of man who would throw himself into backbreaking labor. Once he realized the difficulties and the dangers of settling the frontier, he would head for wherever it was he called home.

In the meantime, she had to deal with him. Her head ached from trying to figure out what he was getting at by harassing her the way he was, and her heart ached, too, from what she had almost done.

No, not her heart, she corrected. Other body parts had been involved in the almost-kiss, but not her heart. Cordoba Hardin was too strange, too exotic to engage a woman's heart. But not other parts. And that was what made him dangerous.

He had secrets, that much was certain. Well, so did she. It was doubtful she would find out what his were, and he would never, ever learn the least bit about hers.

Chapter Five

Calloway's daughter.

Cord felt shaken, far more than the situation warranted. Taking the man's mistress, a woman with a will of her own and no legal or familial commitments, was one thing. A daughter was something else. Especially an innocent like Kate Calloway.

He walked along the street of empty lots and darkened houses, most of them adobe shacks, none so grand as Calloway's home. Like sentinels, they sat quietly beside the dirt road, watching him put distance between himself and the noisy, glittering manor that was the lair of his enemy.

The mistake about Kate had been reasonable. Calloway liked his women young and innocent, liked them very much until their innocence was gone. He sucked innocence out of young women the way juice was sucked from a peach. Kate could have been such a woman. For all her innocence, she was ripe.

But she was still T. J.'s daughter and that made her more of a complication than he wanted to contemplate.

What had brought him to the front of Calloway's home tonight, he was not sure. He hadn't seen him in the three days since spying him on horseback out in the county. Was he getting a closer look tonight? Bearding the lion in his den?

He had been about to go inside as an uninvited guest when Kate came running out, crying. In her distress, she had not seen him, and he had followed her erratic path. What had caused the distress? He had not supposed her a woman given to tears.

Cord wasn't always wise in the ways of women. Once it had cost a life. He had spent most of his adulthood wishing the life had been his.

The tragedy had played itself out not far from where he now walked. He had tried to separate himself from what had happened, cutting it out of him as if with a knife. But the cutting had left him with half an existence, and still the memories wouldn't go away.

Half expecting to hear the keen of a lost soul, the last cries of the lovely Diana Obregon, he waited for the trembles, the dark images, but they did not come, and he walked on, quickening his step until it was almost a run, not stopping until he came to a busier part of the town, with people and open doors and the flickering light from a hundred lamps. He stopped at the nearest saloon.

Ordering a whiskey, he took it to one of the back tables. He thought of the leather packet burning a hole in his coat pocket and downed the liquor fast.

Another drink, and he settled into a rare moment of contemplation concerning Hardin men and the women in their lives. His father, Raymond, had liked women; he had proven it by taking three wives. The first was an unfortunate Irishwoman who gave birth to Cord's half brother Cal, then suffered the disgrace of divorce after Raymond caught her with another man.

Cord was born to the second. Elena Carillo had been a strong-willed Spanish aristocrat. He remembered her as beautiful and distant, someone he could never touch, though he never doubted her love. But he also remembered her as dead, killed while riding a wild stallion. Only eight, he had witnessed the accident. Early on he had learned the cruelty of the world.

Last came a gentle Frenchwoman, who bore a beautiful baby girl named Madeleine and then buried Raymond after his final heart attack.

How different the three wives were, though each had been attracted to the wandering Raymond. Cord saw in himself much of his mother. She had given him the pride and determination that had brought him back to Texas after the long, empty years away.

He saw little of his father in himself, save for the tendency to keep anyone from getting too close.

For a while he pondered innocence and the forms it took in the Hardin women, the second generation if not the first. He thought of the half-sister he had not seen since her infancy. Maddie would be fifteen now, the age when he had run away from home. Cal had done the same when he had reached fifteen.

Was their sister a wild one ready to flee New Orleans? Or did she still have the sweet, loving gentleness she had shown as a babe in arms?

Cal Hardin had inherited Raymond's traveling ways, but he had been fortunate enough to meet his wife, Ellie, on his first journey to Texas, when it was still a Republic. From her letters, Cord knew his sister-in-law still retained an innocence that life on the frontier had not tainted, nor had the years spent with a husband once a loner much like Cord.

If Kate Calloway were given a chance, she might have Ellie's luck and meet a man who could care for her before she lost the innocence in her eyes.

But she didn't have that chance. She was T. J. Calloway's daughter and would suffer his hurt. Cord could not let her get in his way. Otherwise, the concept of justice would be little more than a farce.

She had questioned whether he knew anything about raising stock and working land. Hard work was the one thing that had brought him peace. Until now.

Gradually her fine features began to fade from his vision. Pulling out the leather packet, he set it on the table in front of him. He didn't have to read the fragile note it contained. The words had been seared into his memory the first time they were read.

I am disgraced, the note said in Spanish, *and must take my unborn child to the grave. Do not blame yourself, my love. I alone have brought about my destruction. May God forgive me for my mortal sins*.

The folded paper had been found on the bank of the river where she ended her life, the one word *Cordoba* scrawled on the outside. She had signed the message with the letter *D*. It stood for Diana, but in Cord's mind it also stood for Death. It was Death brought on by his stupidity, by a young girl's foolishness, but most of all by the lust and deceit of a bastard named ironically for the honorable third president of the United States.

Cord's attempt at revenge, undertaken hastily and in a rage, had been futile. He would not now have a repeat of the past.

Diana deserved the best he could now offer her. Dear, misguided Diana, his first love. When he first arrived back in San Antonio, he had visited the poor cemetery where she was buried. But he found only the small headstone that he had purchased long ago, using funds he had saved for their wedding. He had expected to feel her spirit over the grave. But she was not there.

Still, his first love lingered in his mind, perhaps because there had never been a second.

For a moment he made a cursory survey of the gamblers and drinkers around him. A few women were shuffling around the tables, most of them worn down by their trade. The talk was desultory, the laughter harsh and forced. Like most of Texas, the place had a raw, unfinished air about it, as if it couldn't decide what it wanted to be when it finally grew up.

A shadow fell across the table, and Cord glanced up at one of the saloon women. Flat black eyes stared back. She was plump, with a full head of black hair and thick, wet lips. She wore a red embroidered skirt and a once-white Mexican blouse, pulled low on her shoulders, her full breasts close to spilling free. Cord guessed her age as close to his.

"I'm thirsty," she said with a pout, and he noticed a small scar at the edge of her mouth.

She leaned low across the table, and Cord studied the breasts. Nothing stirred inside him. He had been more aroused when Kate Calloway stared at him down the barrel of a gun.

He stood and pressed a coin into the woman's hand. "Buy a drink for yourself, señorita. I ask only that you take it somewhere else."

With a bow, he returned to his chair.

She shook her head in disgust, but she did not give back the coin. "Ain't you the one for fine manners? So I'm not good enough, am I? You ain't gonna get anyone better than me in here." She licked her lips. "I know what a man likes."

Her words were slurred, and he realized she was drunk.

He stared up her. Whatever she saw in his eyes, it made her take a step back. "I don't know what's wrong with you, mister, but if you want to be left alone"—her voice broke and she sniffed loudly—"that's what you got."

To his amazement, she began to cry. Tonight was his night for women and tears.

"You insulting Betty Ann?" A grizzled man the size and shape of a barn loomed behind her. "He insulting you, sugar?"

"He don't want me," she managed through hiccups.

"Ain't she good enough?" the man growled. "I like her real fine. I guess that means you're better'n me."

Cord tucked the leather packet back inside his coat.

"He's going for his gun," Betty Ann shrieked.

Cord ducked as the man lunged for him, falling across the table, crashing with it onto the floor. Cord barely had time to get out of the way.

"Gawddamn it, Al," someone yelled from the vicinity of the bar, "I told you not to get in another fight. Betty Ann, stop him or he's out of here for good."

Al came up with a table leg in his meaty hand, wielding it like a club. Betty Ann jumped on her defender's back, legs and arms wrapped around him, fingers raking his face.

"Stop!" she shrieked, but Al paid her no mind.

Cord had an easy shot at him; instead, he backed off. A bottle flew through the air. The notion of fighting swooped through the air like a contagious disease. Fists flew and tables crashed. Cord counted a half-dozen brawls, which quickly became one free-for-all, with Al right in the middle of it.

At the side he caught sight of Betty Ann edging toward the bar, her eye trained on an abandoned bottle of whiskey. Except for the bartender and a couple of women who were watching their evening's profits disappear, everyone showed signs of having a good time.

Everyone but a shadowy figure who kept to the background and observed.

Cord eased backward, prepared to leave. Al noticed the retreat, and with a roar the big man came after him. He took only a pair of lumbering steps before he was jerked suddenly backward and thrown through the air, landing against the wall and sinking in a quiet lump onto the floor.

Cord stopped and stared with more than ordinary interest at the man who had done the throwing, the shadowy figure who'd decided to join the fray. Short and slim and fair, but compact the way a tornado was compact, he made short work of the remaining fights, tossing a few more bodies, elbowing a few jaws, chopping the necks of those who didn't get the message that the brawl was over.

When he was done, he stood in the midst of broken furniture and fallen men, breathing easy, showing no sign of sweat. He hadn't even lost his hat. Cord expected the watching women to break out in applause. The bartender looked disgusted at the scene.

The man ambled toward the doorway where Cord was standing.

"Lucky," Cord said.

Lucky McKee thumbed his hat to the back of his head. "Captain."

"It's been a long time."

"Eight years."

Cord thought back to the end of the Mexican War, the last time they had been together. They had met in battle, when Cord had been on the run from the trouble in San Antonio. Lucky had been seventeen; he didn't look much older now.

The youthful look was deceptive. He was the most fearless fighter Cord had ever met, and the most relentless. He was also as close a friend as he had ever had. Cord had saved his life once in a gun battle, and Lucky thought he owed him. He didn't, but the younger man didn't see it that way.

"You haven't changed," Cord said, looking over the scene of destruction.

Lucky shrugged. "No need to."

He, too, took in the scene. His eyes were as brown as the South Texas soil and, for all his youthful appearance, as old as the surrounding hills, and they saw everything in a single glance.

"I hadn't planned to get involved, but then I saw you. Any business left untended?"

"Not here," Cord said, and the two walked out onto the street. The sky had cleared, leaving the moon a white disk in the sky. The air smelled of manure, sweetly mixed with the scent of sage blowing in from the brush country south of town.

They stayed close to the row of buildings, avoiding the horse droppings in the street and the occasional rider.

"I thought you would be long out of Texas by now," Cord said.

"I left for a while."

"But you came back." He got no response. "As did I."

Neither man asked for details about the going and returning. For two years they had fought side by side for Zachary Taylor, but neither had talked much about their respective pasts.

Except for once, when drink had loosened Lucky's tongue. It was after a shootout in which an innocent child, a bystander, had been killed. Without giving details, he said he'd been born to an East Texas whore who hadn't been able to name his father. One of the men who bought her had gotten rough, and Lucky had shot him in the back of the head.

He was nine years old at the time. He had been drifting since.

In response, Cord had talked about the hurt he was carrying, told Lucky everything. Neither mentioned the shared confidences again.

"You were in a poker game back there, weren't you?" Cord said. "You were always good with cards."

"It's a living."

Lucky was wearing a white linen shirt and dark trousers, and he had a pearl-handled pistol strapped to his hip. His long, wheat-colored hair was caught with a leather thong at the back of his neck. His brown felt hat was banded in red silk. The boots were a slick gray that shone like snakeskin. Nothing about him looked especially fancy, but everything looked expensive. Gambling must be a good living indeed.

Still, that didn't keep Cord from getting an idea.

"I need a partner. Would you be interested?"

"Yep."

"That's it? You don't owe me anything, as I've told you before. At the least you ought to have a few questions."

"I trust you, Captain. You'll tell me what I need to know."

"It could get dangerous."

Lucky's lips twitched. "That's what I was hoping. You have a way of drawing trouble."

"I'm buying land."

"Tell me how much it'll cost, and it's yours."

"Money's no problem. You've got other skills I may need."

Lucky didn't ask what the skills might be.

"Do you know much about ranching?" Cord asked.

"What I don't know, I'll learn."

"So there's nobody you need to talk to about it." It was as close to prying as Cord was able to get.

"A woman, you mean? None that's stayed around for long."

Though he had been little more than a boy, Lucky had a way that brought women to him, even during battle down in Mexico. Willing women, young and old. It was one of the reasons he had picked up his name.

Lucky flicked his thumbnail against a sulphur stick and lit a cigar. "How about you? Does a woman come with this land?"

Cord thought of Kate Calloway with her red hair and her small, high breasts and the fire of defiance in her eye.

"No," he said, but there must have been something in the way he said it because Lucky gave him a long, careful look.

The cigar tip glowed blood red in the night. "How many men you got working?"

"Two," Cord said.

"You and me."

"Right. There will be more later."

"How much land are you talking about?" Lucky asked.

"A good portion of northern Medina County."

"Sounds about right."

"But there's something I want you to do for me first. Before you ride out." Again Kate came to mind. "It will involve remaining in San Antonio for a while. I want you to find out all you can about a lawyer in town."

"Thomas Jefferson Calloway," Lucky said.

Cord should have realized he would remember.

"And his daughter."

Lucky's eyes narrowed but he made no comment.

"As you ask your questions, do not concern yourself with secrecy. It is not necessary to be discreet." He came as close as he ever did to smiling. "I've kept to myself for a couple of weeks now, but no more. It's time Calloway found out I'm back in town."

Chapter Six

A week later, Kate rode out to face down Cordoba Hardin. The man had finally gone too far. He had to be told a few things, and she was just the person to tell him.

She had no trouble finding the one-room stone house where he was setting up housekeeping. It lay in a narrow green valley two miles south of her own home at Calloway Ranch.

The house sat squat and square in the middle of wild grasses grown tall after the recent rains. Two forty-foot pecan trees provided shade, one at each side of the yard. A single chimney rose from the north wall of the house and a cedar shake roof extended across the front over a railless plank porch. Two sturdy steps led to the porch and lined up with the open front door. A pair of curtainless open windows flanked the door.

It was obvious the house had been constructed to last several generations. A family of German immigrants had built it on the eve of Texas's admission to the Union, back in 1846, but after a Comanche raid through the countryside three years before, they had moved on. Despite being occupied, the place retained its deserted look; the windows were like blank eyes watching for the Germans to return.

Instead of the Germans, Cordoba Hardin had moved in.

Except for a mockingbird singing crazily in one of the trees, she detected no other sign of life. And then the sound of someone splitting wood came from behind the house. Following the sound, she reined Moonstar around the corner; she drew back on the reins when she saw Hardin wielding an ax. And she forgot to breathe.

He was standing in the sunlight, just out of the shadow of the trees. For the chore, he had stripped to the waist. She got a very good look at the play of muscles across his back as he brought the ax down on a log, splitting it evenly in two.

She got a very good look at everything.

She had never been one to view with interest a man's backside, but she did now. He looked far more muscular than he had in the black shirt, or the black suit coat. Maybe he understood hard work after all.

As far as the eye could see, his skin was a smooth copper color, its sheen coming from a fine coating of sweat. He wore the sweat as well as he wore his clothes. Her heart took a couple of extra-fast beats.

She imagined him equally muscular all the way to his toes. And she wondered how far down the copper color went.

Slowly he turned and watched as she reined the mare to a halt. He leaned on the propped-up ax, arms crossed over the end of the handle. His eyes were as blue as she remembered them, startling against the brown of his skin, and she was surprised to see the shadow of a beard on his lean face.

She had thought the courtly man who had bowed to her even at the point of a gun would never be caught needing a shave. She'd also thought he wouldn't know how to chop wood, but the pile he was gathering was even in length and disgustingly neat.

His precision would have pleased the Germans. It irritated her.

She dropped to the ground. Tugging off her gloves, she tucked them in the waistband of her leather skirt and held up her hands.

"Don't worry, Mr. Hardin. I'm not armed. If I were, I'd probably be shooting instead of talking."

He raised one black brow and made the gesture look courtly. "That's why I enjoy the company of women. They are always so reasonable."

"Don't get uppity. The shotgun's right here in the scabbard."

"I appreciate the warning."

Lowering the ax, he reached for a shirt lying

in the grass near his feet. It was black, of course, like the fitted trousers that hugged his hips and long legs.

"Don't bother on my account," she said.

A glint sparked in his eyes. Somehow the words hadn't come out the way she intended.

"I won't bother with the buttons," he said, apologetic. "How's that for a compromise, neighbor?"

He shrugged into the shirt, letting it hang loose and open, providing a wide strip of copper skin for her to contemplate, if she was the kind interested in that sort of contemplation.

Which she wasn't, no more than she studied backsides. Still, he was there and she couldn't resist a glance. She tried to give her attention to the pieces of grass that clung to the dark fabric of his shirt, but her gaze kept returning to the skin.

When her eyes at last met his, he was staring at her as if she was something special to see. He had a way of staring that made her feel undressed. Considering what he had believed about her, that she was a loose woman, maybe he thought he had the right.

For a moment she looked past him to the stone walls of a well rising from the tall grass, and on to a cistern that rose high to catch the falling rain. All the while, she felt him watching her.

Fidgety, she tugged her hat low on her forehead, unconsciously trying to hide her eyes and as much else of her as she could. Then she caught herself. What was she doing? Her anger returned in full force. She saw no reason not to get right to the point.

"You called me neighbor just then. I'm not."

"Don't you live just north of here? As I said, women are always so reasonable."

"Neighbors help one another. You're not helping me. Instead, you're causing trouble."

He didn't look particularly distressed at the news. He took a step toward her.

"It's got to stop," she said.

He took another step.

"What are you doing?" she asked.

He was very close, and she could see the way his damp, dark hair brushed against his face, and the way strands clung to his strong brown neck. Another step and she would be able to count the bristles on his cheek.

"Neighbor or not, invited or not, you are my guest, and you have had a long ride. Water your horse and put her to graze. Then you can join me inside for a cup of coffee."

When he stepped past her, his shoulder brushed against hers, lightly, like a whisper barely heard, and she jumped a foot away. He didn't actually chuckle—he wasn't the kind to do anything so ordinary and obvious—but she knew he was chuckling inside.

Was she supposed to believe coffee was all he was offering? She wasn't a fool. She would simply be on her guard. Making quick work of caring for the mare, she followed him into the house.

But she made sure to take the shotgun with her, resting it on the floor beside the front door.

A narrow bed rested against the wall to the left, and directly in front of her was a long table and a single bench. Otherwise, the room was bare of furniture. Above the stove against the opposite wall, a narrow shelf held a few utensils, a pot, and a couple of tin plates—the basics but nothing more. The floor was bare wood, made of planks that matched the porch.

Devoid of any decoration, the interior held an unexpected kind of rough, efficient charm. The thick stone walls kept the air cool; sunshine through the windows provided a soft, natural light. Both air and light gave the place a feeling of spaciousness beyond its actual size, and a homeyness not obvious from the outside.

Hardin was kneeling before the hearth, poking at the embers of a fire. When he saw her enter, he stood with an ease and grace that brought more irritation. Just once she would like to see him trip and fall on his rear.

He poured a cup of coffee from the pot at the back of the stove. He had not, she noticed, buttoned his shirt.

She took the cup, careful not to let their fingers touch.

"Please sit," he said.

She sipped at the coffee, which was hot and strong and surprisingly good.

"I've come to say something, Mr. Hardin, and I talk better standing."

He poured another cup. "Whatever you want, Kate."

Her name sounded far too intimate on his tongue.

"You're hiring away my men. I won't have it."

"I offered fair wages in both San Antonio and Castroville. The word spread. One of your workers rode over to offer his services."

"Domingo's not the only one who wants to leave. You're paying more than anyone around here can offer, and you know it."

Domingo Gonzalez, one of her recently hired workers, had expressed regret over his quitting, but he had family back in Mexico and he needed all that he could earn. Two others, the best field hands she had, had told her reluctantly that they, too, were tempted to leave.

"I have a great deal of land and much work to be done," Hardin said. "I need help now. Money is the best way to get it."

Kate shook her head in disgust. "How like a man to think that way."

"And how like a woman to think other enticements might make a man do what she wants."

"What's that supposed to mean?"

His only response was to drink his coffee and watch her over the rim of his cup.

A shiver of fear ran down her spine, and something else, a frisson of anticipation, for what she did not know.

"Who are you?" she asked. "Where do you get the means to do what you do? And the gall?"

"I have worked hard for what I have. And as for the gall, I am the son of an Irishman and a Spanish aristocrat. I could scarcely be a timid man."

"Is it the Irish in you that makes you torment me, or the Spanish?"

"Perhaps you give yourself too much importance. Why think that it is you I wish to torment?"

Kate's cheeks burned in embarrassment. She was completely lost in a battle of wits with this man. Most likely she could outride and outshoot him, and for all his muscle, when it came to tilling fields she could probably plow a straighter line. But as for trading quips, he had her beat.

Setting her cup on the table, she turned to leave. No good had been done here today. She must remember to stay out of his way.

She made it halfway to the door before the grip of hands on her shoulders stopped her.

"Let me go, Mr. Hardin."

He did as she asked. "My name is Cordoba. Cord."

She forced herself to turn and face him. "Why should I care what you're called?"

"Why indeed."

He seemed to be thinking something over, to reach a decision about a matter that was very, very serious to him.

"I have spent the past eight years in Spain with my mother's family. Unfinished business brought me back to Texas. Owning this land is part of that business. It is something I have to do."

She wanted to ask what the business could be, but instinct told her she really did not want to know.

She took a step backward toward the door. He reached out to take her hat, tossing it aside, and again his hands touched her shoulders, this time burrowing through her cascading hair. The heat of him shot through her and she trembled, she hoped with fear. Fear was a far safer emotion than any alternative she could name.

"Did you really think that by riding over here you could stop me?" he asked.

"Let me go."

"You don't mean that."

She parted her lips to protest, but the words stuck in her throat.

"Please, no," she managed at last, but to her own ears she spoke with little conviction.

"Please, yes," he said. "We must take care of what you really came after."

His lips were on hers so fast that she had no chance to turn her head . . . if that was what she planned to do.

His arms wrapped around her and held her firmly against him. The only soft thing she could feel was his mouth brushing over hers, then pressing harder, hot and insistent, enticing, intoxicating, filling her with a sweet longing she had never before experienced.

For a moment, he broke the kiss, his whiskered cheek rubbing against hers. The roughness felt good, incredibly erotic, and any protest she should have uttered died in her throat.

She hadn't the will to fight him. When his lips again covered hers, she felt her hands steal to his chest and felt, too, the solid strength of him. Her fingers moved from the smooth fabric of his shirt to the smoother warmth of his skin. Wherever she touched him, she tingled, and the tingles spread.

He surrounded her, enveloped her, and she hungrily rubbed her lips against his. More brazenly, she rubbed her breasts against his chest, seeking release for an urge that demanded satisfaction. What she wanted him to do, she didn't know, but she wanted him to do it fast.

Strange pulses started in parts of her body that had never known them before, as if a vague discontent long with her was about to be ended with a feeling more glorious than she had ever imagined.

She'd gone mad. And then he forced his tongue inside her mouth, taking her by surprise, and she became more frightened than she had ever been in her life. Sobriety came in an instant, and with it the realization that she was doing something very wrong. Worse, she was making a fool of herself.

With all her might, she shoved against him, and he backed away. Eyes once blue stared blackly at her; air once cool suffocated her with its heat.

Stifling a sob, she covered her lips with her hand, fearful that he had marked her mouth in a way that showed her shame.

She had just enough sense left in her to grab her hat, and then she was out the door, whistling for Moonstar, bounding into the saddle, and galloping as fast as she could from the valley, reining the mare toward the safety of her home.

Never could she face him again; she wasn't sure she could face any man. The promise of their earlier encounters had in no way prepared her for what he could actually deliver. Back in that stone house, he had changed her in a way that she knew was profound. With one kiss he had taught her things about herself she did not want to know. For the rest of her life that knowledge would burn as humiliation in her mind.

And as for her body . . . Why did she have to have a body that responded to his kiss in such a way? She felt betrayed, though she was honest enough to admit the betrayal came because she had been so thrilled.

She rode hard, giving Moonstar her head, paying little attention to the way, trusting the mare to take her to sanctuary.

Maybe she was overreacting. He easily could have finished his coffee, then gone back to chopping wood, giving not another thought to her. A man with his dark good looks and self-assurance must have women throw themselves at him all the time, women far more desirable than she.

Not that she had done anything close to throwing herself. But such had been his conclusion when she walked inside his cabin.

We must take care of what you really came after.

He had provided adequate warning. That

was when she should have fled. But she hadn't. She could tell herself a thousand times he hadn't given her the chance, but she wasn't helpless. She could have avoided his kiss.

A more far-fetched thought came to her. Maybe he had been disturbed as much as she. Maybe he was remembering the taste of her with the same exactness that she recalled the taste of him. Cord—she would think of him as Cord this little while—could be chopping wood with a fury born of frustration because she had pushed him away.

But that was too much to believe. The most she had given him was a good laugh because she had been so quick to respond.

Slowing momentarily, she rubbed at her cheek, which must still bear the redness from the brush of his whiskers, and she touched her lips, full and foolishly hungry for another kiss.

And she thought of her sister Jess, who had enjoyed the company of men in a way Kate had never done. Maybe they were more alike than she had ever realized.

The notion shook her.

So lost in thought was she that the Comanche and his horse were directly in her path before she saw them. He appeared so quickly that she saw only the barest details. He sat astride the broad-chested mustang, his own chest bare, his legs stiff against the blanket that served as a saddle, a rifle in his hand.

Mostly she saw the rifle. Too late she remembered the shotgun. In her haste to leave, she had left it by Cordoba Hardin's front door.

She'd remembered her hat but forgotten the gun, both signs of her pitiful mental state.

There was little she could do but rein to a complete halt and pray that, like her, the Indian rode alone.

Chapter Seven

Soaring Eagle stared in surprise at the young white woman he called Fire in Hair. It was not like her to be careless. She was fortunate that it was he who'd crossed her path, and not one of the braves who rode with him in his dwindling Comanche party.

It was only because of his protection that Fire in Hair had not already been raped and killed. But it was a protection that must be carefully guarded. Too easily his people might forget the edict of their old chief.

Like their fathers before them, these brash young men knew all whites were blood enemies. Soaring Eagle knew the same, but he was getting old—getting soft, the young men said. The enemy that rose before him now, the one he could never defeat, was not the white man. It was Death.

"Soaring Eagle," Fire in Hair said, a hand on her heart. "You scared me."

"You are wise to be frightened."

"I'm not afraid of you. It's just that I didn't recognize you right away."

"It is not like Fire in Hair to be unwary."

She looked away, and her even white teeth bit at her lower lip. "I had something on my mind."

"Many years past, my first-born son died of this same kind of mind. A bullet from the gun of a bluecoat taught him too late the cost of this weakness."

Fire in Hair nodded. "You are right to warn me, Soaring Eagle. I must remember to take care. But you surprised me with the rifle. Where is the lance that's always at your side?"

Fire in Hair was clever to ask about the lance. It was with much sadness that he had set it aside.

"The gun speaks with greater power. When the cold winds blow and food grows scarce, only power will bring us meat."

He looked down at the empty scabbard where her own weapon should have been. Whatever thoughts troubled the white woman, they must be severe indeed for her to endanger her life.

"Did you find the salt and tobacco I put out for you?" she said. "I brought back what I could from town."

"Your gift brought much pleasure."

Soaring Eagle knew as well as the woman that the offerings were far more than a gift. In return for them, he had sworn safety for her and the men and women who lived with her on the land she called Calloway Ranch.

His people had grown a taste for salt and a need for tobacco; they did not openly protest the arrangement.

For Soaring Eagle, the offerings were not the lone reason for his protection. Two summers past, when he had been injured in a fall and lay helpless by the edge of a creek, Fire in Hair had ordered her men not to shoot him. Instead, with gentle hands like those of his long-departed first wife, she had tended his wounds and helped him ride to freedom.

For a while she had helped him defeat Death, and for that he had vowed she would live. In his heart he knew the spirit of his wife was in her. He could not see that spirit die.

On this day, with the approach of winter marked in the early turning of the leaves, he should tell her that his strength was slipping. He should tell her, too, about the young braves who wished to kill all whites, angry men who would not be stayed by gifts from the hands of their enemies once their chief had gone.

In private these foolish men scorned him, but they were not valiant enough to do so to his face. When the day came that he was not there to still their cries for blood, Fire in Hair would no longer ride the land free from the threat of harm.

But on this afternoon she had troubles that took her thoughts away from safety. He would warn her another day.

Digging his moccasins into the flanks of the mustang, he rode from her, through the trees, along the bank of the wide creek the white man called Hondo, slipping through the countryside, leaving no more sign of his passage than did the wind that blew at his back.

He did not stop until he came to a far valley with its smaller stream of water and the dozen tents that provided refuge for his people. With the scarcity of the buffalo, much care was taken to preserve these shelters. As he rode close, he felt the weight of his years.

The braves thought he did not understand the troubles of his people, but in this they were wrong. Though he protected Fire in Hair and those around her, he would lead them to stand strong against all other whites. White men talked of land called reservations, places where the Comanches must live without wandering. The Comanches would never submit to such indignities.

Once, many years before, when talks of a treaty had gone wrong, he had been placed in a room of iron bars, a terrible place the white man called jail. He had escaped and vowed he would take an arrow to the heart before he would return.

There was no word in the Comanche language for such a room, but for Soaring Eagle, reservations and jails were the same.

All land was home to the Comanche, and those who would keep them from it, be they Apache or Karankawa or white, must die in defeat.

As he rode slowly into camp, he saw the braves talking by the bank of the small stream. The women moved slowly among the trees and the tents, tending to their chores, and a half-dozen children chased one another around the large pot of the possum and squirrel stew that would be their evening meal.

The braves separated, and one, who was called Night Stalker, walked toward him as he dismounted. Another, Broken Hand, took the mustang and led him to the water's edge.

"We have news," Night Stalker said before his chief could place the gun on the ground for the ritual cleaning that would keep its power trustworthy.

Soaring Eagle was glad to hear the Comanche language once again. Though he had learned the speech of his enemy during the days of negotiation and of jail, he felt at ease only when he used his native tongue.

Soaring Eagle stared beyond him, as if he could see through the clouds and the sky.

"The white men," he said, "have taken their women and their children and returned to the world where they belong."

Soaring Eagle liked to tease Night Stalker with such foolish talk. The brave took himself far too seriously and placed himself as one who would be chief when the old chief was gone. It was sad for Soaring Eagle to acknowledge that the brave, not the wisest nor the most valiant of the Comanches, would one day lead their people. Soaring Eagle's sons were all dead, one from a white man's disease and two from a white man's gun. And there was no one else with such hunger to lead.

But still, Night Stalker moved too quickly to take control.

As always, the would-be chief ignored Soaring Eagle's foolishness.

"A white man lives in the house made of rock," Night Stalker said. "He brings more with him to work on the land."

"Why does this concern Night Stalker?" Soaring Eagle said. "Does this white bring a woman with him? Do they breed children that will be a pestilence for the Comanche?"

"No woman and no children, but Broken Hand has seen him and says that he is strong."

"Broken Hand is an old woman."

"He has the spirit of our ancestors. He sees what we do not see. This one will take the wild horses and the deer and the squirrel. He will bring others like him. They will break the soil and plant their seeds, and the land will be closed to the Comanche."

Night Stalker spoke with a solemnity that demanded a serious response.

"Then we must gather the horses before they become his, enough to trade for guns," Soaring Eagle said, "and we must hunt and lay aside food for the winter. I, too, see what others do not see. Five winters past we came far from our home in the north to find gentle seasons, but this year the north winds will sweep down the land to join us. The white man is foolish and does not read the signs."

With a nod, he dismissed the man who would be chief and took up the rifle. His heart was heavy because the lance had been set aside, as had the bow and the arrows that he had himself carved.

The white man's gun must be the way of the

Comanche. Only with firepower and the will to use it wisely would the Comanche be able to live.

Still, he was filled with sadness to remember the quick smile of Fire in Hair and the trust in her eyes when she looked at him. His wives had borne sons. Had he been blessed with a daughter, he would have chosen the spirit of this white woman to live in her heart.

Chapter Eight

The earthworm curled its fat body around the end of the pointed stick, then uncurled, stretching to its full length, segment by segment, and disappeared deeper into the dirt.

Kneeling close and holding the stick steady, Cord noted each detail. For a while he forgot where he was and what he was doing, digging in the soil in a grassy field a hundred yards and one rolling hill away from the small stone house that served as a temporary home.

For a while, he was back in New Orleans.

Once, when he was a boy, on a day when his mother was busy and his father was gone, he had scooped up a bucketful of such worms from the wet ground behind his house, then headed for the river. He had been very young; it had taken from early morning to late afternoon to catch a string of freshwater catfish, but he had been determined to succeed.

Always, he had been stubborn that way.

His mother turned up her aristocratic nose at river cats, but the family cook cleaned and gutted them, rolled them in coarse cornmeal, and fried them in pork fat, just for him, that first time.

He had eaten every bite she placed in front of him. Since those days, he had dined grandly many times, but he had never tasted anything half so good as those catfish.

After that, whenever he got the chance, he had dug the worms and run to the river. He never mastered cleaning the fish himself without hacking them to pieces. Always he shared his catch with the cook, her husband—the gardener and handyman—and the four children who lived in the one-room cabin at the back of what was called the Hardin estate.

He was forbidden to go near the cabin, so naturally he went there whenever he could sneak away. The faces of the children were polished, like the ebony stones his mother wore in a silver necklace around her neck. Their white-rimmed black eyes always stared at him as if he had come down from the moon and they never asked him to join in their games.

Still, he would go and he would watch them play chase, and he would listen to their laughter and the strange patois that was a mixture of French and English and the sing-song speech of the islands from which their parents had come.

He told himself it was the language that kept

them apart, but in his little boy's heart, he knew the difference went deeper, far deeper even than the color of their skin.

In his own home, there was little laughter, and what was there came from the men and women his mother invited to her grand parties. From his perch at the top of the winding staircase, he had picked up a smattering of French to go with the Spanish his mother had taught him. But he never learned to laugh.

His father was often absent from these affairs. The word was, he was a traveling man.

Cord remembered his home as very large with many ornately furnished rooms and a wide, deep backyard—probably estate was not too grand a word for it—but his father had not paid a dime for its purchase. The money had come from his mother's Spanish inheritance. Why she had married Raymond Hardin, a divorced man with minimal resources, Cord never knew, but he had learned that in affairs of the heart, reason was the least consideration.

He remembered, too, the way his mother used to ride her beloved stallion. Mostly he remembered the last ride, when the stallion failed to clear a high, wrought-iron fence, taking both her life and the life of the baby she was carrying. The accident occurred one week after what proved to be his final catfish feast.

"Your mother's neck was broken in the fall," the attending physician had told him. "She died instantly. She felt no pain."

As if that were consolation for an eight-year-old child. A month later Raymond sold the estate and put him in an orphanage run by

Ursuline nuns. He did not claim him again until after his third marriage. Cord was fourteen, too old to forget and forgive. A year later he ran away.

For one reason or another, he had been running ever since.

He rammed the stick sharply into the shallow hole he had been digging. Such memories hadn't returned to him in a long time. He didn't need them now, any more than he needed thoughts of Kate Calloway to trouble his infrequent rest.

Ever since he'd kissed her, she had been on his mind. He should not have done it, but she had looked so smug, so demanding as she stood in the place he was calling home. She had looked like a woman who needed and wanted to be kissed. And he wasn't carved out of rock.

Whistling for his horse, he rode back toward the house, over the hill and down past all the evidence of the work he had accomplished after Kate's visit. He had thrown himself into a dozen tasks, stacking enough firewood to last through a harsh winter, staking out land for a barn and adjacent corral, clearing pasture land for the horses that would form his remuda.

He had worked hard, so hard that someone watching him would think he planned to stay.

That was one of the reasons he was stirring up so much dust. He wanted word to get around that he was settling in for a lifetime.

The other was to keep a blue-eyed redhead out of his mind.

He would be leaving as soon as his mission

was done; he had no destination in mind, just a place where he could find peace. Maybe he would go back to Spain. After the trouble in San Antonio, after the fighting down in Mexico, he had settled there with his mother's people, on the plains of Andalusia near Seville. Though she was held in disgrace because of her marriage, even years after her death, the son of that marriage was not considered tainted.

It was strange how the time in Spain had left little mark on him, as if he had been only visiting all those years. Once he had considered an arranged marriage with a beautiful and wealthy señorita, the daughter of family friends, but he could not bring himself to take a bride when his emotions were tied up half a world away.

For that, he blamed T. J. Calloway and the unfinished business between them.

And now he had T. J.'s redheaded daughter to agitate his thoughts.

But Kate agitated him in a different way. He kept tasting her and feeling her hands against his skin. And he remembered the hot, hungry way she had stared up at him, puzzled by what was happening, wanting it to happen again.

He thrust the images from his mind. She was T. J.'s daughter, and that made her a forbidden sweet.

As he rode toward his small, sturdy house, he remembered the cabin at the back of the New Orleans estate, and in the remembering decided he needed one more structure, in addition to the barn. He was sitting at the table drawing plans when he heard a horse ride up.

Beside the drawing lay the leather packet with Diana Obregon's message inside. The sight of the packet kept the old wounds raw, and it focused his mind on his task.

Shoving his chair away from the table, he went outside to watch Lucky McKee dismount.

Lucky removed the saddlebags he'd brought with him, handed them over, then thumbed his hat to the back of his head. "If you were thinking T. J. Calloway has had some troubles," he said without preamble, "you were right."

"When?"

"Two years ago. He killed a man."

Cord nodded. "Take care of your horse and come inside. I've got coffee on. You can tell me the details there."

Five long minutes later, after Cord had unloaded the supplies in the saddlebags, Lucky was tossing his hat on the table, its red silk band the brightest spot of color in the room. Rubbing his brow with the sleeve of his white linen shirt, he reached for the coffee cup.

"It was over a woman, wasn't it?" Cord said.

"His daughter."

Cord fingered the leather packet. "Kate," he said, wondering why he felt sick inside. She was nothing to him.

"No, another one. Jessica. Younger than Kathleen Calloway. Wilder, too, according to the talk."

Lucky took a swallow of coffee. Cord let him take his time.

"Calloway got her engaged to one of his friends. The friend kept her for a while, then gave her back, saying he'd decided he wanted a virgin for a wife."

"The avenging father killed him."

"In the middle of town. Both men were armed. The sheriff said it was a fair fight."

Cord wasn't surprised. His trouble with Calloway had been in a public street, and it had been called fair, too.

"What happened to the daughter?"

"She's dead. She was running from the gunfight and got into trouble south of San Antonio—bandidos looking for a good time when she wasn't willing to give it to them."

"She was raped?"

"More than once."

Lucky's voice was without emotion, but Cord knew him well enough to catch the hardness in his eyes.

"When they were done," Lucky added, "they killed her. Calloway put on a big show of mourning and talked about going after his daughter's killers."

"You don't think he was sincere?"

"He left it up to the sheriff to chase them down, but they were long gone by then. And he didn't bother bringing the body back for a church burial. Jessica Calloway is in a Mexican cemetery on the way to Laredo. The other daughter, Kate, went down there and took care of things."

That sounded like the Kate that Cord knew.

He considered the possibilities of the story. "Do you believe that what you were told is the way it happened?"

"No reason not to."

If Lucky believed the events true, then they were true. When Cord asked him to investigate Calloway, he had not expected the injured father story. The part that rang truest in the whole tale was that T. J. had left his child's body in a far-off grave.

After she had been wronged by one of her father's friends.

T. J. wasn't strong on taking care of ruined women, dead or alive.

"The funny thing was," Lucky said, "he came out of it a hero. Folks sympathized with a father whose daughter had gone wrong. He risked his life to avenge her, and for that she ran away. The fact that he didn't go after the killers doesn't seem to bother anyone. It was the sheriff's job, not that of the grieving father."

"Manure doesn't stick to the man," Cord said, "no matter how fresh. I learned that a long time ago."

"It sticks to women. If Jess had lived, she would have been ruined, even without the bandidos. Leastways, that's the word. Some fools say what happened to her was probably for the best."

"You disagree."

"You might put it that way."

Lucky considered his coffee for a moment, then looked at Cord. "You're settling debts."

It was as close to an outright personal question as the young man had ever come.

"I've done a lot of traveling because of T. J.," Cord said. "I've decided it's time to stop."

Green wood popped in the fire. He shoved his

coffee away, tucked the leather packet into the pocket of his coat hanging on a peg by the door, and motioned for Lucky to join him outside.

"I've got plans for the place. Come on out and I'll show you. Do you know anything about adobe?"

"Not much, Captain."

"Well, friend, we're both about to learn."

Chapter Nine

Two days after hearing Lucky's report, Cord headed out to search the creek banks for the particular kind of dirt his new man Domingo said was best for making adobe bricks. In the meantime Domingo was building the wooden forms into which the earth, grass, and water would go. Another worker and his wife would be joining them later from the Calloway Ranch for the final assembly.

The weather had turned summer-warm again, and they needed to get the bricks baking in the sun as soon as possible.

Walking a bank close to Calloway land, Cord didn't see Kate until he was only a few yards away. Hidden by a thick bush growing close to the water's edge, she was kneeling to get a drink of water. Her leather skirt was pulled above her knees, and with her shapeless hat thrown onto the bank behind her, a curtain of red-gold hair covered her face.

He should have let her know he was there. Instead, he watched, wondering what thoughts would occupy a cautious country woman so much that she didn't hear a strange man approach. Her shotgun lay on the ground near her feet, a replacement for the one she had left when she ran away from him. For all the good this one was doing her, it might as well have been in its scabbard.

Kate was far too independent for her own good, and too willing to go out on her own. Hadn't she learned anything from her sister's death?

And what was going on with him that he was worried about her? They were a pair of fools, the two of them.

Still, he held his place and watched as she drank.

Over the rush of water he could imagine the sound of her lips sucking in the cool liquid and the workings in her throat as she swallowed. She had a long, slender, graceful throat for such a small woman. And she had high, rounded breasts. The way she was crouched, he couldn't see them, but he remembered.

She aroused him, and who she was had nothing to do with it. He should have turned and run as if the hounds of hell were at his heels. Instead, he moved closer, making no attempt to be quiet. A twig snapped under his boot. She jumped up and fumbled for her gun, but then she saw him and just stood, drawing in ragged, frightened breaths, her hands limp at her sides.

"What are you doing here?" she asked. "Did you follow me?"

He stepped around the bush, bringing him close enough to see the sprinkle of freckles across her nose. "Don't we always sneak up on each other?"

"It could get you killed one of these days."

"Not likely from one of your bullets. You need to take better care of yourself. I could have had you stripped and raped before you got within two feet of that gun."

If he expected her to pale, he was disappointed.

She tossed her hair back from her face, and he got a good look at the slender line of her throat and the curve of her high, round breasts. To the finest detail they were exactly as he had remembered them.

"You give yourself too much credit, Mr. Hardin. I doubt if you could do what was necessary in less than an hour."

"You seem to know much about rape."

He regretted the words as soon as they were out. Her eyes darkened, and he knew she was thinking of her sister.

"I'm sorry—" he began.

"You're a man. What else should I expect but crudeness?"

What else indeed? She had grown up with T. J. as the closest example of manhood. She ought to consider them all bastards.

He nodded by way of apology and turned to

leave. He needed to get out of there. He was beginning to understand her far too well.

"You never did say what you're doing here," she said.

He shifted back. "Looking for dirt."

"Right. And I'm fishing for whales."

"Did you ever make mud pies as a child?"

"Of course. Didn't you?"

Actually, except for the occasional secret worm digging, he had not been allowed to get that soiled, not when his mother was alive and not when he lived with the nuns. But his past was nothing he cared to share with her.

"Domingo's making adobe bricks. For a shelter for the workers."

"My workers."

"I've hired two men who used to work for you, Kate. They're free to go where they want."

"You're not. You're on Calloway land."

"Are you saying it's reserved for you and your people but no one else? It's a big place. You'll have trouble enforcing such a decision."

"Just you. You're the only one who's forbidden. I just decided. Stay off the Calloway Ranch."

"Why me?"

"You take my men," she said, a little too quickly, a little too forcefully, as if she were trying to convince herself as well as him. "I need them tending the stock and working the fields."

"They already know what I'm paying. If they want to change bosses, they don't need to see me to do it."

"Nevertheless, I don't want you anywhere near me."

She was, he thought, getting closer to the truth.

"Why?"

She leveled her gaze straight at him. "Because I don't like you."

Suddenly Cord could taste her on his tongue. The memory heated him, and he grew impatient with her lie.

"You liked me well enough the last time we were together," he said.

He had meant to sound sharp and taunting, but the words came out soft and caressing. A cloud passed over the sun, and in the resulting shadows he was keenly aware of how alone they were.

All the world held still as she looked at his lips. He hadn't realized she could blush. But of course she could. He had seen her cry, too. A gentleman would be apologizing for any insult he had given her, would be backing away and promising never again to give offense.

But around Kate Calloway, Cord was anything but a gentleman. And he certainly wasn't smart.

"Mr. Hardin—" she began, looking unsure of herself for the first time since he had appeared.

"Cordoba," he said.

"Cordoba's not a man's name. It's a place."

She fingered her hair behind her ear, and he saw that her hand was shaking. Whatever was happening here, it was happening to them both.

"Cordoba was the city of my mother's birth," he said. "Call me Cord."

He wanted a sharp response, another order,

a firm command, anything to make them adversaries again. Instead, she stared at him and whispered his name.

The sound went through him like a shot.

"I don't think of men like you having mothers," she said.

"Why is that?"

"It makes you human."

"Men like me."

"Men who torment women."

"Is that not all men?" he said.

"Some are worse than others."

"How many have tormented you?"

She blinked once, dropped her eyes, then looked at him once again. "None."

She said it without pride, without regret, and he wondered what sort of men she knew who left her unapproached. He also wondered whether she was including him in her count.

"You're too honest for your own good," he said.

The darkness returned to her eyes. "I can lie when I have to."

"Then here's your chance. I want to kiss you again."

He hadn't known he was going to be so honest. He hadn't realized how true the words were until he said them aloud. In that quiet moment he wanted to kiss her more than he wanted to breathe.

She stared at the ground, and he watched the rise and fall of her breasts.

"Do you want to kiss me?" he asked.

"That's an absurd thing to ask," she said, barely above a whisper.

He could not keep the hardness out of his voice. "You can't imagine how absurd. But still, I'm asking."

She took a deep breath. "It's not decent. I'm a good woman."

"Good women like men to touch them. Most are not honest enough to admit it. But then, most are not like you."

She closed her eyes. Standing there, hands at her sides, she looked vulnerable and altogether desirable.

The urge to thrust his hands in her hair became more than he could control. He stepped close. She did not move away. Instead, she looked up at him and let out a long, heartfelt sigh.

"Kiss me, Cord. Now, before I change my mind."

She spoke not like a woman in the throes of passion, but rather like one who was sealing her doom.

Cord feared she spoke for them both.

Chapter Ten

Kate had lost not only her sanity, but what little sense of self and dignity she had ever possessed. The knowledge should have sent her hurrying for her gun.

But Cord had cast a spell over her, and she suspected that somehow she had done the same to him, each of them giving in to something they did not want but could not resist.

Instead of defending herself, she watched as he moved close, his long black hair falling forward to touch her cheeks, his black-shirted shoulders blocking out the world. She didn't dare look at his eyes, or else she would cry out from the tension. It was difficult enough to breathe since each time she inhaled she caught the dark, musky scent of him that was unlike anything she had ever smelled.

So she just watched as his unsmiling lips

came down on hers; she wanted his kiss more than she had ever wanted anything. Adding to her shame, at the last second she stood on tiptoe to meet him halfway.

His lips were firm, exactly as she remembered them, with just enough moisture across their surface to knock the last bit of air from her lungs.

It was spittle, she told herself. He'd licked his lips. But Cord's spittle wasn't in the least repulsive; it helped his mouth glide across hers in a way that had her grabbing at the folds of his shirt.

A little of her spit got caught up in the gliding. Sharing her wetness was the most intimate thing she had done with a man.

His fingers roamed through her hair before taking a firm hold of her shoulders, then moving down her back, rubbing and kneading, all the while his mouth did devastating things to her just by moving back and forth. The pressure was enough to send a shaft of fire from her lips straight down to the bottom of her stomach.

And lower. The heat in her low parts would get her in trouble for sure.

This kiss was better than the first one, and that made it worse, because it came not out of anger or challenge, but because she wanted to know if he really could stir in her all the powerful emotions she had once thought she would never feel.

She had been frightened the first time, but she wasn't frightened now. She was aroused.

When his tongue began to hint at an intrusion, she offered encouragement in the only way she knew how: she parted her lips. The tongue didn't wait for further invitation. His exploration was thorough, making her weak and strong. Her knees turned to butter, her stomach turned to fire, and her breasts were so itchy, she thought she might have to bare them and scratch herself hard.

Or maybe Cord could do it.

The thought was more than she could contemplate without swooning, and she was not a woman who ever swooned.

Just when she started thinking about using her own tongue a little and getting a more complete taste of him, he broke the kiss. But he didn't let go of her, and she sensed he was fighting something inside himself that was very important to them both.

Let him fight all he wanted. She had never felt so excited and humiliated in all her life, and that was about as much turmoil as she could handle at the moment. With her head resting against his chest, she tried to concentrate on breathing. He stirred the powerful emotions all right. She felt like a child who had been offered a whole, hot apple pie and then told to go to bed without any supper at all.

Except that Cord wasn't like hot apple pie. The hunger he could satisfy was of a far different kind, and it wasn't childish in the least.

I'm a good woman.

She wasn't, or if she was, she didn't want to be, not right now. She wanted something from Cord that she couldn't put a name to, needed it as much as she needed her life's blood.

Whatever the need, she knew it was more than just sex.

But that was not a feeling she would ever put into words. If he knew she was thinking such a thing, she might at last see a smile on his unsmiling lips.

They pushed away from each other at the same time, and the thought occurred that maybe he was a little afraid of her. But that was ridiculous. There was no way she offered him harm.

And she wasn't afraid of him. Far worse, she was afraid of herself, afraid the loneliness she carried with her would drive her to a submission she would regret the rest of her life.

But how could she submit to a man who had ceased making demands?

As he stood there, close but not touching, she could do nothing more than hold her place and stare at him, her hair in a tangle, her lips swollen, the fire inside her turning to ash.

"What are you doing to me, Kathleen Calloway?"

His voice was husky and held an edge of anger that reminded her of what she ought to be feeling. Not buttery and fiery and ashy, but as furious as a woman scorned.

For that was pretty much what she was. He had started this whole thing about kissing, and now he was blaming her.

Blame, she didn't need. She got that often enough from T. J.

Belatedly, she found the concentration she'd been after; it came in the form of disgust, not for herself—she would deal with that problem later—but for him.

"What am I doing to *you?*" She raked the hair back from her face. "I thought it was the other way around."

He didn't seem to hear her. Instead, his thoughts were turned inward, and that was about as insulting as a man could be. If he was going to get upset, by damn he ought to be upset with her.

Kate wasn't ordinarily a cussing woman, but Cordoba Hardin was bringing out traits in her she didn't know she had.

"You've kissed me twice, Cord," she said, scarcely aware of the name she had used, "but you won't do it again."

He nodded as if he was in complete agreement, almost as if the kissing had not been his idea in the first place. Her hand knotted into a fist. Hitting him would bring great satisfaction, but it would eventually be something else she would regret.

Nothing became so important to her as putting distance between them. She wanted to scrub herself all over; she felt as if he'd touched more than just her mouth and her hair. She turned to run, but she'd forgotten the shotgun lying behind her on the ground. The tip of her boot somehow got tangled up with the trigger, and the gun discharged just as she tripped and fell.

The pain in her ankle screamed as loudly at her as the blast from the gun. She wasn't sure if her own scream had added to the roar, but she suspected it had. Worse still, she had to endure the bitter knowledge that Cord had been witness to her clumsiness.

Smooth-moving, smooth-talking Cord, who would never trip or fall, or do anything in the least bit clumsy.

He hurried to her side and kneeled. "Are you all right?" he said.

"I'm fine," she said, and she would be, once she was alone.

He offered her a hand. She slapped it away. But when she tried to stand, the throbbing shot down to her toes and up her leg, and she sat down again, hard, and fought the tears in her eyes. He had seen her cry once, outside her father's house. He wouldn't see it again.

Without asking permission, he slipped off her boot and then the thick black stocking that was about as unfeminine as any article of apparel could be. His fingers probed the side of her ankle. Pain stabbed through her; she wanted to kick him with her uninjured foot. Instead, she worked at keeping her cries in her throat.

"The swelling's already started," he said. "I don't know if it's broken or just a bad sprain."

"Put me on my horse and I'll be all right. Moonstar's grazing down the way. All I have to do is call and she'll be here."

He slanted a skeptical look in her direction. "Is there anyone at the ranch to take care of you?"

"Of course. It's my home."

She spoke hastily, almost angrily. It was true that no one was there to hover over her, not anymore, if that was the kind of care he meant. Jess was gone, but then her baby sister had never been a hoverer. The couple who had come out from town with them when they first settled on the ranch were likewise no longer around. Pepe had been killed in a stampede of mustangs a year ago, and Amalia had been called to care for an ailing mother down in Goliad, a hundred miles away.

Still, she could get someone, the woman who served part-time as housekeeper and cook, for one. And Tug would help with whatever else she needed. While the image of her over-muscled foreman wasn't comforting, it did provide her with an answer to Cord's impudence.

"It's my home," she repeated.

But Cord had ceased listening to her. He scooted her toward the creek, carefully, obviously aware that every jar sent more pain shooting up and down her leg, then eased her foot into the water. The shock of the cold did little to comfort her. She tried to jerk free, but he had a strong grip on her upper leg and calf. If he ever decided to have his way with her, there was little she would be able to do about it. Should she decide to fight.

And that was a stupid thought in such a circumstance. He had taken all he wanted from her, and she had given all she planned to give.

Her foot was getting used to the cold water, except where it was lapping at new territory higher on her leg, but enough was enough.

"I'd like my boot, please."

"Your ankle's swollen. It won't fit."

"Then the stocking."

"In a minute."

She lost her patience and whistled for the mare. She would have hobbled to San Antonio if it would get his hands away from her thigh.

Moonstar came at a run, but held back halfway down the bank, her head bobbing, her brown eyes curious as she stared down at her mistress.

Kate glanced at Cord, then past him to the fast-moving stream. Anything was better than looking at the set of his mouth and the line of his jaw.

"I'm all right, really," she said. "Please let me go."

For once, he did as she asked, and her foot sank like a rock into the water, wetting the lower half of her leather skirt. Ignoring the throbbing, she raised her leg and scooted back up the bank. Cord stood to the side, watching, his absurdly provocative eyes showing no expression.

She dared glance at his lips and remembered the kiss, remembered his tongue. Warm shivers shot through her. She had to put distance between them right away. There were wounds that needed licking, and she wasn't thinking of her sprain.

He didn't offer a hand. He didn't show the least sign of sympathy. He just kept watching, and Kate realized how ridiculous she must look.

"Moonstar," she called out, and the mare took delicate steps toward her. When the stirrup was close enough for her to reach, she tried to pull herself upright, but her injured foot touched the ground and she felt as though red-hot fire tongs had been wrapped around her ankle.

Cord muttered what sounded like a string of very ugly words. Then, more clearly, he said, "Enough of this nonsense."

He scooped her up in his arms and whistled for his horse. Moonstar backed away. Smart mare.

"If you'll put me in the saddle, I'll be fine."

His horse, a black Arabian, came galloping out of nowhere, nostrils flaring, proud head high. The gelding was as fine an example of horseflesh as Kate had ever seen; strapped to his back was a black, tooled-leather saddle that matched his magnificence. It matched Cord's boots, as well. Everything about the man went together; every part, every possession was sublime.

What he was doing fooling around with her, she had no idea. What she was doing fooling around with him was equally absurd. Through Jess's experience, she knew men were rats.

While she was looking and thinking, he was placing her sideways on the Arabian, then pulling himself into the saddle behind her, settling her on his lap.

"Put me down," she said, and to her surprise he dismounted, letting her down on the saddle with a jolt that was far from pleasant. At least he was doing what she wanted for a change, though he did it with little gentleness.

She should have known getting rid of him wouldn't be so easy.

He grabbed the stocking and pulled it on her foot, settling it over her sprain so gently that she barely felt a twinge. Next, he whistled for Moonstar, who, traitor to her mistress, trotted up submissively and allowed him to slip the shotgun into its scabbard.

Grabbing her boot, he tied it by a thong to the back of the saddle, thrust her hat into her hand, and was up behind her again, and then under her as he eased her back onto his thighs.

He felt as hard as the saddle, but warmer. No decent woman would sit on a man like this, but they had already proven that decency wasn't much of a concern between them. She doubted he would consider the point now.

Kate gave up arguing. She thrust her hat down on her head, not bothering to twist her hair out of the way. Leaning into him would make her more comfortable; instead, she stretched her left arm across her body and grabbed her right wrist, putting an unnatural twist to her spine. With the way her ankle was throbbing, however, she couldn't moan too much about her back. She told herself the ride wouldn't last forever. He could take her home and all would be well.

Except that he didn't head out in the direction she wanted.

"My place is that way," she said, nodding toward the north.

"I know."

"So why are we heading south?"

"I'm not supposed to ride on Calloway land, remember?"

Kate gritted her teeth. "I changed my mind."

"I can ride anywhere I want, anytime. Is that what you're saying?"

"For now, I meant. You're certainly allowed to take me home."

"Allowed?"

She could feel the tension in him, and the anger, too, both boiling together as if he was about to explode.

"For now is not good enough," he said. "With us, Kate, it should be all or nothing."

His eyes were hooded by his half-closed lids and thick lashes, and by the shadow the brim of his hat cast across the upper half of his face. It didn't matter; she could never read the expression in them anyway.

This time there was no need. His lips were flat, without a sign of a smirk, but she could hear the smirk in his voice.

Maybe she had been wrong about the tension and the anger; maybe he simply liked to torment her; maybe teasing her was his idea of a game.

Silently she counted to ten. She was fast losing ways to keep her patience.

Glancing over her shoulder, she saw Moonstar falling in behind the Arabian, another example of the Hardin males keeping females in line.

"So where are you taking me?"

He didn't answer, and the truth struck.

"Not your place."

"You'll find it adequate. You can recuperate in my bed."

"It's too small."

Where that thought came from, she didn't know.

"I didn't mean to put you there with me. Unless you prefer to share."

She could feel him watching her, though she couldn't see his eyes. She would have blushed, but all her life's blood seemed to have settled in her pounding ankle.

She studied the slowly passing countryside. "I'm used to a big, wide bed, that's all I meant, with a thick feather mattress and clean sheets and a warm comforter to pull over me at night."

"So am I."

She dared steal a look at him out of the corner of her eye. He was staring straight ahead, his profile as finely honed as the rest of him. But it wasn't the way he looked that got her. It was something inside him, something dark and dazzling. At least it dazzled her.

Nobody she had ever met was anything like him. He pulsed with troubles and with secrets. His being here in Medina County made no sense; unlike her, he belonged far, far away, in a land where she had never been.

Ireland? Spain? Those were the lands of his heritage, or so he had told her. What little she knew about either place made her doubt they were where he belonged. Neither seemed mystical enough.

She wouldn't ask him about his true home, or about his secrets. He might ask about hers. Sharing secrets would be about as intimate as anything they had done.

The afternoon sun beat down on her back, and she felt a trickle of sweat run down the front of her neck and settle between her breasts. The heat of her bottom resting against his thighs was hotter than the sun.

And her ankle continued to throb. It held a mountain of hurt. Chewing the inside of her cheek raw, she dared to glance down. The swelling was getting worse. The lower half of her leg would be the size of a watermelon by the time she got it propped up.

In bed.

In Cord Hardin's bed.

Kate knew her troubles had only begun.

Chapter Eleven

Cord had done stupid things in his life, but among the worst of them was taking Kate Calloway back to his place. All in the name of gentlemanly rescue? Hardly. He did not believe that any more than she did.

To begin with, her ankle must feel as if hot nails had been driven all the way to the bone, but she had not whimpered once. He had to admire a woman who could control herself in such a way.

The last thing he wanted in this world was to admire her.

Almost the last thing. The really last thing was to want her. She was T. J. Calloway's daughter, for God's sake. He had known from the beginning that she would get in the way. And had he run? Pathetically, no. Every time

113

she got close, he started stroking her like a sex-mad youth.

The fact that she had started stroking him in return offered little consolation. She was discovering new feelings. Unlike her, he understood the exact nature of those feelings and where they would lead.

He had never felt like this, not even with Diana. And that was disturbing him the most.

Kate had fallen asleep leaning against him, her body at ease in a kind of trusting release she would never feel while she was awake. She was small and soft, and when she turned toward him, she not only rested her breasts against his chest, she rubbed her bottom against some sensitive parts.

He should have been the one to cool himself down in the creek.

He deserved the torment for kissing her. He would shoot off his privates before he kissed her again.

Which was probably overstating his feelings, but not by much.

As he neared the squat stone house he temporarily called home, he passed his new man Domingo working away at the adobe forms.

Domingo stopped work and stared. "Señorita Kate," he said with genuine concern in his voice.

Kate stirred. Cord felt her every shift.

"She's asleep. Her ankle is hurt. I found her near the creek."

He kept the how of the injury to himself, discretion seeming the wiser course for them both.

"She won't be able to ride for a while," he added. "You should go let someone know what has happened."

T. J. Calloway, perhaps? The idea had not occurred to him before. It was hard to believe Calloway would drop whatever he was mixed up with, business or pleasure, and gallop wildly to give succor to his ailing only child.

But if he did?

Cord didn't want him anywhere near Kate. Given all the circumstances, both past and present, that was a less than noble way to feel. But then, T. J. Calloway was not a man to bring out nobility in anyone.

"You want help in caring for Señorita Kate?" Domingo asked.

Yes would have been a smart answer.

"No," he said. "We will manage." The look in Domingo's eyes made him add, "She will be all right. No harm will come to her here."

He was surprised at how much he meant it.

The man looked at him for a long minute, then nodded and went for his horse.

Lucky had gone to scout out men and lumber for the building of the barn. It might take him days. That meant Cord would be alone with Kate.

She woke while he was getting her down from the horse. Her eyes darted wildly, and she began to struggle. He had to cradle her close to keep her from slipping from his grasp. She winced once, then settled down, biting her lower lip but otherwise holding quietly still.

Her weight was insignificant; not so her warmth and the life he could sense rushing

115

through her. He felt his own pulse increase, along with his heat.

He carried her inside, using his shoulder and elbow to open the door, and after pulling the thin plaid cover back to the bottom of the bed, he laid her down carefully.

The mattress was a three-inch pad of worthless horsehair resting atop a six-foot board, which in turn rested atop a storage chest. It wasn't very comfortable, but it was efficient, as was everything the German had built.

He set his hat on the table along with his gun, and looked back at her. She must be feeling terrible, but she didn't complain.

He would have preferred a spate of whining. He did not want her brave.

His lone pillow was about as useful as the mattress. Nevertheless, he put it under her ankle and pulled off the stocking. The swelling had increased, and there was a line of bruising along the side of her foot.

She propped herself on her elbows and looked down at the injury. "I really messed myself up, didn't I?"

Along with brave, she was being reasonable. She should have been blaming him. That would have made her more like a Calloway.

"Try to move it," he said.

"How? Put it on the floor and walk out?"

"You probably don't have to go that far. Just see if you can move your ankle."

She stared at her foot as if it belonged to someone else and slowly moved it up and down, a fraction of an inch, but enough to let him know the bones weren't broken. Tears filled her eyes, but not one escaped to her cheek. She was tough. He muttered a few curses under his breath.

Rummaging in the valise where he stored his clothes, he came up with a black bandanna.

"This is going to hurt," he said as he bent over the pillow.

"Then don't do it."

"It's for your own good."

"I've heard that one before."

Cord wanted to ask her from whom and under what circumstances, but he already knew too much about her.

"I don't know what you plan to do with that thing," Kate said. "Tear it into strips?"

He looked down at the bandanna, twisted tight in his fists. Smoothing the wrinkles, he wrapped the swelling, then tied the ends tight. Last, he removed her other boot and stocking and dropped them on the floor.

She was lying stiff against the mattress, eyes closed, lips flat and tight. He was ungentlemanly enough to look her over. Her good leg, what he could see of it, had a nice, trim curve to it, her ankle absurdly slender, especially when compared to its injured mate.

Her leather skirt was stained from when she had dropped her foot into the creek; otherwise, her clothes looked fresh and smooth against her body. For a small woman, she looked nicely voluptuous, soft and rounded and promising.

Maybe it was just because she was lying helpless in his bed. Maybe it was because he had not been with a woman in a long time.

Whatever the cause, she still looked good to him. And very tempting.

The next few days were not going to be easy. He would stay away from her as much as he could.

She caught him looking, and he threw himself into being busy. He folded the cover so that she could rest her arms on top of it. Her long-sleeved shirt matched the blue of her eyes, and her hands looked delicate and pale against the plaid. Yet when he touched them, he found the delicacy was only an illusion. She worked hard. It was evident in the firmness of her palms.

The sight that stirred him the most was the way her misshapen hat had fallen back, leaving her hair to spread across the sheet like a spill of late-day crimson sunshine.

It was a curious comparison when the man doing the comparing wanted nothing to do with the woman whose hair he was contemplating.

He hung the hat on a peg near the bed, then grabbed his own hat from the table and dropped it on top of hers, adding the holster on top of them both. While he worked, she stared at him the way a woman looks at a stray dog who might yet prove dangerous.

From the beginning, he had known she was smart. Nothing she was doing had changed his mind.

He stepped back. "I would have undressed you, but I decided you would object."

She blinked once, but she did not look away. "That's the most intelligent thing you've said today."

The words were as saucy as ever, but she didn't put much spirit into them.

He went about making coffee, then stirred the pot of beans and ham on the stove.

"Do you cook?" she asked.

"Lucky."

She frowned, and he watched a pair of small, vertical lines crease the smooth skin above the bridge of her nose.

"I'm lucky you cook?"

"Lucky McKee is my partner." He thought of how to describe him. "He is a man of many talents," was the best he could do. He stared at Kate, who had folded her arms beneath her head. "Including a way with women."

"More than you?"

Immediately she looked as if she wanted to swallow the words.

My way with women can be fatal, Kate. Do not let yourself get too close.

If he told her such a thing, she would believe him. And she would want to know more. Eventually she would have to know all. It was not a revelation to bring either of them joy.

Letting the question go unanswered, he stirred the potatoes that were roasting at the edge of the fire. They would have cold biscuits, too. A veritable feast.

"I'm a great deal of trouble," she said. "You should have taken me home."

He pulled a couple of tin plates off the shelf by the stove.

Kate was persistent. "The accident wasn't your fault. I'm the clumsy one. You shouldn't feel guilty."

119

"I don't," he said, and meant it. He didn't know why he had brought her here, but guilt had nothing to do with it.

"I don't believe you," she said.

"That is your mistake. There was no reason to run from me. We had done everything we were going to do."

Her eyes filled with anguish and she came halfway to a sitting position. "That's a terrible thing to say." And then she caught herself. "Maybe not terrible, exactly. It's certainly not wrong, but—"

He dropped the plates on the table with a clatter and strode to the bed, planting his hands on either side of her and looking her straight in the eye. For the first time since he had met her, she looked cowed.

"I just this moment realized why I keep kissing you. It's the only way I can shut you up. If you want to be kissed again, Señorita Calloway, you have only to keep talking."

Anger flared in her eyes, but he got what he wanted: quiet. He didn't hear another word from her—not during supper, which he served her in bed, not when he was settling on a bedroll in front of the fire, and not during the long hours before and after midnight when he stared sleeplessly at the glowing coals.

But he heard her breathing, and he heard her sigh. Never in his life had he spent the night in a room with a woman. The experience had a strange effect on him, making him feel at once suffocated by her presence and desolately alone.

120

Chapter Twelve

Kate woke early the next morning, as the first rays of sunlight were filtering through the open windows of Cord Hardin's home. She was alone, and for a moment fluttery panic made her forget where she was. Sitting upright, she started to shift her legs to the side of the bed.

A jolt of pain was all the reminder she needed to bring back memories of yesterday— memories of Cord, of what he had done to her and she to him, and worst of all, how she had made a fool of herself.

With a moan, she fell back against the mattress. She ached all over, not just in her ankle, and she had to relieve herself. Right away.

As if he could read her mind, Cord came in with a small pan.

I just realized why I keep kissing you. It's the only way I can shut you up.

She pulled the cover over her head, but the echo of his words refused to go away. If he would just leave, she could survive almost anything. Even her memories.

"Kate," he said, as though she were a recalcitrant child. "You can talk now."

She growled. The restless night had been bad enough, hearing him toss by the fire for hours, and then listening as he went outside in early morning, she supposed to try for sleep. Now he was back and as rude as ever.

Throwing back the cover, she stared at the pan. "I can't use that thing," she said.

"Then I'll help you outside."

How reasonable of him. She considered her choices. Behaving childishly was not one of them.

Tossing the cover aside, she gritted her teeth and shifted her feet to the floor. The pain was bad but bearable. He knelt before her, but she slipped her good foot into the stocking and boot without giving him a chance to help. Her bad foot looked as swollen as ever, and with it lowered against the floor the throbbing was getting worse.

Before she could put her standing muscles to work, he scooped her into his arms and carried her out to a brilliant day, doing so with an ease that made her feel, if not exactly loved, at least coddled. It was a sensation she had never experienced before, not even when her mother was alive.

Immediately, the throbbing eased, or if it didn't ease, at least she didn't mind it so much. Despite herself, she took a deep breath of the clean air, lifted her face to the sun, and came close to smiling. She felt him watching her. She changed the smile to a scowl.

She ought to be scowling. Coddled. How absurd. She stirred restlessly. He wasn't coddling her, he was making up for an accident he considered his fault, no matter how much he denied it. It was just her luck to be kidnapped and rendered helpless by an honorable man.

Where that idea came from she didn't know. He wasn't completely honorable, as she knew too well. He was seldom even polite anymore.

How was she supposed to think clearly? He was holding her too close, and he smelled of the soap he had used to shave, plus the clean clothes he had changed into, and his copper skin was tight and smooth across his cheeks. He had a good, sharp profile, too. Ordinarily, she didn't like long hair on men, but she liked it on him.

Anyway, the hair ended at his shoulders. It wasn't nearly as long as hers.

Which reminded her that she needed to bind her hair up beneath her hat. Unbound hair made a woman look lascivious. Jess had told her that. If there was any way Kate did not want to look right now, it was lascivious.

Not that honorable Cord would notice. He might have been carrying a sack of potatoes for all the attention he was paying her. The thought occurred that if she started chattering, he might kiss her again. It was reason enough to keep very, very quiet.

He walked her right up to the door of the privy, which was behind a clump of bushes a long way from the house. It would be an uncomfortable distance on a cold winter's night.

But it wasn't winter and the sun was shining brightly.

"You don't have to take me inside," she dared to say. "I can hop."

He shrugged, and she felt the play of muscles beneath the arm she had draped across his shoulder.

The hopping went about as badly as she had expected, her awkwardness outmatched only by the onslaught of pain.

When she was done, he carried her back to the house and she didn't object. She vowed she would not drink a single drop of coffee or water all day. She didn't want to go through the hopping again.

He served her cold biscuits and ham in bed, using a small slab of wood as a tray, just as he had done last night, and by the time she was finished eating, she heard someone ride up at the front of the house.

After a couple of minutes, Domingo knocked at the door. Cord gestured for him to enter, and he did so, hat in hand.

"Señorita Kate," he said with a nod.

She smiled at him, waiting for the sound of another rider, someone to rescue her and take her home. All was silent outside the room.

Her former worker was short but broad and

strong, although not in the excessively muscled way of Tug Rafferty. His strength was less obvious, but he could work hard, always without complaint, and she missed him at the ranch.

He wore his hair longer than Cord's and his skin was darker, his features more sharply defined. She suspected he had Indian blood in him, but she couldn't guess his age. All she knew was that he had a family in Mexico to whom he sent money.

"I hope you didn't worry anyone too much," she said. "It's really not much of an injury."

He glanced at her stocking-covered ankle, propped on the pillow, then looked down fast, as if he had done something wrong.

How polite. How discreet. Cord could use a little of his manners.

"I bring a message from Señor Rafferty," he said. "He will let your father know what has happened."

"There's no need to bother T. J.," she said, alarmed.

What she really wanted to say was how sorry she was that her father had to know. She wanted him to think of her as invincible when she was out in the country.

Or did she simply want him to think kindly of her, at those times when he didn't need her for something, like handling pigs and cows or greeting guests.

Lying around in bed certainly left a woman open to strange, unsettling thoughts.

She chanced to glance at Cord. He wasn't looking at much of anything, just staring into space, as if he saw a vision no one else could see.

125

It wasn't a cheerful vision. His eyes were cold and dark, dark blue, like the sapphire she had seen on the finger of a woman at her father's last party. She'd thought the jewel out of place on the woman's work-callused hand.

But the coldness looked at home in Cord's eyes.

"That will be all, Domingo," he said.

With a worried glance at Kate, the worker left.

In the stillness that followed his departure, she shivered, though the room was pleasantly warm.

"T. J. will take care of me once he finds out what has happened."

Slowly Cord brought his gaze to her. She wished she had never spoken.

"Will he?"

"Of course," she snapped.

But she wasn't sure. This was the first real demand she had made of him, the first need for rescue. And it wasn't even a stated demand, but rather one implied. There wasn't much telling how Tug would relay the news. Her foreman was neither the most sensitive nor the most articulate of men.

Besides, Domingo might have reported she was in no danger where she was. In truth, Cord was taking better personal care of her than anyone at her own ranch would do.

But such care was not the only consideration. There were forces around her in this solid stone cabin she didn't understand. She'd felt them the first time she saw Cord, aiming a rifle at her father from the top of the hill. Today, with the talk about T. J., they had returned.

She had allowed herself to forget the feeling. No matter how much she fell under Cordoba Hardin's spell, she must not forget it again.

Chapter Thirteen

T. J. smiled at the man sitting across his desk and smiled, too, at the man's wife.

"I am pleased, sir, that the sale went through much as you wanted," he said. "The price was somewhat higher, I know, than you planned to pay, but still, houses of this quality are difficult to find in San Antonio. And it is what your wife desired. We must please our women, do you not agree?"

The man started mumbling something, but T. J. had already shifted his attention to the daughter, standing in front of the window behind her parents' chairs.

Sunlight streamed over her yellow hair, turned-up nose, and full lips. It lighted, too, the not-quite-plump frame that showed so well in profile in the tight-waisted blue cotton gown.

She was eighteen years of age and already full-bosomed, losing her baby fat in womanly ways.

Prime stock, to use terms a cowman would understand.

She glanced over her shoulder at T. J. She didn't smile. She just looked. But he could see the interest in her eyes. And he could feel the tension racing through the air between them.

He rested his hands in his lap. Much more of her look and he would be too aroused to stand.

"Have we signed all the papers?" her father asked, and T. J. had to struggle to remember his name.

Samuel Netherby, that was it, and his good wife Margaret. The Netherbys were moving here from Houston to open up a mercantile store.

"All is taken care of, Mr. Netherby. You can move in anytime you wish."

"Good," piped up his wife. "I'd like to start measuring for curtains as soon as I can."

The Netherbys were upright, God-fearing people. They would be an asset to the some-times raucous town. Netherby was also a voter, the kind who studied issues and supported whomever he considered the better man. He was also the kind who could be fooled.

Unfortunately, he was as boring as his wife.

Not so their only child.

"Rebecca," T. J. said, "I hope you are as pleased with your new home as your parents."

Her deliciously full lower lip puffed out. He could see she wanted to say something sharp, but she glanced at her father and shrugged.

"It's fine," she said.

"It's lovely," her mother said.

Rebecca rolled her eyes but kept quiet. She would not be one to follow closely the edicts of her parents, but rather would find enjoyment in having her own way. In secret.

The Netherbys stood.

"We've taken enough of your time," Mr. Netherby said.

"And there are those windows waiting," Mrs. Netherby said.

T. J. came around the desk and shook their hands. Rebecca moved close to him and held out her hand. He took it and squeezed. She squeezed right back.

Reluctantly, he let go of her and stroked his beard.

"Welcome to San Antonio, Miss Netherby," he said, already thinking of a few ways he could make her feel at home.

She licked her lips, then swished out behind her parents, hips moving from side to side.

He had been right about her. She was a knowledgeable young woman who not only knew but also enjoyed her effect on men. Alone, T. J. tugged at his paisley vest and rested a hand on his stomach. Though he'd put on a few pounds in recent years, at fifty he was still a fine figure of a man. And he still knew how to please women of any age.

But he preferred them young and tender, like meat off a young calf.

Rebecca Netherby would indeed be a prime cut.

His musings were interrupted by the slam of the outer door to his office, and he watched in surprise as Tug Rafferty strode inside. Immediately, he lost his public face.

"What the hell are you doing here? You know we're not supposed to be seen together off the ranch."

"It's Miss Kate," the foreman said.

T. J. shook his head. "What's she done now?"

"Hurt herself."

"Badly?" he asked.

The concern in his voice was not feigned. She was his daughter and he was not without affection for her. He also needed her, both on the ranch and occasionally in town. But he needed her healthy and full of energy.

"All I know is her ankle's hurt and she can't ride. The bastard that's been buying up half the county found her by one of the creeks."

"She was riding by herself? I told you to watch her."

"I can't keep up with her. I got chores to do."

T. J. looked at the foreman in disgust. His job was more than helping to run the ranch. He was supposed to make sure Kate didn't get in trouble, the way her sister had done.

But the girl wasn't interested in men. And they didn't seem interested in her, which was both a comfort and an aggravation. She was too much like her mother. She didn't know how to have a good time.

Still, he needed her if he was going to make a run at being governor. And he needed her at the ranch. He had to give her credit. She ran the place smoothly, and she managed to make a profit when most farmers and ranchers were barely getting by.

And now, damn it, she was hurt.

"By the creek, you say. Who was it that found her? Oh, yes, our mysterious newcomer."

"He took her with him to his place and sent word where she was. I rode in as fast as I could."

T. J. turned back toward his desk and took his chair, not bothering to ask Rafferty to sit. There wasn't a chair that would hold him without breaking.

Cordoba Hardin was an enigma, and that was something he detested in a man. He'd ridden into town and started buying up property that should have become part of the Calloway ranch, putting in more money than he could ever get back. T. J. had been furious when he first heard about the sales, but he'd calmed down. The man was overextending himself with all that land. One way or another, a smart lawyer would get some of it back.

And T. J. was nothing if not smart.

But the land wasn't the worst of it. There were rumors Hardin's partner had started asking questions about T. J.

There was nothing bad to find out, nothing that hadn't been smoothed over, including the trouble with Jess. He looked at women like Rebecca Netherby, but he kept it to just looking, unless he made certain no harm would come to him. He was not a man who liked to take needless risks.

About the only thing he knew for sure was that Hardin had money. Lots of it. And political campaigns were expensive. Once he got into office, he could start getting some of those expenses back, and more.

But he had to have the election money first, and that was something that oftentimes came hard. If Jess had handled her betrothal better, he wouldn't be in the situation of needing money. But she hadn't. He didn't allow himself to think of her for long. He had one daughter left; she was the one who could help him now.

Joseph Wharton was casting moon eyes at Kate, but the fool wasn't rich enough to do his campaign much good. This was not necessarily a problem. If his daughter could attract one man, she could get another. And she was laid up in a rich man's home. His small home. They were bound to at least look at one another.

Kate wasn't homely, far from it. It was possible she could catch herself a wealthy husband after all. Owning the land Hardin had acquired would be his first choice, but having it in the family was close behind.

It all depended upon Kate coming up with some womanly wiles. Her trouble was, she didn't know what to do with what she had.

Put a woman like Rebecca Netherby in such a situation, and she would be coming out of it with at least half of what Cordoba Hardin owned. Hell, the fair-haired Rebecca would probably have faked the injury to begin with.

Several thoughts came to him, ways in which both Kate and Rebecca could prove useful.

He smiled to himself as he reached for pen and paper. All his daughter needed was a little instruction. What better person to give it than the father who was doing nothing wrong in asking for her help?

He wrote fast, then handed the sealed message to Rafferty.

"This is for Kate. Take it to her, and don't bother to wait around for a reply. The girl will do as she's told." Again he smiled. "But first I need to gather a few items to go along with the message. Wait here for me. I won't be long."

"I'm to leave her with Hardin?"

"Until I say bring her home."

"But—"

T. J. waved aside his protest. "I've got a better idea. Wait a day before you go see her. And don't give me any argument. Remember who you work for, Tug. If she sends for help, you let me know. But I don't think she will. She's got to have at least a drop of Calloway blood flowing through her veins."

Humming to himself, he went out to find the ripe and lovely Miss Netherby and enlist her help. She would know, better than her mother, what he wanted, without his telling her. Of course, Mrs. Netherby's assistance would also be requested, but it was her daughter's help he was after.

It was probable she could find exactly what was needed in her parents' mercantile store. In describing the situation, he must remember to be distraught. It wouldn't do at all for people to suspect he was glad his only child was hurt.

Chapter Fourteen

Kate sat naked in bathwater fast growing cold, her right leg extended in the air, her knee resting against the side of the big tin washtub. Three feet away, the dying flames flickered in the fireplace, putting out far too little heat, certainly not enough to offset the temperature of the water.

Worst of all, her ankle was throbbing the way it had the day she'd fallen. Probably because last night, after Cord left, she had tried to walk and had twisted it again. He didn't know, and she could see no reason to tell him.

Still, it was not a condition that offered peace of mind. Especially with him waiting outside and her inside—cold, naked, and unable to figure out how to stand without another re-injury.

The way he had been treating her the past

two days, he probably wouldn't be interested in offering to help. He probably had naked women around him all the time, out there in the world where he really lived. Healthy women who could prance around and do pretty much anything he might ask.

She didn't want him interested in her, didn't want his taunting presence, but still, the way he was behaving wasn't doing her much good. He avoided her as if she were carrying a terrible disease. After that first night, he even slept outside.

He fed her and he carried her to the privy, but he didn't talk and she, in turn, didn't talk to him. He said he kissed her to shut her up. She didn't want him to think she was inviting another kiss.

So why had she complained about feeling dirty? She should have known Mr. Efficient would fetch a tub, fill it with water heated by the fire, and then leave her to maneuver on her own.

Oh, he'd lingered a minute, looking as if he wanted to offer help, and for a moment she'd sensed a familiar interest on his part. But he had muttered something that was probably obscene and certainly uncomplimentary, and then he had left, after setting her on the bench by the tub.

Getting undressed hadn't been difficult and getting in hadn't been too bad, though she'd done a fair amount of splashing, soaking the floor. But getting out seemed impossible. Her muscles must have died while she was lying in bed.

"Are you all right in there?"

It was Cord, speaking from right outside the door. She held very still. "I'm f-fine."

He was silent for a minute.

"You're having trouble getting out."

She pulled herself up on one knee. The ridged bottom of the tub cut into her flesh, and her still-swollen ankle waved in the air.

"I'll be all right."

"Call when you decide otherwise."

When cows gave birth to pigs. What if he came in and caught sight of her body? She was scrawny, but she was available, and Jess had said with some men that was enough.

Maybe Cord's secret was that he was a rapist who was trying to rid himself of the habit. Maybe he had given up having women altogether and the reason he had brought her back to his bed was to test his resolve.

And maybe the chill was getting to her brain, rendering her incapable of rational thought.

She gripped each side of the tub and pushed, twisting her good foot under her, but the foot slipped and she sat down hard, splashing more water onto the wooden floor.

Unfortunately, she also yelped.

Before she could protest, he was in the room, pulling a shirt out from the storage chest beneath the bed, handing it to her without looking, keeping his back turned.

"Put this on," he said. "Now. I've got work to do. You're holding me up."

So much for his plans to ravish her.

She stared at the shirt—black, of course, like all his others. "I'll get it wet."

He glanced at the floor. "You've managed that with everything else. Why start worrying now?"

She started to tell him that if he had taken her home instead of here, none of this would be happening. But she figured he had already seen that for himself.

Instead, she again balanced on her good leg and grabbed the tail of the shirt from him, unfortunately dragging it across the water on the floor. She pulled it on, folded the long sleeves up to her wrists, and was in the process of lining up buttons and buttonholes when he turned.

"A gentleman would have waited until I was done," she said, folding her arms over her chest.

He had probably seen a flash of skin—she could tell by the look in his eye—but all he did was back away, sit at the edge of the bed, and gesture for her to proceed.

Her fingers turned to butter and she swayed precariously on her knee. His eye traveled down the length of her bad leg which was still propped on the side of the tub. He lingered at her ankle.

"What did you do to yourself?"

"Bathed."

He shook his head in disgust. "Your ankle's swelling worse than ever."

She tried to look innocent. In all her life, save in one very important area, she had never been able to lie to anyone and get away with it, but that didn't mean she shouldn't try.

"What did you do, attempt to walk?" he asked.

"Actually, I was practicing the polka in case you asked me to dance."

He was on her like a hawk on a rabbit, lifting her from the tub, holding her close while she fumbled to keep the shirt closed, feeling the wet fabric against her skin. For all its fullness, it followed the lines of her body far too well.

Her hair dripped on his arm, wetting his shirt as much as her borrowed one. Her legs stretched out disgracefully bare for his view, and she was embarrassingly aware that beneath the wet shirt she had nothing on.

The scowl on his face, which wasn't really quite a scowl, told her he was aware of it, too.

"You can throw me back," she said, flinging her hair away from her face, sending out a spray of water that wet him even more. "I'm not much of a catch."

He stared at her toes, then moved up her legs to where the shirttail lay halfway up her thighs. He lingered before moving on to the twin mounds that were her breasts, to her throat and slowly up to her eyes. She was short, but the journey took an eternity. By the time it ended, her stomach was pulled so tight that she thought he must surely be aware of her muscles at play.

Water from her hair had caught in his eyelashes, and there were droplets like polished crystal beaded in the blackness of his hair. His skin had darkened from his hours working in the sun, and though he had shaved, dark bristles were visible across his cheeks.

His lids were lowered, hiding his eyes, and she concentrated on his lips, pulled tight, and then parted, slightly, and she could hear his quickening breath.

She would have to leave the breathing up to him; she'd forgotten how. Blood pounded in her ears. She lifted her chin. He touched his lips to hers. She let out a long sigh, mingling her breath with his.

Stepping backward, he once again sat on the edge of the bed, only this time he brought her with him. Resting her feet on the mattress beside him, she shifted to wrap her arms around his neck, abandoning the unbuttoned shirt to open as it would, which it did, helped by the way he bent his head to lick her throat.

They both moved slowly, quietly, with only Cord's ragged breathing disturbing the stillness. It was as if they had no choice except to do what they did.

Her breasts were full, tight, filled with a surplus of nerve endings, each of them tingling at once. She was tingling all over, and when he kissed his way down to the valley between her breasts, kissing to one side and then the other, she could hardly hold herself still.

She settled for a low moan that seemed to come from her soul, thrusting her hands into his hair, surprised by its fineness. He kissed his way back to her lips, pausing to look into her eyes, as if he were looking for something he couldn't find. He made her want to cry, though she did not know why. Mostly, he made her want to press her body against him everywhere she could.

She started with his lips, touching her tongue to them, urging him to let her inside.

On this day Cord was not a man to deny her, and for the first time she tasted him as he had tasted her.

He tasted like coffee, and he also tasted the way he smelled, a little musky, dark and moist and intoxicating. He sucked at her tongue. She held herself tightly against him. A hand stroked her knee and moved to her thigh, and she felt heat building higher between her legs. Fingers slipped under the tail of her borrowed shirt. Instinctively she parted her legs, and when he stroked between them, she squeezed them closed again to capture his hand, wanting to hold it there forever.

When his tongue brushed against hers, then invaded her mouth, she didn't know where to concentrate, he aroused so many places about her body. Everything seemed to pulsate at once, and she felt her hips move in a rhythmic fashion, the memory of which would bring her shame when sanity returned.

For the while, she would revel in her madness. Especially in the mad way his hand managed to steal higher between her legs. She forced herself to relax and ease the path he had chosen.

She held herself very, very still, which took more control than anything she had ever done. She wanted to encourage him, to let him know she wanted whatever he could give her, not totally understanding what that could be but knowing it was right and inevitable.

She was wet in a way that had nothing to do with the bath water and everything to do with his touch. He broke the kiss, but he did not pull his hand away. She tightened her arms around him, burrowing her head into the crook of his shoulder, feeling his energy and his body heat, trying wildly to pull them both inside her as the pulsing he had started quickened.

She was barely aware of the noise on the porch and of the knock at the door. But she knew Cord was moving his hand, smoothing the shirt over her thighs and holding her close, as if he would protect her.

A small cry escaped her throat. All the blood that had been coursing through her rushed to her head and she grew dizzy, her face still pressed against the side of his neck. If she could have one wish granted her that moment, it would be to die.

The cause of her distress was brutally clear. They were no longer alone. She could feel the presence of someone else, maybe a dozen someones, and she forced herself to look up, to learn the identify of whoever was witnessing her shame.

A stranger not much older than she and not a great deal taller took a step into the room, dragging a large lump she recognized as a man. He glanced at the tub and the trail of water leading to the bed, gave one brief look at the couple sitting there, and looked away, shaking his head as if expressing regret for his intrusion.

He raised and lowered the lump.

"I found him skulking around," he said, keeping his eyes straight ahead. He spoke as if nothing he saw was out of the ordinary, his manner a kind of apology for interrupting the most private moment of Kate's life. "Sorry to disturb you, Captain, but I wanted to make sure you two were all right."

Cord mirrored his attitude. "You did right," he said, his voice thicker than usual but otherwise calm.

Kate disagreed with him, but she didn't think this was the time to start an argument. Reason told her it was the time to run, if only she had two good legs. What she had were two bare legs and two bare feet—she who had prided herself on her modesty. Not even Caprice had seen her so undressed.

The men in the room, with the possible exception of the lump, were far more worldly than she.

She dared a more direct peek at the newcomer. He had a lean, almost babyish face, dark brown eyes, and long yellow hair, which he bound at the back of his neck with a leather thong. His white linen shirt was full-sleeved and his trousers looked tailored for him. He was too pretty for a man, yet he didn't look soft. Not with that hardness in his eyes and the grip he had on the lump at his feet.

This had to be Lucky McKee. A man of many talents, Cord had said. Perhaps he was also a strange kind of blessing in a very strange disguise. She could not begin to guess what further shame he had saved her from.

The lump stirred and managed to look up.

Kate, who should have been rolling away from Cord's lap and pulling the cover over her head, felt too far gone in depravity to do anything other than observe.

"Tug," she said in surprise.

"You know him?" said Cord, in a conversational tone, as though he didn't have sitting on his lap a naked woman half-covered by a very wet, unbuttoned shirt.

She nodded.

Lucky tipped his hat, but didn't let go of Tug. Neither did he look her way. "I'm Lucky McKee, ma'am. You must be Kathleen Calloway. I'm sorry to interrupt."

"It's no problem," she said, wondering where all the calmness was coming from. Inside her was a turbulence that would put a thunderstorm to shame. Especially since Cord was casting a strange, watchful look her way.

He didn't know she was at her best in a crisis. And this was as critical a moment as she had gone through in a long time.

Maybe she was more worldly than she had realized.

"I hope he isn't a friend of yours," Lucky added.

"He's my foreman. Tug Rafferty."

"Then I'll get him cleaned up for you. Awake, too, if I can."

Tug groaned. Lucky grabbed him by the back of the collar and half-dragged, half-carried him back outside, closing the door softly behind him. He had to be outweighed by at least fifty pounds, but in the dragging and carrying, he didn't appear to break a sweat.

His departure was as much a shock as his entry, for now Kate and Cord were alone and no longer in the throes of passion. From being overheated to the boiling point, she went right back to being cold.

Easing her hands from Cord's shoulders, she folded them ladylike in her lap, remembered the partially open shirt and pulled it closed, gripping it so tightly that a grizzly couldn't have torn it from her grasp.

Her hair was wet, limp and dripping, her skin gooseflesh from the chill in the air, and her less than voluptuous body was bared where even strangers could see. It was not her finest hour. But she held her head up high.

"I'm sorry, Kate," Cord said. "I took advantage of you."

He spoke as if she'd had no say in what happened between them. But then, men always assumed they were in charge.

"I thought it was the other way around," she said. "I promise not to entice you again."

That shut him up. It shut her up, too, there being nothing else so absurd she could think of to say.

"How's your ankle?" he said at last.

With a start, she realized she hadn't once thought of it since he'd lifted her from the tub.

She concentrated on it now, which was easy since it started throbbing again as much as ever.

"Fine," she said.

He eased her from his lap and set her on the bed, then proceeded to take off his shirt, which, when compared to the one she was almost wearing, appeared relatively dry.

"Put this on. It was clean this morning. Right now it's the best I can do."

She was about to accept the offer when he jerked the shirt back, removed a small leather packet from the pocket, and tossed it on the table. She barely noticed what he did, so absorbed was she in looking at his bared chest.

Lots of muscle, a dusting of black body hair, and sleekness. Definitely sleekness.

He looked better naked than she did. It was a lowering thought.

Studiously keeping his eyes averted, he picked up a pair of buckets from beside the doorway and began to scoop out water from the tub. While he made trips outside, she changed shirts, then buried herself under the covers, propping her foot up on the pillow, taking care of herself. And watching him through slitted eyes when she thought he wouldn't notice.

When the tub was emptied, he dragged it outside, returning to stand in the doorway. She knew he was looking at her. But she did not return the look. It was bad enough breathing in the scent of him from his shirt without staring into his eyes.

He started for the bed; she held her breath, not knowing what she wanted him to do. When he picked up the wet shirt she had discarded on the floor, she tried to sigh in relief because he hadn't touched her. But the sigh came out pitifully weak.

Slinging the shirt over his shoulder, he closed the door, and she was alone. Tears began to burn her eyes. It couldn't be time for the monthly inconvenience. She wouldn't allow it. That would be a humiliation she could not bear.

No, these tears came from another source. She was not handling Cordoba Hardin any more skillfully than she handled T. J. Hadn't she learned anything from Jess?

Temporarily she had forgotten the lesson her father had taught her long ago: never was a woman more meant for virginal spinsterhood than she.

Chapter Fifteen

Cord concentrated on the hard-packed dirt behind the cistern. Earlier in the day, when he had attempted to turn the earth in preparation for a vegetable garden, the ground had resisted. It didn't dare resist him now.

An image of Kate sitting naked in the tub flashed across his mind, not for the first time.

Ramming the shovel into the soil, he lifted, turned, and rammed again.

She has short legs, he told himself, trying to find something to criticize about her.

Short but nicely shaped, all the way up. . . .

Wiping the sweat from his brow, he rammed the shovel into the earth again.

He felt her nuzzling against his neck for protection when Lucky walked into the room.

He scratched where she had nuzzled, as if he could scratch the memory away.

Protecting her was the last thing he wanted to do. If he had any sense, he should want to use her, then send her back to her father. Not pregnant, of course. He would never harm a woman in such a way, no matter who she was.

But he wouldn't keep her around. Never that, either.

He rammed and turned the soil again.

"Captain."

He looked over his shoulder at Lucky. "What is it?" he snapped, then caught himself and shrugged an apology.

Something close to a grin pulled at Lucky's lips. His friend did not smile readily. He must have finally found something amusing.

"Miss Kate's foreman has come around," Lucky said.

"Is he in with her?"

"He's still sitting on the front step, shaking his head. I hit him harder than I thought."

"He shouldn't have been skulking. Don't worry about it."

"I'm not."

Dropping the shovel, Cord splashed himself with water from the well and shrugged into the still-wet shirt he had given Kate for a short while. Given and tried to take back while she was still wearing it.

Carefully he buttoned every button, tucking the tail inside his trousers. The fabric clung to his skin. Kate's hands hadn't been clinging. Not even her damp hair—

"Let's go," he said.

"I'll hold back," Lucky said. "The talk will probably go better without me."

Among his many talents, Lucky bore a sensitive streak that he did not often show.

Cord grunted, rounded the house, and watched as Tug Rafferty lumbered to his feet on the porch, shook his head, and grasped one of the posts that held up the roof. Cord had not appreciated the bulk of the foreman before. But he wasn't surprised Lucky had made short work of their fight.

"You want to see Miss Calloway," Cord said, coming up behind him.

Rafferty glared down at him, then looked around hurriedly. Searching for Lucky. Cord doubted Kate's foreman would be in the mood for a rematch any time soon. Time would have to go by, confidence return—and then he would get taken down again.

"It's just the two of us," Cord said. "And your boss inside."

Rafferty's eyes narrowed, but he didn't say anything. Walking around him, Cord held open the door. "Miss Calloway," he called out, "you have company."

Inside, she muttered something he took as a welcome. Stepping aside, he gestured for Rafferty to enter and followed close on his heels.

Kate was sitting up in the bed, trying to smooth her tangled hair, her reddened eyes looking everywhere but at him. His shirt hung loosely on her shoulders, making her look small and young and all the more vulnerable.

Something twisted inside him. He had made her cry. He had made her do other things, too, although he had not needed much effort. It was an ungentlemanly thought, but she didn't bring out in him much that was gentlemanly.

Still, he had not thought to make her cry. No matter who she was.

"Tug," she said. "Are you all right?"

"He sneaked up on me," the foreman growled.

Cord doubted it. If there was ever a man who didn't need to sneak, it was Lucky.

"But are you all right?" she said.

Rafferty grunted.

"I brought some things from your father," he said. He glared at Cord. "And a message. I'm to make sure you're the one that gets it."

Cord suspected the delivery was to have been discussed and made in private, but it was a subtlety Tug Rafferty wouldn't recognize. He wondered just how good a foreman the man was.

The idea of a message made him glance at the table, and he cursed himself. The leather packet with Diana's letter was lying there. For the first time since finding it by the river, he had let it out of his possession.

Because of a Calloway.

He cursed himself again, this time saving a few curses for Kate, not caring how vulnerable she looked.

Tucking the packet inside his shirt, he went outside to find a leather-trimmed carpetbag sitting by the front door. Lucky again.

He took it back inside. "Is this what you brought?"

Rafferty grabbed it from him and dropped it on the floor beside Kate.

Unbuckling the leather strap, she opened the bag and reached inside, pulling out a lace-trimmed white chemise that looked too small even for Kate. She dropped it as if it were on fire; then, peering inside curiously, she rummaged through the bag's contents. But she didn't pull out anything else for the watching men to see.

Instead, she closed her eyes and sighed.

Keeping to his ungentlemanly ways, Cord strolled over and felt around inside the bag, pulling out a moss-green silk gown that was as far from Kate's usual cotton-and-leather attire as it could be.

"You won't be needing my shirts anymore," he said.

She slapped the gown from his hand, then sat back on the bed. "Where's the message?" she asked.

She had a way of getting to the point.

With a sideways glance at Cord, Rafferty pulled a folded and sealed piece of paper from his pocket. She ripped it open and read fast, then looked up at her foreman with a mixture of horror and disbelief, her not-so-good poker face showing itself again.

"Do you know anything about this?" she asked.

Rafferty shook his head, but the shake wasn't very convincing.

She glanced at Cord. "I'd like to talk to Tug alone."

It was not a request. For a small woman, she could come up with a voice and a tone that would make a boulder quake.

Cord went outside, the sounds of an argument following him down the steps. He would have stayed close to the front door and listened, but he knew that somehow, in some other way, he would find out what the argument was about.

No more than five minutes passed before Rafferty slammed out of the house. Lucky was waiting for him with his horse. His fed and watered and brushed horse, Cord was sure. His friend never took his violence out on an animal, a woman, or a child.

Without a word, Rafferty grabbed the reins from Lucky's hand and took off. Cord gave Kate a quarter hour before he went back inside.

The bed was covered with clothes as fine and fancy as the camisole and green silk—petticoats and more dresses, and a pair of stockings the color of Kate's ivory skin. Ignoring her father's largesse, she was staring into space, his message crumpled in her hand.

"A new wardrobe?" he asked.

Her eyes focused on him, and she looked ill at ease. He suspected her embarrassment was not caused by something that had already passed between them but by something new.

"They're not mine."

"Then you'll keep wearing my clothes."

A warning growl very much like that of a wildcat sounded in her throat.

"Miss Rebecca Netherby picked them out," she said. "I don't know her, and clearly she doesn't know me."

Something dark and ugly clawed at Cord's insides.

"Miss Netherby must be one of your father's women friends. He has them, does he not?"

A daughter loving and close to her father would have questioned his interest. Kate simply shrugged. "I imagine. He's a man." Slowly she raised her eyes to him, and he saw a look of such despair on her face, he forgot his own ugly thoughts.

"Look," he said, "I'm sorry—"

"Don't you dare apologize. You took advantage of me, but I didn't exactly scream for help." Her jaw squared and she lost the look of despair. "Be assured I will next time."

He wondered if she were stating a fact or wishing it were so. Once he had thought there would never be a next time, but he had been proven wrong. Around Kate Calloway, he was not in control.

Which meant he'd better get her away.

"If you can take the pain, I can bind your ankle and take you home."

She stared at the crumpled paper in her hand. "I know I'm a bother." She seemed to be thinking of more than just him. "Pain frightens me," she said, biting at her lower lip.

She was lying, but Cord let her talk.

"I guess I'll stay a few more days, if that's all right. I've got the clothes"—she glanced at them as if they were reptiles curling on the quilt—"so your shirts are safe. Just put me on the porch. I can sleep outside."

Meekness didn't suit her, any more than lying. She didn't do either very well. At that moment Cord knew he had to read the note. And that meant not pushing her to leave.

The chance did not come until the next morning, when Lucky carried her out to sit on the porch in the sun. As always, she had slept in Cord's bed, and she had slept alone.

After cooking breakfast, Lucky had spread a blanket by one of the posts, where she could sit and support her back, rest her bound ankle on a second, folded blanket, and sip at a cup of coffee.

Again he was showing his sensitivity, treating her as if she were a treasured friend, or a pet that needed care. It wasn't anything like his usual attitude toward women, which was either a much more personal kind of friendly or a polite, get-out-of-my-way restraint.

Good for him, Cord thought with more irritation than charity. And good for her.

She was wearing the green gown, which had fitted sleeves, a low, rounded neckline, and a tight waist. He caught a glimpse of the flesh-toned stockings and the lace trim on a petticoat peeking out at the hem. Soft black leather slippers covered her feet, and he wondered if her ankle was bothering her. Everything else about her was certainly bothering him.

But he did not ask. Instead, he watched her from the doorway for a moment, then went inside to change the covers on her bed. He found the note inside the pillowslip. Reminding himself she was a Calloway under orders from T. J., he read it fast.

Good girl for getting inside Cordoba Hardin's home. He's a man I am very much interested in, although I know little about him. Stay as long as you can. Find out about who he is, his money, where it comes from, why he is here. At my request, Miss Rebecca Netherby has selected a wardrobe that should aid you in your task.

I ask very little of you, Kathleen. Do this for me.

Not one word was there about worry over her injury, or sympathy because she was in pain. There wasn't even a comment about who was caring for the Calloway Ranch, a place he supposedly loved.

Too well Cord understood fathers who did not care about their offspring. Raymond Hardin had been a selfish bastard most of his life, but next to Calloway he seemed like a saint.

What Cord did not understand was her following orders the way she was, not cheerfully, not enthusiastically, but following them nevertheless. He had never done anything his own father had asked, not after age eight when he went to the orphanage and Raymond went back to the road.

Kate should have been furious at the way T. J. was using her. Instead, she had announced she would stay, and then she had put on one of Miss Netherby's gowns. He almost wondered if she had fallen on purpose. Her father certainly hinted at the possibility. And she was the one who had asked for the bath, then acted as if she were trapped without any clothes.

Who truly was the trapped one here?

Cord's mistake was that he kept forgetting she was a Calloway. Even if she was innocent of all that he suspected, she owed her allegiance to his enemy, a killer in Cord's mind, who wouldn't hesitate to sacrifice his only remaining child for some purpose yet to be determined.

Why was Calloway interested in him? Because he had sent Lucky to ask questions about the prominent San Antonio lawyer and landowner? It certainly wasn't because he was investigating a potential suitor for his daughter. That would have required unselfish thought.

It also seemed unlikely that T. J. remembered Diana's death, or if he did, Cord's connection to the incident. Maybe he had gone through so many such occasions, he got them confused.

Cord folded the paper and returned it to its hiding place, then backed away from the bed, leaving it the way he had found it. His own message in its leather holder burned against his chest.

Grabbing the rifle beside the door, along with several boxes of ammunition, he strode outside and down the steps. He didn't bother to glance Kate's way. It mattered not the way the dress fit her or how the green made her skin look golden, and it didn't matter that her hair was brushed and gently curled, its soft redness catching the light and making the long curls glow like sunset.

He didn't need to look at her to know how she appeared. His first glance had burned the image in his mind.

Lucky was standing in the area that might eventually hold a barn. Cord waved.

"If you hear gunfire, don't worry. It's just me

getting in some target practice. I feel the need to shoot something, and right now tree limbs seem the safest things around."

He felt two pairs of eyes on him as he walked around the cabin. He hurried past the well and cistern, past the horse trough he had built while keeping away from the cabin. When he came to Domingo laying out stacks of adobe brick, he kept on walking without saying a word. Like Lucky and Kate before him, the man watched his passage in silence.

Cord didn't stop until he was standing in the trees clustered near the small stream that ran close to the edge of his land a quarter of a mile away. The stream was a tributary of the larger Hondo Creek, and he thought it the most beautiful part of the ranch.

He wasn't looking for beauty now. He wanted to destroy.

Loading the Smith-Jennings rifle, he took aim at a thin branch hanging over the water fifty yards upstream. He fired and missed.

The trembling caused the bad shot. One reminder of T. J., and it returned. He wiped his brow and gripped the stock of the gun.

Kate the Duplicitous was another, stronger cause. Kate who did her father's bidding without understanding anything.

Perhaps it was time he let her know what all of this was about. It would be far more information than T. J. ever could have imagined when he wrote his orders.

"A long time ago I loved a child-woman named Diana," he could say. "In my ignorance I told her we must wait until vows were said before making love. Your father was not so fastidious. Except when it came to caring for her and their child. This he could not bring himself to do. He had a reputation to maintain, and she had acted like a whore."

T. J.'s daughter would not believe him, but that would not stop the revelation.

"She drowned herself."

Kate would be all sympathy, but still she wouldn't believe.

"After I found her, I went to kill him. But he had friends who held me down. In the street, for all to see. When I accused him of causing her death, he took the note she had left and read it aloud. Unfortunately, the note was ambiguous. I was the father of the unborn child, he said. The truth was there for all to hear. And he pistol-whipped me until I could not stand, even after the friends released their hold."

Cord had been a proud young man brought to public shame, and he had run. This he would also tell, the most shameful part of his story, but Kate would have long quit listening or even trying to believe.

He closed his eyes and felt the blows as he had done so many times before, in Mexico, in Spain, and now here in this idyllic spot, spoiling its beauty, as the memories spoiled everything.

Since that time, how many other women had Calloway ruined? What other sins blackened his soul?

The questions were the reasons for his return, along with the long overdue deliverance of justice.

If perhaps, under a barrage of detail, Kate

did begin to believe him, something inside her would die, the way it had died in him.

Where was the honor is destroying her so soon? He would leave that task to T. J. Calloway, after Cord had brought him to ruin.

Taking up the rifle once again, he fired and reloaded, fired and reloaded, again and again, until the ammunition was gone and the trembling along with it—and, too, a dozen limbs and a hundred leaves that had once hung over the beautiful stream.

Chapter Sixteen

Kate hated the deception. T. J. had no right to ask it of her. It was wrong. Cord deserved something better than a spy watching him. He might as well have put a serpent in his bed.

Two days of wearing Rebecca's clothes was driving her crazy. But the long skirts and petticoat covered her ankle, which wasn't very swollen anymore, covering the evidence that she could walk. If she had to, she could probably run.

It was best she didn't see Cord very often. If she did, she could imagine what she would say.

"How much money do you have?"

"Why?" he would reply, his eyes watching and unnerving.

"I just wondered." Airily spoken. "My father needs contributions if he's to run for governor in two years and he thinks you might be of some help."

Cord would stare at her as if she had lost her mind.

But she wouldn't be able to stop, not if the truth were to come out.

"That's why I'm still here," she would say. "It's the reason for the clothes. He wants me to learn all I can about you, and he doesn't think I dress the way a woman should. Especially a woman who needs to lie to a man and get away with it."

She was ready for the confession part of the conversation. The trouble was, Cord didn't stay around her very long, and never when it was just the two of them. It was almost as if he knew her purpose. But that couldn't be. She had kept the note hidden for a short while, and then she had tossed it into the fire.

The truth, the only truth she could see, was that he didn't like her very much, not for conversation and sharing confidences.

For groping she wasn't too bad, but she wasn't anything he couldn't resist.

All this was going through her mind while she sat on the front porch watching Cord and Lucky put together a coop for the chickens the younger man had brought from one of the neighboring farms. It was early, not much past dawn, but she had not been able to sleep, and apparently neither had anyone else.

Lucky set a smooth, steady pace. Cord was working fast, as if he had more energy than he could contain. Or maybe the energy was anger.

It almost looked it. This time she couldn't be the cause.

Of the two, Cord was more skilled with his hands. The observation did not come as a surprise.

He had already started putting together his herd, one bull and a half dozen cows, and she had overheard him talking to Lucky about a sow that would be needing a pen.

It wasn't much information to pass on to T. J.

This was not a problem for her. She didn't plan to tell her father anything. He already viewed her as a failure at so many things; he might as well add spying to the list.

She took a deep breath. It was time to tell the men she was leaving. She was about to lower herself from the porch to the ground and limp over to them when Cord stopped his work and started walking toward her, unbuttoning his shirt as he moved close.

She looked away. She wasn't interested in anything he had to show.

His long strides brought him to her side far too soon. She studied the tops of his tooled leather boots.

"You're not talking much, Kate."

Surprise made her look up at him. Something was glittering in his eyes that held no warmth. Anger. No, something closer to fury.

She dropped her eyes fast.

"Neither are you," she said.

"Don't you want to know what I'm doing?"

"You're building a chicken coop."

A less than brilliant response.

"I mean what I'm doing here, in Texas. I've got money, far more than I need to set up this place. That's something you ought to remember. I could live anywhere. Don't you want to know what brought me to this isolated land?"

This time when she raised her eyes, she kept looking at him. Again she wondered if he had read T. J.'s note. It was addressed only to her, but she doubted that would stop him.

"Your reasons and your money are none of my business," she said.

"That doesn't mean you don't want to know about them. I keep thinking you will ask, but you don't."

She dug her fingernails into her palms. He had read it. He must have. But she couldn't accuse him of it; that would bring everything out into the open. She wanted to get away fast, without a confession. She hadn't done what T. J. wanted, except wear the Rebecca clothes. If she was supposed to make Cord dizzy with desire, enough to reveal all, both the clothes and she had failed.

This morning she was wearing a blue calico gown that matched her eyes and came almost too low on her bosom for decency. Her hair was brushed and shiny and she had thought, despite her guilty conscience, that she looked rather nice.

She must be the only one who thought so. Neither man had bothered to compliment her, although Lucky had given her an extra long look. As far as she could tell, his partner didn't know she had anything on at all.

And didn't care.

Why was he so furious? As far as she was concerned, she had done no one harm, except herself. If he had any sense, he ought to find the situation laughable.

From embarrassment and guilt came a new sensation: vexation.

"If you're so intent on revealing all," she said, "how much money *do* you have? And what *are* you doing here? You're obviously not happy with anything you've done since coming to Texas."

And that includes almost making love to me.

"You're right," he said. "I haven't had a really pleasurable experience in a long time."

She felt as if he had struck her. Tears burned in the back of her eyes, but she would burn in hell before she'd let them show.

It didn't matter whether or not he had stolen a look at the letter; he had no right to say anything so cruel. She hadn't written it, and she hadn't done anything about the instructions it contained except change clothes.

She did not like Cordoba Hardin. Not at all.

She was about to tell him so when he took the steps in one stride and disappeared into the cabin. A few moments later he was out again, bare-chested, a clean shirt thrown over his shoulder.

Then he was down the steps and around the corner, leaving her alone. She looked around for Lucky, but he had disappeared. Wise man.

After his work, Cord was cleaning up. But not for her.

Slowly she lowered herself to the ground, tested her ankle, and found it strong enough to get her in the house and then get her gone. She hoped Moonstar was within whistling distance. One more night in Cord's bed and she would be a raving lunatic.

The steps weren't easy, but she was so enraged and hurt and intent, she barely paid attention to the pain. Inside the house, she started unbuttoning the front of her gown. Her shirt and leather skirt were around here somewhere. The Rebecca clothes she would leave as payment for the care she had received. Maybe Cord could find a woman to give them to, one who would do them more justice.

But the clothes weren't enough, not after all the trouble she had clearly brought him. He was getting a sow, wasn't he? The appropriate payment for her to send him was a big, fat, rutting boar.

She had the dress unbuttoned and was easing it down her shoulders when she saw his discarded shirt on the table. Picking it up, she thought about throwing it in the fire. Instead, she did something very foolish and very unplanned. Holding it close, she smelled the dirt and sweat embedded in its fibers.

Kate had worked with and around men all her life. Unlike Jess, she wasn't driven to fantasizing and erotic feelings when she was near them. As a lot, they didn't seem anything special—just a little more muscled than her and given to swearing more and chewing tobacco and drinking hard liquor when they got the chance.

They were certainly less sensitive to anyone

else's feelings. And most of them couldn't carry on more than a two-minute conversation without breaking out in a sweat.

Jess had always admired the difference. Not so Kate.

Yet here she was breathing in Cord's smell. And not his just-bathed smell, but the working one.

She was about to return the shirt to the table when something fell from a pocket onto the floor. It was the leather packet he carried with him. She picked it up, fully intending to put it back on the table.

Then she remembered how he had read her father's note.

You don't know for sure, her conscience told her.

For once, Kate didn't listen to her inner voice.

Opening the packet, she saw an often-folded piece of paper inside. Swallowing, she pulled it out. *Cordoba* was written on the outside in a feminine hand. The ink was faded, but she could make out the name.

Before her conscience spoke again, she spread the letter open. It was written in Spanish, a language she could quickly translate.

I am disgraced and must take my unborn child to the grave. Do not blame yourself, my love. I alone have brought about my destruction. May God forgive me for my mortal sins.

It was signed with a scrolled letter *D*.

171

She had no clue as to when the note was written, or where. It could have been in Spain. Or it could have been in Texas, a long time ago. Whenever or wherever, the contents were plain enough to understand. Cord had ruined a woman, probably someone young, and she had felt the need to take the life of herself and their child.

Had she followed through on what was in the note? Kate knew that she had; otherwise why would Cord have carried it with him for so long?

She felt all hollowed out and heavy at the same time, as if a huge weight had settled on her heart and crushed all the energy out of her. She hurt for the woman and she hurt for herself, although she had no idea why.

And as for Cord—

She didn't know how to feel.

"Were you looking for something to read? You should have told me. I could have found something more appropriate."

She looked up to see Cord standing in the door.

The light was behind him, casting a shadow across his face, and she couldn't read his expression.

But his words were cold and his voice hard, like the hammer he had been using at his work.

The letter shook in her hand. She tried to speak, but she didn't know what to say. In the terrible silence that stretched between them, she looked at the delicately written words once again.

"Come on, Kate, surely you have questions. Don't you want to know what this is all about?"

"Did she really—"

"Take her life and that of the infant? Yes. By wading into a river when she couldn't swim."

Kate swallowed a cry. "How long ago?"

"Eleven years."

"You were nineteen. And she was—"

"Sixteen. And you were, what, thirteen? Surely you heard about it. It happened in San Antonio."

"Jess and I had moved to the ranch. It was a year after Mother died." She couldn't look away from the note. "She was just a child."

"Not so much. She was woman enough to bear a child of her own."

Yours?

She couldn't bring herself to ask.

But she knew. Somehow she knew.

He crossed the room and took the paper from her, folding it carefully and putting it back in the leather packet, then setting it on the table beside his shirt.

"Her name was Diana Obregon. Apparently the name means nothing to you. Don't you want to know if the baby she took with her was mine?"

Sometimes he frightened her, so easily could he read her mind.

"You don't have to say the words," she said.

"Of course I don't. I am a ravisher of women. A destroyer. The truth is there to read on your face. You should never play poker, Kate. Everyone would know what you held in your hand."

173

He let his gaze slowly trail down the length of her and more slowly return to her eyes. Too late she remembered that the front of her gown was unbuttoned and pulled down on her arms, exposing the curve of her breasts and the lace-trimmed camisole that barely covered their tips.

She hadn't the strength to cover herself. It was difficult even to breathe.

"I see that your ankle is well," he said.

"It's—"

"Well enough to run? That's what you ought to do. I might ravish you as I obviously did Diana and then cast you aside. Would T. J. take care of you? Would he welcome our child? There's no need to give me an answer. Again, it's there on your face."

She closed her eyes for a moment. "This is something I didn't want to know."

"And I did not want you to. But it's what comes from reading other people's messages."

"I could say the same to you. So what are you going to do? Ravish me the way you've threatened? Maybe my father would have difficulty accepting an unwanted child, but he wouldn't let you get away with rape."

"Don't be too sure. Your sister Jessica found out just how safe she was under his care."

Kate cried out and stared up at him with a new kind of horror. "What do you know about Jess?"

"What everybody knows and chooses to ignore. And don't worry. You're safe from my unbridled lust. Unless you keep parading around half naked."

He kept throwing words at her like stones, bruising her in places he could never see, and she could come up with no effective defense.

"I was inside when I began to get undressed," she said, too limply to express the torment he aroused. "I thought I had privacy."

"So did I. Damn you, Kate, for getting involved in something that is none of your business."

He spoke coldly, without emotion, and that made the curse seem all the more profane. A terrible rage built in her, a rage against all the injustices men visited upon women, a rage for herself, for Jess, for the lost Diana and her child.

She struck his chest with her fists, and struck again, but he didn't move. Baring her nails, she went for his face, acting on instinct, little knowing what she planned to do.

He caught her wrists and twisted her hands behind her, pulling her hard against him.

"It's time I gave you something you can tell your father. Be sure to mention it's what you asked for by remaining here. A gentleman always gives a lady what she wants."

Chapter Seventeen

Kate knew she could not free herself by force, but she refused to be frightened, and she refused just as fiercely to be aroused. The rage gave her that choice.

"You read the message from my father." She said it as a fact, not an accusation. "What makes my sin so much worse than yours?"

"It's not. I would say that makes us well matched."

He spoke as if the idea gave him no more satisfaction than it did her. But he did not let her go, instead continuing to hold her close against him with her wrists imprisoned behind her back.

And he looked at her, solemnly, almost curiously, as if she were someone he had never seen before, all the anger and the scorn in him gone. The looking lasted a lifetime and drained

her of the rage far more effectively than anything else he might have done. When he bent
his head to hers, she didn't have the energy to
fight him, nor the will.

He kissed her, lightly, almost without passion, yet the kiss started a yearning within her
that was sweet and tender and at the same time
stronger than all the wild hunger he had loosed
in her before.

Stronger, too, than the anger and the sense of
being wronged and misunderstood. So many
extreme emotions, and all in the space of a few
minutes, left her dizzy.

Nothing made sense, nothing, beginning
with what she knew about him from his hidden
letter and ending with the almost sympathetic
look in his eyes.

"I told you that since my return nothing has
brought me pleasure," he said. "I lied." He kissed
her again, lightly. "This brings me pleasure."

He spoke haltingly, as if he had to drag the
words from deep inside. Had he been the devil
himself embracing her, she could not have
mocked him or argued, or even pulled from his
grasp.

"It brings me pleasure, too," she said. "And it
also frightens me."

"It should. It frightens me."

Cord frightened of her? That made no sense.
She had no power over him, and no will to do
him harm. Not really, God help her, not even if
he brought harm to her. She didn't know if this
feeling was her weakness or her strength.

"If I should make love to you," he said,

"admit at least to yourself that it would not be rape."

"How could it not be? We don't even like each other."

"Poor innocent Kate. You know nothing about how lust works against all other emotions."

He blew at her hair and kissed the side of her neck. She could not suppress a shiver.

"I like the secret places of your body," he said. "Here"—he kissed her neck again, pressing his lips against her throat and then the rise of her breast— "and here."

It was a gentle assault against which she had no defense. No one ever treated her gently. She did not know how to react, except to wonder if he could hear the pounding of her heart.

"You are not what I need, Kathleen Calloway," he said, "but you seem to be what I want."

He looked back into her eyes. "Or maybe I have it reversed. You've twisted need and want within me until I can't tell one from the other."

"I don't under—"

He stopped her with a kiss. Long and slow.

"Neither do I," he said. "But this I know. You're too expensive. I can't afford your price."

He let go of her wrists and cupped her face in his hands. This was the moment she should pull away from him. He had said hurtful things that made no sense. Expensive? She had made no demands upon him of any kind. Except that he leave her alone.

Cord was using her and rejecting her at the same time in a way she couldn't comprehend.

But he was doing something far worse. He was making her long for something she knew he would never give, and physical love had nothing to do with it.

And he was doing it gently, which made it all the more cruel.

She could not bring herself to believe he was a truly good man; she did not know if one existed anywhere. But he stroked her heart. And he made her long to brush the hair from his forehead and ease the pain in his eyes.

Except she couldn't. Because he didn't want her to.

He dropped his hands to her shoulders and began to adjust her gown. She looked away, and her gaze fell to the packet on the table, and she remembered the letter inside.

Once he had brought ruin to a young woman and an unborn child. Whatever had brought him back to Texas, she knew it was mixed up in that long-ago tragedy.

You're not what I want, he had said, and then, *You're too expensive*.

Pride took hold where common sense had failed. Pulling away, she finished straightening her gown, slipping each button in place with great and deliberate care. When she looked up at him, she did not flinch.

"You speak in riddles, Cord, and if I asked you to explain, I know you would not give me the courtesy of an answer. I apologize for reading your private message, but I thought because you read mine, I had the right. Which makes me as wrong as you."

"We're even, then." He spoke without expression, without moving, without any sign that what she said had any effect on him.

"Not quite. You are on your own land, and I am not. As you noticed, I am well enough to ride. If I can find my clothes, I would like to change into them and go home. I know the way, and it's early enough in the day for me to get there hours before dark."

"No."

"What do you mean, no? You don't want me around any more than I want to be here."

"You've forgotten one element in all of this. Your father."

"You mean I'm supposed to stay here because that's what he wants me to do?"

"Not exactly. He wanted a report on me, and he ought to get it. I'm taking you to town so that he can ask me for it himself."

Kate had thought she was confused before, but she hadn't known what confusion could be.

"He doesn't need a report. He was wrong to ask."

She ought to feel a twinge of guilt because she was openly criticizing T. J., but she had engaged in deception far too long. She wouldn't put herself on Cord's side either. All she wanted was to be free of both of them for a while.

Cord tucked the leather packet inside his shirt pocket. "Your clothes are in the chest under the bed. I'll get the horses ready and we'll leave."

He walked out, leaving unspoken the hundred protests she wanted to make.

Moving methodically, as if method would bring sanity to her world, she packed the Rebecca clothes and donned once again the plain blue shirt and leather skirt she had worn the day by the creek. The boots felt far more comfortable on her feet than the delicate slippers her father had sent, and the ugly black stockings far more serviceable than their flesh-toned thin replacement.

She was getting her way. She was leaving. Considering her father's demands of her, there was a kind of rightness in being taken to him. Not that she would stay for the confrontation between the two men. Cord would see soon enough that T. J. wanted him as a political supporter and nothing more. She was a detail that both of them could soon forget.

So why did she feel so desolate? Why did she feel so lost?

She was about to go outside when Lucky entered. He nodded at her, then went to the back of the room, where he took a loaf of bread from the shelf over the stove. He placed the bread on the table, along with slabs of dried beef.

"You'll need food for the ride," he said.

Slicing the bread thickly, he wrapped the slices and the meat in a heavy cloth, then tucked the bundle inside a saddlebag that had been left beside the hearth. He worked as if he had done such tasks every day of his life, and perhaps he had. He was a far better cook than anyone at her own ranch.

She thought of the way he had handled Tug Rafferty, with seeming ease, just as he had handled the packing of the food. Lucky was as much an enigma to her as Cord.

"The Captain is an honorable man," Lucky said, as if she had asked.

"Did you hear us talk?"

Lucky shook his head. "I know there was trouble between you. I saw his eyes."

"He says I show my feelings too easily. I didn't realize he did, too."

"You have to know what to look for." He stared across the table at her, and she was again struck by how young and handsome he was. And yet, in ways she didn't know, he was far older than she.

"I doubt if I'll be seeing him again," she said. "After he takes me into town, that is."

"Is that what you believe?"

"Very much. Except in passing, which will probably be inevitable since we're both in the cattle business. As for anything more personal, we've said all we have to say."

And done all they were going to do. But Lucky didn't have to know that. Already he knew too much.

"He saved my life in Mexico. I was surrounded by the enemy and he rode in and rescued me. He could have been killed."

Kate thought back to the day by the creek. "He likes to rescue people." And then she thought of Diana Obregon. "But not everyone."

She turned to leave.

"He's an honorable man," Lucky said. "This you should believe if you're to understand him."

"Honor is a quality that men speak of more than women. We have to be more practical. We are the givers of life and the nurturers. We have to survive if anyone is going to."

"No matter what happens, don't give up on him."

She didn't try to hide her surprise.

"I don't think he cares how I feel about him. It's clear how he feels about me."

She didn't wait for any more unexpected remarks from the strange man who was Cord's partner and friend. Putting her ankle to the test, she hurried outside and found Cord behind the house watering the horses from the trough he had built during her stay. Canteens of water hung from each saddle. Moonstar's white coat shone, and she looked well fed and cared for. The mare bobbed her head in greeting when her mistress came in sight.

Kate hurried over and caressed her horse's head, rubbing at a spot between the eyes where Moonstar liked to be rubbed.

"I missed you, girl," she whispered. Moonstar snorted in reply.

Feeling Cord watching her, she looked at him, and then at the blood bay gelding he rode.

"Does your horse have a name?" she asked.

"No."

"He should."

"Why? I may not keep him."

The remark disturbed her far more than it should have.

"Is there nothing permanent in your life?" And then she felt regret. "I'm sorry. I shouldn't have asked."

She thought a minute. "How about Sunset?"

Cord's eyes narrowed, as if he were studying

her more carefully than ever, and then he shrugged. "Very well. Sunset is as good as any other name."

Kate could have sworn the newly named Sunset bobbed his head in acceptance. She felt satisfaction. Here was one male she could please, even if he did have four legs.

"And the ranch. Haven't you named it either? Or do you not plan to stay?"

This time she did not apologize for the asking.

"It has no name."

This one came easier to her.

"The cabin was built the year Texas became a part of the United States. The Lone Star State, it's been called. How about the Lone Star Ranch? It suits you and the place."

"I don't know about the *star* part, but *lone* definitely suits."

They looked at one another for a moment. Lucky might be able to read what Cord was thinking by looking at his eyes, but Kate was lost. All she knew was that he looked unapproachable.

When she started to mount, she saw her hat tucked between the saddle and blanket, where he must have placed it.

"Oh, I forgot this." Twisting her hair on top of her head, she tugged the shapeless leather into its rightful place, then settled into the familiar comfort of the saddle. If Cord was watching, she didn't care. He watched everything she did, watched and judged.

He wouldn't have her around to watch for long.

Lucky came out with the saddlebag packed

185

with food. He handed it up to her, but Cord came over and took it. She passed it on without a word. He could feed her by hand if that was what he chose to do. She would eat, politely thank him as her mother had taught her, and count the hours until she could say good-bye.

After he had tied down the saddlebag, he went back into the house. When he returned, he was carrying the carpetbag filled with fancy clothes.

"I planned to leave that," she said.

"I've got no use for it." Cord glanced at Lucky, who was standing by the corner of the house, looking as though he had no part in the proceedings. "How about you?"

Lucky shook his head.

"It seems they are yours," Cord said as he strapped the clothes to the back of Kate's saddle.

She sat very still as he worked, being very polite. She knew what he was doing. He was ridding himself of all evidence she had ever been there.

They were close to two hours down the trail to San Antonio, with the sun halfway up the sky, when she felt other eyes on her besides Cord's. Someone was watching. He felt it, too. They were riding side by side along a flat, grassy stretch of countryside, but there was a wall of trees to the west behind which an army of men might hide. It was those trees that got his attention.

"Your gun's ready," he said, as if he were talking about the time of the day. "I made sure before we headed out."

"Good."

"Have you ever shot anyone?"

"Once not long ago I considered it."

His lips twitched.

"Then you should have no problem pulling the trigger if we should run into trouble."

This was when she should have been truly frightened, or angry, or alarmed. But she was turning into a strange kind of woman. She had felt far worse when Cord found her with his letter earlier in the day.

Suddenly she remembered Lucky McKee's words.

He rode in and rescued me. He could have been killed.

At last fear came, not for herself but for the man who rode at her side. He was complicated and secretive and usually not very likeable, but the world would be a drearier place if he were gone.

"Don't do anything foolish," she said. "Take care of yourself. I'll take care of me."

Chapter Eighteen

" 'Pears to be just the two of 'em. We can take 'em easy."

The bearded man spat a ribbon of tobacco juice beside his cracked and dusty boot, then squatted to a more comfortable position behind his cover, a thick, low evergreen that grew at the edge of the trees.

Close beside him, his smooth-shaven companion grinned, showing space between teeth the color of river-bottom dirt. "The woman's mine."

"Like hell she is."

"We can both have her. I want the first dip. You got the last one down in Goliad. By the time I got to her, she weren't barely breathing. I like 'em to fight."

Bearded One grunted.

Smooth Face stroked the barrel of his rifle.

Soaring Eagle watched them both from deeper in the woods. He watched, too, as Fire in Hair and the man beside her rode across the field of grass. He was the white man who had come to the stone house, the one who brought worry to Night Stalker. Soaring Eagle, too, saw danger in the man. But he rode with Fire in Hair and must be kept safe.

Behind Soaring Eagle, a half-dozen Comanche braves also watched and waited, but without the patience of their chief, or an understanding of the promise he had made to the woman.

But they heard the rattle of death that sounded in Soaring Eagle's chest each time he breathed. This, they understood.

"We got to get closer," Smooth Face said.

"We can shoot him from here," Bearded One said.

"She's got a gun, too. The way she's riding, like a man, she can probably use it."

"What if she is a man?"

Smooth Face grinned again. "From the size of her, she'd be a boy. I've had them before. I can do it again."

Bearded One spat again. "Let's shoot for the horse."

"That'd be a waste. Ours're plumb wore out. We got to move around closer, take 'em by surprise." He giggled. "The bastard'll be sittin' in shit by the time he sees us."

Again, Bearded One grunted.

Night Stalker came up behind Soaring Eagle and crouched low beside him. Like the other braves, he wore red war paint streaked across

190

his cheeks and down the part in his hair. The braids of his young man's thick hair lay heavily against his bare brown chest, and his knees did not make the sound of crackling leaves when he bent them, unlike those of his old chief.

Like Soaring Eagle, he watched the two men crouched in the shadows of the bush.

"They kill the white man and woman," he said, as if the killing were done. "We take the horses and guns."

He spoke low, using gestures to enforce his words. Too eagerly, Night Stalker wanted to make the choices, practicing for the day he would lead the people who remained in Soaring Eagle's once mighty band.

"I will decide what is to be done," Soaring Eagle said.

He took no time to remind the young brave that the woman was Fire in Hair and would be protected from harm.

Night Stalker knew. He pretended to forget.

The two white men who would do her harm stood and walked backward, deeper into the shadows, their small eyes on Fire in Hair and Stone Man.

The men were large, clumsy in the way of their people, and they fouled the air with an odor that would linger in the woods until the full moon.

They mounted their horses in the midst of the braves, but they saw no danger. Bearded One set the trail. If it continued as it began, the trail would follow the line of the trees, bringing the two into the path of Fire in Hair.

Soaring Eagle held back, knowing the plan

as if Bearded One and Smooth Face had spoken the words aloud.

Broken Hand, the friend of Night Stalker, the seer of visions, joined him.

"We must use our guns against these whites," he said. "If we do not, bad times will come to the Comanche."

The Comanche would find these bad times the rest of their days, but this Soaring Eagle did not tell his brave.

"We will use our guns. But against only these two."

His rheumy eyes stared at Broken Hand, and they did not move away until the brave nodded slowly.

At a signal from Soaring Eagle, a whistle like that of a bird in its nest, the Comanches mounted and followed their chief, their ponies making no sound that rose above the rattle he heard in his chest.

He raised a hand, ready to command the braves to attack. Suddenly the horses of Fire in Hair and Stone Man burst into a run toward the protection of the trees that lay in their path.

"*Ei-yiii,*" Night Stalker yelled.

Without waiting for the command of his chief, he rode past him, cutting through the trees into the open meadow. He raised his weapon to fire, but Soaring Eagle carried with him one last flash of the swiftness that had served him well all his life.

The swiftness flowed from him to his horse, and he rode like the wind after the rash young brave, blocking his path and swerving his pony away from the targets he wished to protect, into the path of Bearded One and Smooth Face as they burst through the trees.

"Injuns!" Bearded One shouted.

Soaring Eagle fired once across the meadow. The bullet found its mark, and Bearded One fell. The cracked boot caught in the stirrup, and his horse dragged him across the uneven ground. The horse, with its unwanted burden, disappeared into the trees.

Another shot exploded, this time from the gun of Stone Man. Smooth Face collapsed and bounced against the ground. He lay as still as the dirt on which he fell.

Another signal from Soaring Eagle, and the braves went for the horses of the fallen men. Even Night Stalker obeyed.

Soaring Eagle rode on toward Fire in Hair, halting when he could see the fear in her eyes and, too, the recognition and the beginning of relief.

Stone Man showed no similar sign, and his rifle shifted. Soaring Eagle stared down the barrel, and in the narrow darkness saw the bringer of death.

"No," Fire in Hair screamed.

She reined the white mare into the path of the man. Stone Man's horse reared, and the shot passed without harm over the head of the chief.

The three horses came to a halt, Soaring Eagle's horse a tree's length from the other two. Once before the woman had saved his life. She had done it again, and this time at risk of her own.

The mare turned in circles, and Fire in Hair brought her to a halt. "Soaring Eagle is my friend." The voice of Fire in Hair was broken, but there was spirit in it, too, and spirit in her wild, wide eyes.

Stone Man stared at the chief with eyes the color of a hot summer sky. His raven hair fell straight to a shirt collar the same black as his hair. His skin was not so dark as that of the Comanche, pale enough to be called white, but Soaring Eagle sensed that the same strong heart beat within him that beat within the Comanche chief.

The white man did not move his eyes from Soaring Eagle, even though the chief lowered his gun and laid it across his legs. He stared without emotion. The chief looked at him in puzzlement. He had no knowledge of white men who did not feel.

"Get behind me, Kate," Stone Man said.

Soaring Eagle had been told the white woman's name, but it sounded harsh to him. Fire in Hair carried no harshness within her. She was brave and good, like the wife of Soaring Eagle, the first wife, the one who had died long ago.

"No," Fire in Hair said, "I'm not moving. I told you he's my friend. No matter what you think of me, you have to believe I know what I'm doing. I promise, Cord, the Indians will not hurt us."

Stone Man stared at the woman, and then at the Indian he knew to be his enemy. Slowly he lowered his gun.

Fire in Hair smiled at Soaring Eagle. The wildness was no longer strong in her eyes, and the bravery had returned to her voice. But he still sensed the remains of fear within her. It would not soon leave her heart.

"Thank you for saving us from those men," she said.

Soaring Eagle saw the empty expression of Stone Man turn to disbelief and then disgust.

These were emotions the chief could understand. Stone Man had shot one of the outlaws. He could have shot them both. Soaring Eagle was not needed as a protector, any more than he could be trusted.

Such would always be the way between their two peoples. Stone Man was wise to understand.

Soaring Eagle felt the death rattle sound deep in his chest, where the air he breathed could no longer travel. A great sadness settled in his heart. He stared at Fire in Hair for the last time, and he returned her smile.

Then he reined away and rode to join the braves, who had done what he asked and gathered the horses of the two fallen men.

He would not stay with his people long. Like him, they knew his time had come. He would ride to a place high on a hill and await the final stroke of his heart. And then he would be buried, not with his horse as in the old days, but with the tail and mane. In these times of hardship, horses were too valuable to sacrifice in such a way.

So, too, was the gun he carried with him today. He would choose the lance he had carved when he was a young brave, and the bow and arrows, to rest with him in the ground.

He would become a part of the earth, and his

spirit a part of the sky. There was much consolation in this knowledge, yet there was a sadness in him as he rode, not for himself but for the people he would leave behind.

For all his strength and willingness of spirit, Night Stalker could not stay the winds of trouble that would plague the weakened Comanche tribe.

He felt sorrow, too, for Fire in Hair, who would not understand that he was gone. With his leaving, she would be left alone.

Stone Man wore courage and strength in the manner of the Comanche. But Soaring Eagle did not know if they were enough to save the woman whom he called his friend.

Chapter Nineteen

Kate and Cord took time to bury the bodies of the gunmen in a shallow grave, marked with stones in case the sheriff or, far less likely, a caring family wanted to move either of them.

In his usual manner, he insisted on doing most of the work. She kept busy gathering the stones. It was very important for her to keep busy and not to think. When they were done, with no biblical words said over the graves, they rode on toward town, Cord close at her side, silent and grim.

In her mind and in her heart, Kate was still back in the field, watching the armed men gallop toward them, waving guns, and then hearing the whoop of Comanches echoing over the thud of hooves.

She didn't know how Cord had felt, or how he was feeling now, except disgusted with her.

But she knew he would not believe her if she told him the truth—that her fear had been not for herself but for him. She scarcely believed it herself, and she certainly didn't know why it was so. The fact remained that worrying about him had been as instinctive as drawing breath.

A mile from the field of death, and still her heart pounded. Closing her eyes, she let Moonstar have her head. A scene of violence played out in her mind, of Cord firing at the Indians and they at him, of blood and fallen bodies, of Cord lying on the ground.

A small cry escaped her throat. Quickly she glanced around and saw him staring at her, solid and strong and unhurt. She swallowed and looked straight ahead, willing her imagination to leave her in peace for a while. Reality was bad enough.

They rode along the ridge of a deep ravine, and in the distance clouds began to form. The silence between them roared in her ears. If she talked, maybe she wouldn't think. Cord certainly believed she couldn't talk and think at the same time.

"Soaring Eagle really is my friend," she said, satisfied that her voice held little hint of her lingering terror. "I helped him once when he was injured, and I put out tobacco and salt when I know he's in the county."

She got no response other than one of the glances that told her absolutely nothing concerning his thoughts.

"I know Indians can be dangerous. I wouldn't ride around so freely if it weren't for him."

Again, no response, this time not even a glance.

She was about to launch into how she and Soaring Eagle sometimes crossed paths, when Cord reined to a halt, twisted in the saddle, and stared at her. His hat was pulled low on his forehead, but not so low that she couldn't see his eyes. For once she had an idea what he was thinking. As usual, it wasn't nice.

"I am truly relieved for you, Kate, since the chief obviously has influence with the other tribes around here. Are there any other special friends I should know about—an outlaw band for instance?"

At last the terror began to subside, replaced by irritation. It was a far more familiar reaction to his taunts, which, while irritating, weren't completely unwelcome. They weren't exactly soothing words and a gentle, comforting caress, but at least they slowed her pounding heart.

"You don't have to get sarcastic," she said.

"Maybe I do. I lost about ten years of my life back there, and you—" He shook his head in disgust. "Forget it, Kate. Just let it go."

He sounded like T. J., but she kept the thought to herself.

He spoke little the rest of the ride, except to indicate when they would take relief stops, mostly to care for the horses. In her mind she imagined a conversation in which he asked why she considered a Comanche chief her friend, listened and believed all she had to say, and then went on to comment about how brave she was.

Instead, she heard, "We'll stop here," or "I'll water the horses," and once, "Are you ready for food?" The latter was asked halfheartedly, and she accepted with an equally halfhearted nod. She still had her father to face. She would need her strength.

Four hours was a long time for so little talk, but still, she endured it. Across all those miles of trees and shrubs, of creeks and gullies and cliffs that lay between the newly named Lone Star Ranch and San Antonio, she knew he was watching for Indians and outlaws, protecting her as best he could.

More than once she wanted to reach out and touch him, to whisper his name, to tell him thanks, to say she understood how he had risked his life to save hers when Soaring Eagle rode down upon them.

But like him, she kept her thoughts to herself. She would have cut off her hand before she reached out to feel his warmth and his strength.

At last they came to a row of adobe shacks that marked the western edge of town. The sun, round and golden red, hung low in the sky, seemingly pushed down by the bank of dark clouds above it. In the lengthening shadows, a chill had taken command of the air.

"Where will we be more likely to find your father?" Cord asked. "At home or in his office?"

It was the first time all day that he had asked her opinion about anything; unfortunately, he chose a question she couldn't answer. She didn't know much about her father's day-to-day habits. On her few trips into town, she was always at home helping Caprice prepare for some social event, and then hiding out while the event wore on well into the night.

Maybe Rebecca Netherby could take over her hostess chores. Maybe T. J.'s disappointing daughter could stay at the ranch. Maybe she would never have to run into irritating men again. Except Tug. He would always be there.

It was a depressing thought.

Maybe Lucky would visit her. There were times when she had thought he was her friend. But mostly he belonged to Cord, if friends could be said to belong to each other. The way it was supposed to be between husband and wife. The way it never was.

"You don't have to deliver me in person," she said.

He glanced at the sky. "It's getting late. Let's try home."

He said it as though she had no choice.

At the street corners, he made the necessary turns, moving steadily and surely toward his destination, as if he made this trek every afternoon of his life. His face appeared carved out of wood that had been polished to a fine sheen. His hair hung straight to his collar, looking freshly combed, and she remembered how fine it felt to the touch.

But he wasn't completely rested and at ease. There were creases around his eyes that she hadn't noticed before, and his lips were a thin, tight line. If he sat any more rigid in the saddle, he would lock into place and have a hard time trying to dismount.

He was thinking about Diana Obregon. She knew it without his saying a word.

In the middle of feeling sorry for herself and being angry and wanting to run away, she suddenly realized that she had seen their situation only from her own viewpoint. No matter what he had done to bring about the girl's death, he had suffered. And he was suffering still, else why had he returned?

It had to be the laying of ghosts that brought him back to Texas. That was why he had bought land and sought to settle down. He was simply searching for peace.

And then she had ridden along, giving him no more peace than he had given her.

She thought of the way she felt when he held her, the first soft, protected wave of pleasure, and then the explosion of burning and wanting. She remembered, too, the sense of loss when he let her go.

"Did you love her?" she asked.

The question surprised even her. She hadn't realized any such idea was on her mind.

Cord kept his eyes directed straight ahead. She didn't get so much as a twitch of his lips.

"I'm sorry," she said. "I was thinking maybe it happened close to where we're riding. The river's only a block away."

She was only making things worse. At best, he would ignore her; at worst, he would tell her what she asked was none of her business and he would be glad to get rid of her.

"Would it make any difference if I said I loved her very much?" he said.

She covered her surprise with a shrug. "It would make a difference to you."

For a moment he looked at her, riding so close at his side. Like him, she sat straight in the saddle, but she forced her attention on the narrow dirt street in front of them. If there were other riders around, or wagons, or people on foot, she didn't see them. With the coming of night, she and Cord were alone.

Thunder rumbled in the distance. It was an appropriate sound.

"Let it go, Kate. However I felt, I'm not going to feel that way again. About anyone."

She blushed, so fiercely that she could feel the heat waves coming from her face. Why she had ever wanted him to talk, she couldn't remember.

"I didn't think you would," she said, too fast, then added, "Don't worry. I'll let it go."

He had rejected her plain and clear. She ought to shut up. She ought never to say a word to him again. So, of course, she hurried on.

"Anyway, it makes no difference to me. Whatever your attitude, it won't make me feel any better about myself."

If he had any sense at all, he would hear the sincerity in her voice. Apparently he did, because he didn't come back with a response. Instead, he kept riding in silence, down the quiet, lonely street.

Something seemed to be building inside him, something ugly and hidden. A sense of foreboding struck her. They should not be here. Trouble, bad trouble, lay in their path, worse than all they had left behind.

The ominous feeling was crazy. She was riding toward her father and her home, which should both offer refuge. But one thing she had learned in life was that what should be oftentimes never was.

Had she the power, she would have slapped reins and ridden out of town as fast as she could, praying that Cord rode close behind her. It was the day, she told herself, the brush with death, the long ride, the confusion he stirred in her heart. But she knew it was all that and something more.

A block farther on, she spoke up. "I need to leave Moonstar at the stable." It was a stalling tactic, but it wasn't a lie. She had to say it again before Cord heard her.

He nodded, and she led him to the small private stable where they boarded the Calloway horses, a short two blocks from the house. The stable boy met Kate with a smile, but she could give him no more than a cursory greeting as she handed him the reins. She knew the boy was staring at her and at Cord, then back at her, wondering what was going on. She could have told him she was wondering, too.

"I can walk," she said when the two of them went back out to the street, the gelding Sunset in tow.

Cord lifted her in his arms and set her in the saddle; then, with the carpetbag of clothes in one hand, he took the reins and headed back down the street. Either he was concerned about her ankle, or he wanted to be in control. The truth probably was a mixture of both.

She stared at the back of him, at the way his

hair lay against his neck, and the pull of the shirt across his shoulders, and the steady length of his stride. He looked tall and lean and lonely, and he said nothing, not even when they came to the house.

In the twilight the two-story, brick-and-wood home looked almost cozy, with lights flickering in welcome from the windows. A white picket fence ran across the front of the house, and there were beds of flowers on either side of the steps. On one of her visits Kate had planted the flowers, but it was Caprice who weeded and watered them and saw that they lived.

She looked at Cord, wondering what he thought of the place she seldom called home.

A horse and carriage were tied up by the fence. She thought through a list of possible visitors. It was probably Joseph Wharton. She almost welcomed the thought of his presence. At least he would be a friendly face, and with him nearby she could put off the inevitable confrontation with her father.

Cord put his hands on her waist and helped her to the ground. In the dim light she looked up at him, unable to think of anything smart or quick or impudent to say.

But she did have one request. "Do me one more favor, please. Don't mention the outlaws or the Indians."

He continued to hold her by the waist, standing between her and the house, making her feel protected, and she found herself leaning into him, keeping it slight, so that maybe he wouldn't notice.

205

"The sheriff will have to be told," he said. "Word will get around."

"I know what you're thinking. T. J.'s a lawyer. He'll hear. But he won't. He has a way of looking at things"—she struggled for the right words—"from a narrow perspective."

"Why don't you want him to know?"

Because he would make a big show of protecting his daughter and wanting her to stay in town and using the incident to further his own public image. In private he would criticize her for subjecting herself to danger when she knew how important she was to him. He wouldn't have to add the importance lay as a manager of his land and his stock, and as a hostess when a suitable occasion arose.

All this she could have told him. But it wasn't what she chose to say.

"I've already caused enough trouble. Let's leave the attack alone."

"If that's what you want."

He stared at her a moment, and she thought he might be going to kiss her. He didn't, but he continued to look at her. When she could no longer meet his eyes, she concentrated on the silver clasp at his throat.

"You've been very brave today," he said.

She felt as far from brave as it was possible to feel.

"I may not have mentioned it earlier," he added, "but I know of only one other woman who could have gone through so much and kept going without breaking down."

One other woman. It couldn't be Diana, although he had said there were no other women in his life. With a man like him, there had to be. The stupid thing was how his words hurt, at the very moment when he was trying to pay her a compliment.

"Ellie—" he began.

"Oh." The word was more a sigh.

"My brother's wife."

"Oh," she said with more spirit. "I didn't know you had a brother."

"Half brother. We didn't grow up together."

There was a finality in his voice that warned her not to ask more.

He straightened her collar, as though he were taking care of her for the last time, and backed away. Putting distance between them, he became another man—the grim, determined Cordoba Hardin she had often seen before, his body rigid, his eyes hard.

"Now it's my turn to ask a favor of you. Whatever happens inside, Kate, do not get in the way."

Before she could ask what he meant, he opened the gate and led her down the front walk, past the flower beds, up the stairs, and through the front door.

Chapter Twenty

When Kate and Cord walked into the entryway, Joseph Wharton was standing by the parlor door close to her father, looking as if it were his birthday and his gift had just arrived. For once she didn't mind the warmth of his greeting. It was far different from the expression on T. J.'s face.

His lips were pursed in the center of his full, gray-streaked beard, and his small brown eyes glowered at her.

He was furious. It was a far more common effect she had on men than welcome. An unwanted suitor and a Comanche chieftain were the only two she could think of who ever seemed genuinely glad to see her.

Do not get in the way, Cord had warned her. He should have told her in the way of what, and he should have mentioned how.

209

"What a pleasant surprise," Wharton said.

T. J. was not so gracious. "I thought you couldn't ride."

Kate could hear Cord stirring behind her. "I got better," she said hurriedly.

T. J. looked at her skirt and shirt, saving his harshest glance for her hat. "Where are the clothes I sent?"

Cord dropped the carpetbag on the floor. "Here."

He snapped out the one word. Kate glanced over her shoulder at him. He hadn't loosened up any, but his grimness had turned to the unreadable expression she was more accustomed to.

He was still wearing his hat; the eyes peering out from under the brim ought to set everyone he stared at to trembling. Whatever he was thinking, or feeling, was as much a mystery to her as ever, but he was putting out strong vibrations, like a wire pulled tight.

It was as if he had two people inside him, one gentle, one harsh, neither anyone she truly understood.

The sense of foreboding she had felt earlier sharpened into a clawing certainty that the troubles of the day had barely begun. T. J. gave no sign he noticed anything amiss, other than his daughter's unwelcome presence.

"You must be Cordoba Hardin," he said. He chuckled in his false-friendly way, once again the politician. "Forgive me for being so rude. I'm Thomas Jefferson Calloway, this wayward young woman's father."

Wharton cleared his throat.

"And this is an associate of mine," T. J. added. "Joseph Wharton by name."

Wharton was looking back and forth between Kate and Cord, as if he was trying to figure out from just observing whether anything was going on between the two of them. In a way he reminded her of the stable boy.

Her father showed no such concern. T. J. was nothing if not consistent.

"Aren't you going to ask how Miss Calloway's feeling?" Cord said.

Kate started and suddenly grew more frightened than she had been when the outlaws rode down on her.

Why was he talking like this? And how in the devil could she stay out of the way of anything when he was the one who brought her up? If only she could back up time and go outside and tell him he had delivered her as he promised and was free to leave. She should never have let him into her home—but then, at what point was she given a choice?

Pulling off her riding gloves, she tucked them into the pocket of her skirt. Her hands shook, and she squeezed them together at her waist.

"How considerate of you to think of my condition," she said, trying to keep her voice light, and added, very politely, "Mr. Hardin."

Thank him, get him out, then deal with what she had to face. It was the best strategy that came to mind. Not that she had much influence on what was going on.

Cord's hands, already shorn of gloves, hung

straight and steady at his sides. He was staring at her father with such intensity that he probably hadn't heard anything she said. He had other things on his mind, issues she couldn't divine. But she knew what T. J. was thinking: how much money could he get out of this man?

In truth, T. J., my ankle's almost well, but Mr. Hardin took advantage of me so you wouldn't want to take any money from him or solicit his support.

Cord wouldn't mind if she said it—he probably wouldn't even hear—but her father would be enraged, not by him, but by her, figuring somehow that she had been at fault.

"Kate is strong," T. J. said.

I've got good teeth, too. He might as well have been talking about a horse.

She looked back and forth between the two men; ignoring Wharton, finally settling on her father. It was clear she wasn't important anymore, merely a temporary point of contention between two men who had weightier matters to deal with. Somehow she had to separate them. She didn't know why, but it seemed the most important thing she could do.

"Could I see you alone?" she asked her father.

When he didn't respond, she added an almost desperate, "Please."

Brushing past Wharton, she strode into the parlor. With each step, her limp grew more pronounced, but no one made any comment. When T. J. joined her, after making a great show of apology to the other men—"You know how women can be"—she closed the door.

He jumped on her right away. "Kate, you're

behaving badly. We have guests, and you know how I feel about hospitality."

She was in no mood to defend herself or seek his approval, as she so often was.

"That was a terrible thing to ask of me," she said.

T. J. did not insult her by pretending to misunderstand.

"We can talk about this later. And please lower your voice. We wouldn't want anyone to hear."

"What difference would it make? Cord knows about the letter."

"You told him?"

"Of course not. I was too ashamed. But he knew I got it, and he saw the clothes you sent. He's not stupid."

"I did what any man in my position would do," T. J. said, straightening his paisley vest. "You were in a position to help me. I always need your support."

"I was alone with him out there in the country."

"It was my understanding that one of your former workers was present."

"Oh, yes, Domingo the chaperon. I don't think the good ladies of San Antonio society would think him adequate."

"You've never wanted to be a part of society, Kate. Be honest."

She felt the urge to pace, but that would show her limp all the more and make her look weak. Instead, she stood still and held her ground.

"You're right. So why send those clothes? And who is Rebecca Netherby?"

"Come, come, Kathleen. You forget who is the parent here and who the child."

"I'm a woman, in case you hadn't noticed."

He stroked his beard, and his small brown eyes stared at her thoughtfully. "Did Mr. Hardin?"

That stopped her. This was not an ordinary conversation between father and daughter, but then, with Kate and T. J., none of them were.

"He didn't ravish me, if that's what you mean."

"Did he show interest?"

"Since he slept outside, he was most interested in getting me back here so that he could reclaim his bed."

"Humph."

It was not an encouraging sound. If anything, T. J. sounded disappointed.

"So you found out nothing?" he asked.

It was all he cared about. She stared at him in disbelief as the bitter truth finally struck her. She'd been slow to understand, but she was catching up fast.

T. J. truly would not mind hearing that Cord had attacked her, or allowed her to seduce him, or concluded a successful seduction himself. To him, she was a commodity to be traded when she could bring the most value in return. He hadn't solicited her help in that letter; he had demanded her body and soul.

Her head reeled. Surely she was being too harsh on him.

She knew she was not. Wanting his love and approval all her life, she saw now she would

214

not get them, not in the way she wanted, with no conditions attached.

For some reason she didn't understand, she thought of Jess and of how she had been betrothed and of how things had turned out, Jess running, her former lover and fiancé shot dead by an avenging father. How different matters were between father and daughter now.

A profound sadness settled on her. And she began to lie.

Remembering the letter Cord carried with him, she said, "I found out nothing. Except he has a partner who knows how to cook."

The thoughtful eyes turned hard. "Didn't you wear the dresses?"

She took off her hat and shook out her hair, which tumbled in long curls against her shoulders.

"Look at me, T. J., really look at me. You can wrap me in ribbons and tie me in lace, but underneath all that I'm still Kate Calloway. That's enough for me, and it ought to be for you. Give up on Cordoba Hardin as a political supporter. He's got other things on his mind. And don't get that look in your eye. Those things do not include me."

He moved closer and stroked her hair. She flinched. Except to take her hand on occasion when someone was watching, he hadn't touched her in years.

"You have more to offer than you believe, if you would only take a little advice and try to change. Why, this very day Joseph Wharton brought up the subject."

He spoke as if somehow the attention of his fellow lawyer gave her a validity she didn't otherwise possess, as if she was nothing other than how she was perceived by men.

Too much had happened to her today. With the reading of Diana Obregon's letter, she had invaded Cord's privacy, and with his tender assault he had invaded hers, in a way she still did not understand. As if that weren't enough of a trial, outlaws and Indians had attacked. At every turn, Cord had scorned her.

Until tonight, for a moment. But that moment had ended far too soon.

And now her father was scorning her, too.

Maybe she ought to describe the first time she'd met Cord, tell in detail how he'd put T. J. in his gunsight and held him there for a while. But her father, consistent where she was concerned, would come up with an explanation that put the blame for the incident squarely on her.

She knew nothing that would refute what he said. T. J. wasn't overly concerned with the premonitions of her sex.

She wanted to scream. Instead, she evened her voice.

"Please excuse me." She tugged the hat back on her head. "I'm going to go upstairs and ask for a hot bath, and I'm going to let Caprice baby me as much as she will. Do what you want about Cordoba Hardin. You will anyway. What I say is of no concern."

She didn't wait for permission. Leaving the parlor, she caught the man who would be her suitor standing alongside the man who wanted

216

no part of her, an awkward silence hanging between them in the entryway. It had been too much to hope that in the absence of host and hostess, both men had gone.

Cord had removed his hat, and even after a day of hell, looked very much the gentleman—hard, unbending, untouchable for sure, and as dangerous as ever to her, but still a gentleman, a man of honor whose private torment did not show.

"Thank you, Mr. Hardin," she said, "for all your care. I have assured T. J. that you were always considerate and treated me with the respect that was my due."

It was close enough to the truth to satisfy any righteously indignant father, should there be one in the room.

Playing the polite lady in her slouch hat and split leather skirt, trail dust sprinkled liberally about her, she nodded to the three men and walked grandly up the stairs, past the purchased portraits of unknown men, and into the far-too-frilly bedroom she used when she was in town, giving no hint of how much the effort cost her.

Caprice was waiting for her inside.

"Help me get off these boots," Kate said. "I think my ankle has started to swell again."

Before she could make it to the nearest chair, or take Caprice's outstretched hand, she collapsed on the floor and burst into long-overdue tears.

Chapter Twenty-one

T. J. seethed with a rage that was hard to control, especially with the headache this new stress had brought on. The pain throbbed above his right eye, but he couldn't worry about it now, not with his daughter giving him so much trouble. She needed a good thrashing. If either of the two men with him knew how arbitrary she could be, and how disappointing, they would agree.

But it seemed an inopportune moment to bring up parental woes. He kept the rage to himself. Losing his composure would serve little purpose and might possibly bring great harm. Apparently Kate had not totally alienated Cordoba Hardin. After all, he had brought her home and, somewhat sharply, mentioned her well-being.

But she had certainly failed to charm him.

She wasn't Jessica. For a brief time, he had allowed himself to forget.

When she had disappeared at the top of the stairs, he gestured toward the parlor. "Shall we have some brandy? It's the least I can do for you, Mr. Hardin, after all you have done for me."

"Good idea," Wharton said, leading the way. "I've been worried sick about Miss Calloway since I heard of her accident. We didn't get the particulars of how it happened. Perhaps you could fill us in."

T. J. was about to speak up and say they should hold such questions for another time, but Hardin's expression suggested such a move would be unwise.

"Hear, hear," he said, filling glasses at a side table in the parlor and passing them around. "I suppose it was a simple fall."

Hardin waved the brandy aside. "Not so simple for her ankle. She fell on a creek bank."

"Kate's not the most graceful of creatures."

"It was understandable, given the uneven surface."

T. J. refused to allow the sharpness of the man's tone to discourage him. "Were you two together?" he said, trying not to sound too eager.

Hardin shifted his gaze from the brandy glass to T. J. He looked neither angry nor distressed, but there was something in his eyes that caused T. J. to stir restlessly.

"Only by chance," Hardin said. "When I came to her aid, she was gamely trying to stand. She insisted on it and did not readily accept my help."

Hardin sounded almost complimentary. Perhaps Kate had not been the total disaster he had feared.

"How like her," he said.

Wharton nodded. "She's very brave."

"Yes, she is," Hardin said. "Sometimes too much so."

He spoke with the firmness of conviction, and T. J. took heart. Even the headache began to ease. Always the cautious one, Kate must have been wrong about the inadvisability of approaching Hardin for support. The man did not sound distant in the least. Blunt-spoken, maybe, on the edge of confrontational, but that was probably just his way. As a lawyer, T. J. had often faced his kind in court.

He set the rejected glass back on the side table. "You are not a drinking man, Mr. Hardin?"

"Not tonight."

"I understand you're interested in our local politics," Wharton said.

"What makes you think that?"

The question was sharply asked. Wharton glanced at T. J., no longer sure of himself.

"Something our host said." Wharton took a swallow of brandy. "I must have misunderstood."

T. J. cleared his throat. Wise or not, the issue of politics had been raised, and he could not let it rest. It was clear Wharton was too spineless to pursue his cause.

"Let's not speak like weak women here, Cord. I trust I can call you Cord. Joseph and I both know you were asking around about me. It is common knowledge that I am interested in the governor's race two years from now, after Pease steps down. Tonight is not too early to seek active support."

"We need men who think the way we do," Wharton said. "Like our own new city government here in San Antonio."

T. J. finished his glass of brandy and took up the one he had poured for Hardin. He would have preferred talking in generalities, waiting to bring up specifics of his platform at a more favorable time, but Wharton was giving him little choice. The man was a fool. He should have asked him to leave.

"And how does the government think?" Hardin asked.

"Several of our officials are followers of the American Party," T. J. said. Might as well be honest. Hardin probably knew the truth anyway.

"Aren't they called the Do-Nothings?" Hardin asked.

"It's a terrible name," Wharton said. "It came about because wrong ideas have been put forth about the party, and there were those who felt they should do nothing until the truth was known." He chuckled. "Hence the name Do-Nothings."

"Tell me, Mr. Hardin," T. J. said, "were you born in this country?"

"New Orleans."

T. J. laughed softly. "I've been there once. It's close to the United States."

Hardin did not react to the small joke. The man clearly had no sense of humor.

"I didn't think you were foreign-born," Wharton said.

"Why not?" Hardin asked.

Always a sharp retort, always a question. It was one thing to be occasionally confrontational, but Hardin came close to being rude.

T. J. stirred uneasily. There was something about the man he didn't like, didn't trust. An unwillingness to bend, maybe. It was the best way he could put it. In politics, a man needed flexibility if he were to succeed.

But he didn't want the man to run for office. Financing a campaign would be political enough.

"You seem American," Wharton said. "Plain-spoken, sensible, you know."

Hardin's expression seemed to say he didn't know what the lawyer was talking about.

"Look," said T. J., "we've had a lot of new-comers flooding into Texas—hell, all over the United States—and they're bringing in elements we're not sure belong."

"Such as?"

Wharton spoke up. "Irish, Germans, Catholics for the most part. America wasn't founded as a Catholic country, and there's no reason for her to go that way now."

T. J. kept watching Hardin's eyes, waiting for something to show besides steadiness. He liked a man who was nervous. It showed he was unsure of himself. A man like that could be converted to almost anything.

"Perhaps you're not a religious man," T. J. said.

"Why would you want to know something like that?" Hardin said.

"You're absolutely right. Why indeed? A man's religion is between him and his God, though there are those who say the mark of any man can be found in what he believes."

"And what do you believe, Mr. Calloway?"

The question seemed innocent enough, but again T. J. caught the sharpness in it, only this time it was more pronounced.

"I believe in hard work and a church that lets a man worship in the manner of his choice. We don't need foreigners telling us how to pray."

"What do you pray for?"

T. J. lost his patience. "God damn it, Cord, we're not talking about what I believe. We're talking about you."

"*We* are not talking at all. You're doing most of it. You're a hypocritical bastard. But then, I knew that a long time ago."

He spoke so softly, it took T. J. a couple of seconds to realize what he'd said.

"See here, sir, you are a guest in my home, but you have no right to speak to me in such a manner."

"I've got the right, and I've got the will. Would you prefer we have our talk out on the street?"

"Mr. Hardin," Wharton sputtered, but one sideways glance from Hardin shut him up.

T. J. was not so intimidated. This time when rage hit him, he did not keep it to himself.

"I should have known what to expect from a man who brought my daughter home long before she was well. If I were a man of violence, I would demand satisfaction."

"You like satisfaction, all right, don't you, T. J.? But not the kind that comes with honor. Nubile young women are more your style."

Wharton gasped. "Surely you don't mean that, sir."

T. J.'s rage settled into a steady, pounding hate. No one talked to him that way. No one.

"I'll shoot you between the eyes, by God, if you do not leave here immediately."

"I thought pistol whipping was more your style."

With a roar, T. J. went for him, throwing all his bulk behind the attack. He drew back a fist. Hardin caught him by the wrist, twisting his arm until he thought it would snap. He went down on his knees, giving in, trying to make the pain go away.

It worsened. He tried in vain to catch a whimper in his throat. When he brought his eyes up to Hardin, he saw a revulsion that truly frightened him for the first time that he could remember. Hardin could break his arm and feel no regret.

But he didn't. Instead, he let go and T. J. fell back, sitting hard on the floor.

"Get out," he hissed.

"Don't ever come at me again," Hardin said. He settled his hat low on his forehead. "I will kill you if you do."

He left quickly, leaving the parlor door open and the front door as well, as if offering the humiliating scene for the world to view.

"Well," Wharton said with a shake of his head, "I've never seen anything like that. The man has clearly been misinformed."

He offered T. J. a hand.

T. J. ignored the offer. "You get out, too. And don't mention what happened here. To anyone."

"No, of course not, T. J. It's just that I've never seen anything—"

"Out!"

Wharton hurried from the parlor. T. J. barely heard the front door close, and then the sounds of the lawyer climbing into his carriage and riding away.

Slowly he pulled himself to his feet and tested his arm. The pain would be a long time in going away. It was something else to feed his hate.

With shaking hands, he brushed off his clothes and smoothed his hair, all the while letting the hate for Hardin build inside him. He had just cause. The man had bought land meant for the Calloway Ranch; he had spurned a Calloway woman, and treated her father with more contempt than he would have shown a slave.

For all of this, Cordoba Hardin was a dead man. The only issues in doubt were where and how he would meet his end. Most likely it wouldn't be soon. Such matters had to be taken slowly and with great care, much in the manner a man approached seduction. T. J. had never resorted to murder, not openly. He knew there was another method he could use to get his way. Once before he had played the part of an avenging father. He could most certainly play it again.

Already he was easing into the role. To think he had entrusted his daughter to the hands of such a scoundrel. She was upstairs. She needed to be told a few things.

He took the steps two at a time, his anger returning, this time injected with an air of righteousness. He slammed into her room and found her sitting in a porcelain tub in the middle of the rug. She was alone, but Caprice hurried in and handed her a towel to wrap around herself.

"You are never to see Cordoba Hardin again. Do you hear me? Never."

She blinked at each bellowed word.

Caprice moved closer to the tub, but Kate waved her away.

"I take it he turned down your request for money."

"Don't sass me, young woman. The man's a bastard. He is never to set foot in this house again. Trust me, I'm doing this for your own good."

With that, he whirled and went back downstairs to pour himself another glass of brandy, and then another. He took the decanter to his desk and settled heavily into his chair. Minutes ticked by on the mantel clock. He rubbed at his right temple. The rage was slow to leave.

Gradually the liquor mellowed him and allowed him to think. He had lost his temper far too much tonight. He needed to make amends.

But not, of course, where Hardin was concerned. For a moment, he wondered about the man's comment on nubile women. Could he know something? No, he was simply guessing. Many men of fifty and older preferred the tender flesh of maidenhood.

It was Kate he needed to assuage. He had been harsh with her, too blunt, letting her know what he had wanted to happen. Kate was a simpleton when it came to sex. She wasn't Jess—wild, fun-loving Jess, who had been like her father in her approach to life.

T. J. felt a tightness in his chest, the tightness that always came when he remembered his younger daughter. Sometimes he thought that maybe the wrong girl had died, but that was a monstrous thought, and he wasn't a monster. He simply saw the way of the world and made certain of his place in it. There was nothing wrong with that.

Poor Kate. She might even have formed an attachment to Hardin. It was hard to believe, but he had to consider all the possibilities.

The complexities between men and women were more than she could handle. Whatever his faults, Hardin was no doubt a man of appetites, and there was nothing about Kathleen Calloway to satisfy him.

No, the whole idea of Kate seducing him had been in error. She was owed an apology—she would see it that way—but the manner of it must be carefully chosen. T. J. needed her too much for further alienation. She would come around. She always did.

He was meditating over his approach when she walked into the room. She was wearing her plain white wrapper, and her hair was damp. She had no sense of how a woman ought to look.

"Do you want to tell me what happened after I left?" she asked.

The girl had no subtlety. T. J. bit back a reprimand.

"He attacked me. I thought my arm was broken"—he cradled it carefully—"but it's only badly bruised."

She started forward with a soft "Oh, no," and then she backed away and looked at him in an unsettling, undaughterlike way. "Why? What did you do?"

Indignation would serve little purpose at the moment. He took a calculated risk in forming his reply.

"You were right. He knew about the contents of the letter, and like you he misinterpreted my request. I wanted you to make friends with him, Kate, that was all, and show him the strong, good side of us Calloways."

She folded her arms in front of her. "That's not what you indicated to me earlier. You wanted to know if he was interested in me as a woman. Nothing was said about being his friend."

"Tsk, tsk, Kate. You judge me too harshly. I failed to make myself clear. Naturally, as a parent, I was concerned that nothing untoward occurred when you two were alone."

"Oh, T. J.," she said with a sigh, "getting a straight answer out of you is like uncurling the springs on a wagon. You still haven't told me why this—this alleged attack."

Spoken like a lawyer's daughter. It was clear she listened to him some of the time. A tug of affection warmed him. He must not forget that his blood ran in her veins.

"He said unkind things about you."

Kate's sharp intake of breath inspired him.

"Naturally, I came to your defense, but the man is twenty years younger. He grabbed me and shoved me to the floor." He stopped and shook his head. "I would prefer not to recall the details." He stared straight into his daughter's eyes. "But I can never forget what he said."

She blanched. "What was it?"

"He called you something no lady should hear."

"I didn't know you considered me a lady." She dropped her hands to her side and took a deep breath. "What did he say?"

He had to fight to hide a smile. He had her now.

"He called you a whore."

She gasped. "I don't believe it."

But he could see she almost did.

"Neither did I, not even when I heard it plain and clear. Oh, he didn't come right out with the word, not at first. But he said you were acting like a woman with something to sell and that I was the one who did the arranging for you."

"That could have meant anything." She sounded desperate, wanting to believe what she said.

"I thought so, too. But then he asked what kind of father I was asking my daughter to whore for me. You did not, he said, do a very good job."

T. J. was rather proud of that last part. It showed an inventive mind.

"When I tried to defend you," he continued, "the man became irrational. Ask Wharton. He'll support what I've said."

She looked away, as if he had slapped her, and there were definitely tears in her eyes. Perhaps he had gone too far. A shaft of pain traveled down his arm, worse than the ache over his eye, and he forgot the voice of conscience. He had not gone too far, not at all under the circumstances. If she had any thoughts about some kind of alliance with Hardin, she would forget them now.

"I regret telling you, but you wanted to know."

She hugged herself and stumbled toward the door. He had almost forgotten about her limp. Hardin had probably shoved her. It would be in character. But he would pay. He would most assuredly pay.

"I could call him out," T. J. said. "Hardin is too much for me in a wrestling match, but I'm still a fine shot."

"No," she said quickly, "please no." And then more slowly, "From his viewpoint, I guess that's what I am." She looked back over her shoulder, and for a moment she was the Kate he saw more often, the defiant daughter who questioned him at every turn.

"If you're lying to me, I'll never forgive you."

"I'm not lying. I swear it on my honor as an attorney and as a father."

She looked as if she wanted to say something, but she held back. She also looked as if she couldn't totally believe him. Still, the doubts were planted in her mind, and that was enough for him to play on over the next few days.

"Would you like a drink?" he asked as he poured himself another brandy.

She shook her head. "I'm going to stay here a day or two resting up, and then I'll be leaving."

"For the ranch."

"Not right away. It'll be a few days more before I get there."

He didn't have to ask her where she would be during the time. The place was one they never spoke of, but tonight the liquor had loosened his tongue.

"When did this come up?"

"I decided just now. But it's been in the back of my mind for a while."

"The place is a cemetery, Kathleen. Not a shrine."

"It's important to me."

"You're a fool, talking to a pile of dirt. Your sister's gone. Dead and buried. She's not there to listen."

"Sometimes she does."

"That's crazy talk. I don't want to hear it."

He glared up at her, but the liquor was beginning to take over, making her look out of focus. For a moment he thought it was Jess standing there, Jess with her rich brown hair and her wide brown eyes and the figure men had begun to notice when she was no more than twelve.

The focus cleared. He looked at Kate, and

then he looked away. "Haven't we had enough trouble for one night?"

"I never give you trouble."

"Like hell you don't." A mistake. He was supposed to be an indignant father. It was a role he must now play all the time.

"I'm sorry, Kate," he said, softening his approach. "It has been a long day. But you shouldn't cross me. I'm the father around here."

"I know. And I'm the daughter."

She spoke barely above a whisper, and he had a hard time hearing her. Not that she was saying anything important.

"Don't worry about my seeing Cord again," she said. "That's something neither of us has to worry about."

She started to leave, then stopped in the doorway.

"There's something else about Jess. She not only listens to me when I talk, sometimes I can hear her talking back."

Chapter Twenty-two

Cord stood on the bank of the San Antonio River and stared into the dark, slow-moving water. Around him all was quiet, the air still and thick with the promise of a storm.

On this first return to the river, he had expected the trembling to hit him, the way he'd expected it when at last he came face-to-face with Thomas Jefferson Calloway. In each situation he had remained calm, almost coldly without emotion.

Here, it should have been the worst. From this grassy slope, eleven years ago, a passerby, a stranger, had seen Diana in the water and pulled her to shore.

A short distance upstream, in a secluded bend of the river, he and Diana had liked to spend hours, just the two of them, holding hands, kissing, planning for the future. Cord had been hurrying to that spot, looking for her, when he came upon the man working over the lifeless form. He had never learned the man's name.

She had left her letter to him on the bank at the river's bend, where she knew he would find it. By the time he did, her father was with him. Like the rest of the world, he blamed Cord for her death. Eventually he closed the small shop he owned near the Alamo and was gone, as quickly as his daughter.

Cord had wondered if he would be able to find the right place on the river. On this cloudy night he had come to it as if guided by an unseen hand. But when he looked into the darkness, it was not Diana's face he saw but that of Kate Calloway.

Kate looking up at him with anger, with hope, with hunger, with all the emotions that played so clearly across her face.

Kate bursting from the parlor after the private talk with her father, thanking him as if he had truly taken care of her, then striding up the stairs as if her ankle were not paining her, her back straight, head held high.

Kate the brave, Kate the beautiful, though not in the traditionally pale, fragile manner most women craved. Kate pulsed with life, met with defiance those who threatened harm, explored with explosive hunger the possibilities of her womanhood.

He had never met a woman like her. But he could not forget who she was, daughter of the man who, if not Diana's killer, had brought her to her death. A man of vile appetites and vile politics, a man who craved power, a man who had to be stopped.

In the stopping, the daughter would be hurt.

On this riverbank, Obregon had cursed him. It seemed that the curse remained with him still. Worse, it extended to an innocent who had crossed his path.

The knowledge brought an anguish he did not understand any more than he could deny it.

He stayed by the river a long while, and then he took a room for what he knew would be a restless night. A storm struck around midnight, but the thunder and lightning were no more volatile than the images that tore through him. The next morning, with the weather now crisp and cool, he went out with a renewed vow to ruin Thomas Jefferson Calloway.

He began at the courthouse, where he went through deed records, ostensibly to check on a fictitious property he was thinking of buying in town, in truth seeing what Calloway actually owned. And whether he was as powerful as he claimed.

For the Medina County farm and ranch-land, he would have to go to the county seat of Castroville.

He found nothing but the deed to the house in which Calloway lived, and even that still had a mortgage on it. The office space he used near the courthouse was leased.

The clerk, a talkative young man who liked to brag about all he knew, watched him for a while, then offered additional help.

"We got us some fine opportunities right here for a man with money to invest," he said.

"Fine citizens, too," Cord said.

"Yessiree," the clerk said, and went on to name a few, none of whom meant anything to Cord.

"I'll need an attorney."

"Got those, too." Again, he provided names. Not once did he mention T. J., although Joseph Wharton was on his short list.

"There was one in particular that was mentioned to me."

"Now, you know, Mr. Hardin, I can't go around recommending anyone. I'm a public servant. That would be against the public trust."

"T. J. Calloway."

The clerk fell silent.

"Is there a problem?" Cord asked.

The clerk pulled at his string tie. "No, no. Around here, Mr. Calloway is as prominent as they come."

"But?"

"I don't know what you're getting at."

"You're holding something back. I can hear it in your voice."

"It's a personal matter. Now about that property you were interested in. Where did you say it was? I'll have to know exactly if I'm to help with a title search."

Cord took a handful of coins from his pocket, picked out a ten-dollar gold piece, and laid it on the counter. It was a considerable sum for anyone, a fortune for a young man starting out in the world.

"I assure you that anything you say will be

kept in the strictest confidence. It will also be appreciated."

The clerk glanced over his shoulder, stared at the coin, and slid it toward himself and into his pocket. Leaning close, he spoke in a lowered voice.

"A friend missed a payment on some land he was buying, planning on putting in a restaurant, what with all the new people coming to town. When he realized what he had done, he took the money to Calloway, who was handling the sale. He wouldn't take the money, said he'd already sold the place to somebody else. My friend found out he'd doubled the price."

"It doesn't sound as if there's anything illegal in what Calloway did."

"That's what I tried to tell my friend. But he checked the original bill of sale. He had thirty days to make up any missed payments. Calloway claimed he'd come up with the money after the thirty days, but he lied. Wasn't anything could be done about it. There weren't any witnesses to the late payment. He lost everything he'd already invested. That was in the original contract, something he hadn't noticed. Ruined him. He left town."

"Are there any other such instances of misdealing?"

"Could be. You paid for one, and one's what you got. If I were to come up with others, they'd cost you."

"I'll keep that in mind," Cord said.

Outside the courthouse, he thought about what he had learned. It wasn't much, but it was enough to tell him Calloway was a danger to more people than just naive young women.

He started to leave, but an idea drew him back inside the building, to the same clerk who had helped him before.

"About those lawyers you named. Is there one among them who is young, eager, idealistic?"

"Could be."

"Someone not connected to Calloway."

"As I said, could be."

Cord leaned across the counter and smoothed the lapels of the clerk's coat. The man started to back away, then looked into Cord's eyes and held still.

"Consider that giving me his name is your civic responsibility. As a clerk of the county, you do understand civic responsibility, don't you?"

He could see a protest forming, but the clerk seemed to think better of it and hastily scribbled down the name on a small slip of paper.

"The address of his office, too," Cord said, and got it. "I'll remember your cooperation."

The office was close to the courthouse, in a row of adobe buildings that dated back to Spanish colonial times. He spoke with the lawyer for an hour and left, satisfied.

Next he went to a bar on Houston Street, near Military Headquarters, where farmers and ranchers were known to gather when they came to town. Here he talked cattle, describing the Spanish long-horned breed that had long ago been the foundation of the Texas Longhorns, the Swiss Browns he had imported to his ranchero outside Seville in order to improve the breed, the feed, the methods he had used in handling and slaughtering the stock.

He even discussed the uses of cowhide, showing off his boots, the tooling on which had been done by his own hand. He promised to show a half dozen of the men how it was done. He meant it, too. It was clear to him now that he would be in Texas a while, and he wanted more than acquaintances. He wanted men on his side, should there be a showdown with T. J.

He talked, too, about the crops he would be planting, asking about the best seeds, the best soil, the best time for tilling and sowing. He stayed at the bar the rest of the day, drinking little, finding himself falling into the talk and forgetting about why it was taking place.

These were good, hardworking men with interests the same as his. He could almost forget he would not be settling anywhere around here, once he eventually started his real home.

He met the ones in particular Lucky had talked to about building the framework for a barn and made plans for the work to start within the week. In all the talk, he showed them he was not out to take over the narrow markets for cattle and crops. He was here to expand them. While he talked, he meant every word he said.

Early the next day, at the largest livery stable in town, he bought a horse and wagon and ended up hiring one of the stable hands to take it to the Lone Star. He had just finished buying supplies at a newly opened mercantile store, having made arrangements for them to be delivered to the wagon, when he was reminded of his true purpose. Calloway walked in with a young woman on his arm. Kate was close behind.

He stepped into the shadows at the back of the store to observe. The woman was fair-haired and ripe of figure, and very young, several years younger than Kate. Her dress was a deep green that had been carefully fitted to her body. When she looked up at Calloway from under a matching bonnet, she batted her eyes. Rebecca Netherby, Cord would guess, the female who had helped Calloway pick out Kate's new clothes.

Kate wasn't wearing them now, having stayed with her normal attire, adding a fringed leather jacket because of the chill air. The shapeless hat was back in place, hiding most of her hair. From a dozen yards away he could make out dark smudges under her eyes. She wasn't sleeping well.

"Mr. Netherby," Calloway said to the middle-aged man behind the counter, "as promised I have returned your daughter safely."

Whatever Netherby's response, Cord didn't hear. He was watching Kate. She was picking out a supply of food, cheese and crackers from a barrel near the counter, and a twist of licorice from one of the jars nearby. She thought a second and added a second twist.

She picked out other items Cord couldn't make out, mostly because he was watching the determined look on her face, the dark circles, the almost indiscernible limp as she walked.

"Wrap that up tight," she said as she

counted out coins for payment. "It's going in a saddlebag."

"Leaving for your father's ranch?" Netherby said.

Calloway turned for a moment from the upturned face of Rebecca. "It's where she ought to be going," he said.

Kate ignored her father. "I'll be heading out there, Mr. Netherby. In a couple of days."

She took the package and looked at her father. Cord could read nothing in the look.

"I told you I'll be all right. I've made this trip many times before."

"You ride back into town when you're done, before you go to the ranch. That way I'll know you've not come to harm."

He preened as he talked, the proud parent doing right by his child.

She looked at him without giving an answer and left the store quickly. With the Netherbys talking to Calloway, Cord followed undetected and watched as she mounted and took off down the road that led south of town. He waited until she was out of sight before riding after her.

What he was doing made no sense. She was free to ride where she chose. But she had a habit of getting into trouble when she was out and alone. She was none of his concern—that much had been established between them— but still, he rode after her. And he made sure she didn't know he was there.

South of town, the road flattened to a gently rolling terrain, and he had to drop back to keep from being seen, using her trail of dust as a guide. The landscape became more desertlike, with stretches of cactus-covered rises stretching out in either direction, and patches of live oak and mesquite trees. Occasionally an ox-drawn wagon passed, coming up from Mexico a hundred and fifty miles to the south.

When a stagecoach passed, stirring up thick clouds of dust, he had to pull over to the side for a couple of minutes, and then head out fast to make sure he didn't lose her. He kept thinking he ought to turn back, that he had no business doing what he was doing, but he still rode on.

She stopped by a creek once to water and feed Moonstar, but she didn't bother eating any of the food she had bought. Instead, after letting the horse graze beside the creek for a quarter hour, she was under way again.

When she left the main road for a lesser trail, he almost missed her, barely catching sight of Moonstar's backside as she galloped around a bend in the trail into a grove of silver-leafed oak. He moved slowly after her, watching to left and right. This was prime country for outlaws and Indians. He had already been through one attack with Kate; he didn't want another.

The trail came to an abrupt end in the middle of the woods at a run-down building that must have been built when Texas was still a part of Mexico. The roof was falling in, and the adobe walls were streaked and stained. A rusted-out washtub lay at the corner, and a half-dozen chickens squawked and pecked at the dirt.

Several horses were tied at the front, including Moonstar. The saddlebags Kate had brought with her were gone. Cord could make out a stable at the rear of the building. Laughter and the music from a concertina came from inside. A sign hung crookedly from a single hook over the front door, identifying the place with one word: INN.

He tied Sunset beside the mare. The ride had taken two hours. He took time to walk around, but he found nothing beside the inn that might have brought Kate to this unlikely place. The back door was blocked by a pile of trash and looked as if it had not been used in years.

She had to be inside.

He gave her a quarter hour to get to whatever business had brought her there, and then he went through the front door. The main room was thick with stale smoke and the smell of stale bodies and cheap liquor.

He saw about what he had expected: a straw-covered dirt floor, a few tables, a half-dozen men drinking or playing cards, and at one side, mostly ignored, an old man wearing a serape over his shoulders, his weathered hands squeezing at the concertina as he sat back in his chair, eyes closed, lost in the music.

The musician's skin was papery brown and heavily lined, and he had the high, sharp cheekbones of a Mexican *paisano*. He was good at his trade, but he wasn't good enough to bring Kate all the way out here.

And anyway, she wasn't in the room.

Two doors at the back of the inn were both closed. The rooms, he guessed, that made the place an inn. She had to be behind one of the doors.

No one paid attention to him. He was just one more stranger passing through. He walked up to the bar, which was little more than a long board resting on a couple of barrels at the side of the room. A few bottles and some glasses sat on the board. The bartender, looking very much like the musician only without the serape, watched him with little interest.

Cord nodded in greeting. "A short while ago a woman came in here."

The bartender shifted his dark eyes around the room. "I do not see her. Are you thirsty, señor?"

Cord pointed toward the nearest bottle. The bartender poured the pale liquid into a glass that hadn't seen soap and water in a while.

Ignoring the liquor, he pulled out a gold coin.

"This is too much," the bartender said. "You want the bottle, señor?"

"No. Take the money. I need very much to find the woman."

The bartender pocketed the coin. "If you wait, it is possible she will appear."

But Cord had wasted enough time. He started for the back of the inn. He was halfway across the room when one of the doors opened and Kate walked out, hat in hand, her coat and the saddlebags draped over one arm.

She was looking down and didn't see him at first. One of the card players staggered to his feet and stumbled toward her, muttering in Spanish about how it was time a woman showed up.

She was about to answer the man when she glanced past him and saw Cord. Her gasp was audible across the room. The laughter and the music stopped, and she stared at him with wide and terrified eyes.

"No," she said hoarsely, and then again, "No."

Before Cord could move, she ran past him and darted out the door, leaving him little choice but once again to follow.

Chapter Twenty-three

Kate ran, dropping everything she carried, taking no time to mount Moonstar. She had to get away. She knew nothing else, could think of nothing else.

She ran into the trees, fear and desperation giving her the strength to keep going, even when she could hear Cord crashing through the woods close behind. When she came to the muddy bank of a small stream, she slipped. He caught her before she fell.

"Let go of me," she gasped, struggling to pull free, but he held her tightly by the arms.

"No," he said, pulling her back onto the grass, away from the mud. She pushed at him as she struggled for breath.

"Kate," he said, and again, "Kate."

The sharpness in his voice got through to her and sanity returned. She quit fighting him. All the energy drained from her body. She stood limply in front of him, feeling his powerful hands on her arms, and at last summoned the strength to look up at the familiar set of his mouth, the coppery skin, the frown of displeasure, the bristled cheeks, the probing eyes.

A totally unexpected rush of anguish and yearning washed over her. She hadn't seen him in two days, two agonizing days, but it seemed a lifetime. He looked so dark and forbidding, stern and judgmental, poking into things that were not his concern. But all she could think of was how she loved him.

And hated him, too.

She grew dizzy from the thinking and the feeling. Nothing made sense.

He shouldn't be here. He'd washed his hands of her, had said terrible things to her father, enough to bring on a rage the likes of which she had never seen, and now he was following her, checking on her as though she had committed a crime.

She was wrong. One thing made sense—the hate. It was the love that was insane. Until this moment she hadn't realized how she felt. It shamed her and at the same time filled her with a warmth that threatened to explode in her heart.

She looked down. He must not read the warmth in her eyes. If he had said only half of what T. J. reported, he scorned her in a way that was especially cruel.

"What's going on?" he asked.

"You have no business here. I do."

"What are you talking about?"

"Men. That's my business, isn't it? That's what you told T. J. I figured you followed me to get more proof."

"What in hell are you talking about?"

"Let me go. I won't run. I'm so clumsy I might fall again, and we know where that can lead."

When he eased his hold, she rubbed at her arms. She took a backward step, too, but she did it slowly so he wouldn't think she was running and grab her again.

Looking around, she was surprised they had come so far off the trail. They were isolated from the world, just the two of them. For a moment she thought how wonderful that could be, if only matters were different between them.

"You were kind to me outside my father's home. At least, you talked kindly. Why did you tell him the things you did?"

She could see him stiffening and drawing back.

"Whatever I told your father was between the two of us. Stay out of it, Kate. You are not involved."

He spoke coldly, and it was clear he meant every word. In that, he wasn't very different from T. J. Sadly, it was her fate to connect herself to unfeeling men.

"I could tell you the same thing," she said. "You are not involved with whatever I'm doing here. Go away."

"No, not until you tell me what all this is about. What business? What proof?"

How dare he intrude himself on matters so

private she had never told anyone, not even Caprice? And certainly not T. J. Her father was the last person in the world she would tell.

No, not the last. That honor now belonged to Cord. The man standing before her could indeed have called her a whore. Maybe T. J. hadn't lied. How strange it was to love a man and not understand him at all.

"There are men waiting for me. Men who aren't afraid to stop what they start."

"I'm a little confused, Kate. You're trying to tell me you sell yourself?"

He sounded as if what she said was the most ridiculous claim in the world.

"Not to everyone. I'm very particular in certain regards."

She knew her hair was falling wildly about her head and shoulders, making her look as debauched as she was trying to sound. She ran her fingers through the long strands, pulled herself into a proud stance, and turned to leave.

"I don't believe you. This whole thing is absurd."

She stopped and looked at him once again. Tears burned in her eyes.

"Is it really absurd to think a man would want me? Really want me for more than just to tease? Am I too small? Too thin? Too anything? I know what it is. You don't think a man would be willing to pay for—"

He grabbed her so fast, she couldn't finish, his fingers working quickly, expertly, to unbutton the top of her blouse.

"Show me you're not lying. Sell yourself to me."

When he thrust a coin between her breasts, she drew back her hand and slapped him. He let her. Then he kissed her, and all the fury that had been building inside her exploded into passion, all control burned to ash.

She pulled him down to the grass and wrapped her arms around him, holding the kiss, afraid only that he would pull away, once again changing his mind. But this time he didn't pull away, except to take off his holster and gun and lay them to the side, but he did it so quickly, she didn't have more than a second to miss him.

This time he sucked at her lips so hard that he drew them into his mouth, and then he found her tongue. She shivered and ran her hands across his shoulders, catching the back of his hair in her fingers, the fine raven hair that gave him such a forbidding look.

He didn't feel forbidding. He didn't taste forbidding. Her heart sang because this time she knew he wouldn't stop.

"I'm not stopping this time," he said.

A nervous laugh rose in her throat. "You always read my mind."

He lifted his head and cupped her face. "How could I? I never know what you're thinking."

She stared at his lips. "I guess we don't know each other very well, do we?"

"Are you sure you want that to change?"

She answered by brushing her tongue across his lips.

He groaned, and with a smoothness that was both thrilling and frightening finished unbuttoning her blouse. Her chemise was the kind that tied down the front. He made equally quick work of the ties. When he saw the coin resting between her breasts, he flicked it aside and replaced it with his lips.

Kate felt innocent and ignorant and worldly, all at the same time, but she wanted him to think only that she was worldly.

"Don't let that coin get too far," she said, her voice husky.

"Please me and I'll double the price."

She didn't know if he was making a game of this, but she didn't care. Nothing he said right now could hurt her, not if he continued to do the things he did.

Which, of course, was exactly what happened, only he made things better. He ran his tongue across her nipples. He cupped her breasts with his hands and kneaded her flesh with fingers that were gentle and probing at the same time.

It was as though he couldn't get enough of the feel and taste of her. He made her burn everywhere, in places he hadn't touched, places she knew would not be ignored for long. She tried to unfasten the buttons of his shirt, but she wasn't nearly as smooth and sure as he. He helped her. She thanked him by kissing his throat and licking her way down to his nipple, tasting the salt on his skin, feeling the sharp intake of breath as she kissed him the way he had kissed her.

She was acting on instinct. This had to be the

way a worldly woman made love. It felt too right to be otherwise.

Cord wasn't quite so gentle when he unfastened the waistband of her skirt and slipped it down her hips, taking with it her plain cotton undergarment. He made up for the roughness by being quick. Suddenly she was lying beneath him with nothing on but her boots.

When he settled beside her and looked at all he had uncovered, she had to scream at herself to keep still. But her hips wouldn't obey. The redness of her private hair had always been as personal a concern as anything about her. She had thought that when she married, she wouldn't let her husband see it in case he might laugh.

Cord wasn't her husband. And he wasn't laughing. Not at the slight shifting of her hips, nor at the hair.

Putting one arm beneath her head as a pillow, he stroked down her side, all the way to her boots.

"I can take them off," she said.

"Don't you dare." She hardly recognized his voice.

When his fingers made their way back up her body, he took an inside path, easing up her leg until he came high on her thigh. The torment was too much. She could no longer make any pretense at holding still.

Shifting to her side, she kissed his chest, the only thing she could reach, and she draped one leg over his hips while her hands worked at the silver buckle at his waist.

He helped her. Gently, as if she was a treasure, he eased his arm from beneath her and finished unbuttoning his shirt, pulling it open before he eased his trousers down lower on his legs. He did not get undressed the way she was, but he exposed the parts he wanted to. She was too caught up in passion, and too struck with an unexpected tension to protest.

She knew what was going to happen, but knowing and experiencing it were a universe apart. He barely gave her time to notice that his skin was, indeed, a golden brown below his waist, before he was kissing and stroking her again. When he ran his fingers through her private hair and then between her thighs, she cried out from the sweetness and the shock.

"You're ready, Kate." Spreading her legs, he settled his body on top of hers and rubbed his hardness against her. "And so am I."

Covering her mouth with his, he started slowly to move inside her, and then with a sigh he thrust hard. The pain was sharp and unexpected, but she covered the involuntary jerk of her body by raising her hips and wrapping arms and legs around him in an embrace as strong as a vise.

He hesitated for a second and pulled back, but with a groan once again joined their bodies, and this time the entrance did not hurt so much. Rhythm seemed to matter very much in the pattern of movement he created. Nature helped her catch on. The pleasure she'd experienced when his fingers touched her was slow in returning, but then it was there, building and quickening.

Suddenly he pounded hard into her, shuddered, and with a powerful embrace gradually grew still. She was left wanting more. But she wasn't worldly enough, even in pretense, to let him know.

So she held him as he held her, and when he kissed the side of her face, she kissed the side of his. She knew a kind of joy because she understood without being told that she had brought him satisfaction. He hadn't done quite the same for her, not completely, but that gave her a strange kind of compromising pleasure.

It could just be that she was better at making love than he.

But of course, she loved him and he didn't love her. Therein lay the difference. Her pleasure was quickly gone.

At last he pulled back enough to look down at her. She waited for compliments.

"You should have told me," he said.

He didn't sound in the least complimentary. If anything, he sounded angry, as if she had done something wrong. She closed her eyes to hide the hurt.

Maybe she had made a mistake. But she wasn't about to tell him. Speaking at all was difficult, the way she was still shivering and tingling inside and wanting more of what she should never have tasted.

Instead, she took a deep breath. Whatever she said in the next few minutes would be the most important declaration of her life.

Chapter Twenty-four

Kate kept her eyes downcast. She found it very difficult to look at a man who knew so many personal things about her. In this regard, loving him only made the embarrassment worse.

Now was the time for a little of that hate she had felt a short while ago, but naturally, when she was most needful, it was gone.

"What is it I should have told you?"

Cord brushed the hair back from her face. "That this was your first time. That you were a . . . a maiden."

He was putting the matter as delicately as he could, speaking gently, softly, for the first time since she'd walked out of the back room at the inn. It was a tone she would have liked while they were making love.

For all his gentleness, he was still making an accusation. She would have denied her inexperience, but he spoke with such certainty that she knew he knew. She had done something wrong when up until the end everything had seemed so right.

"It was my concern," she said. "I didn't see why it was any bother of yours."

"Good God, Kate, I've always told myself I'm a man of honor, and here I've—"

He broke off, but not soon enough. She heard the disgust that had edged into his voice. With him, gentleness didn't last very long.

"I didn't realize this was just about you," she said.

She shoved him off her. This time he moved with ease, and she sat up with her back to him and covered herself with her arms. He touched her shoulder. She shook his hand away.

"That's not what I meant," he said. "You deserve better than this."

"It's what I thought I wanted. I'm beginning to understand how wrong I was."

He kept silent, for which she was grateful. It was very, very difficult to come up with ripostes when what she really wanted was to be alone to scream.

The only relief she got was an absence of tears. She had never been so dry-eyed in her life.

"Why?" he asked. "Why did you let me do this?"

"Didn't we do it to each other?"

"Not exactly."

He was mistaken, as he was so often, but she had no more energy to pretend she was strong.

"Don't worry about it, Cord. I'm not trying to

trap you, if that's what you're worried about. My temper got the best of me."

"That's what all that talk about business was? Temper? What is it exactly I'm supposed to have told your father?"

You called me a whore.

After what had just happened, she couldn't bring herself to say the words.

She stared at her hands. "He called you irrational. You said he'd used me to influence you." In a lower voice, she added, "You said I wasn't very good at being a distraction."

It was the closest to the truth she could get to explain the fury she had felt when she saw him. It had nothing to do with her panic, but it was the best she could come up with while she sat in a patch of grass on the cold ground wearing nothing but boots.

And nothing she said was a lie.

"Your father fights dirty, doesn't he?"

"He's not the only one."

He was silent so long, she wanted to look over her shoulder to make sure he was still there. But he was. She felt the tension in him, and the heat.

"Look, Kate, the trouble between your father and me goes back a long way, to when I was here before. He doesn't remember it, but I do. It has nothing to do with you."

But of course it did. In his fury, her father had made her a part.

"You wanted an explanation and I gave it to you," she said. "It's the reason I got angry, and then other things took over. If I have to explain those other things, you're not the man you pretend to be."

"They got to me, too."

If he planned to start in with the compliments, it was a little late.

She sat up straight. He'd looked at her naked backside long enough. He had, that is, if he was still interested enough to look. Until today, she had thought men liked virginal women, if she thought about the subject at all. Cord apparently would have preferred her more experienced. That way his honor would have been satisfied as well as his passion.

He had possessed her body. That would have to be enough for him.

"Could you give me a few minutes alone? The stream's right here. I'd like to clean up a little bit and get dressed. Then I'll show you why I rode out to the country."

It was a suggestion even he could not protest. She listened for a moment while he got dressed. It didn't take him long. All he had were a few buttons to contend with, a shirt to tuck in, and probably some grass to brush off his clothes, while she . . .

A glance at herself told her she had much to do. For one thing, she would have to wash off the spot of blood on the inside of her thigh.

Suddenly she realized how cold she really was, and uncomfortable, her bottom itching, her skin turning to gooseflesh. It was late October; ever since the storm of a few nights ago, the air had been chill. Strange she hadn't noticed until now. She made quick work of the bathing, settling for a splash or two of water, and hastily pulled on her clothes.

When she stood, he came up behind her and

pulled pieces of grass from her hair. She shook him off and without a word started in the direction of the inn. But she didn't go all the way there. Instead, she veered off in the direction of a low hill that sloped away from the trees, several hundred yards south. Cord matched her step for step.

"Your ankle's healed. Good." It was all he said on the trek.

There were other parts of her that were sore, including her heart, but she kept that piece of news to herself.

A few rickety crosses lined the top of the rise. There were other, unmarked graves, a dozen or so, and one small, incongruent marble headstone on which was engraved:

JESSICA ANNE CALLOWAY
September 24, 1835–October 18, 1853
May she at last know peace

She and Cord stood for a while before the headstone.

"T. J. says I come out here to talk to dirt."

"Have you ever considered moving the grave closer to the ranch?" Cord said.

"It was dug here. And here's where it will stay."

There was a better reason, of course, a perfect reason she could give him that would bring no argument. But if she told him, he would have other things to say. Where Jess was concerned, the opinion of a man, any man, was the last thing she wanted to hear.

A breeze ruffled her hair, and despite herself

she shivered. "Could you give me a minute alone?" she asked.

He stared at her a moment, then backed off and retreated to the foot of the hill. She watched him—she couldn't help it—but when he glanced back up at her, she looked away quickly, embarrassed, as if he had caught her doing something wrong.

Her eyes swept the South Texas landscape, vast and for the most part unoccupied by permanent settlers. It was scrub-brush country, both to the southeast leading to the Gulf of Mexico, and to the southwest down to the Rio Grande, to Mexico itself. Forbidding though the miles could be, she loved every one.

She loved Jess, too.

She stared at the slab of marble and thought about her sister, concentrated on her, trying to forget what had happened in the woods. But Cord had destroyed her peace of mind. She had to get him away from here, back to town, out of her life.

He watched her walk down to where he stood. There was an air about him that said he'd come to a decision. She knew in her heart that for her it boded ill.

"Are you all right?" he asked.

"Of course," she said and hurried past him.

"I mean really all right. I have to take care of you."

That brought her to a stop. She turned to look at him. He looked about as distressed as she felt.

"I thought you'd already done that," she said,

knowing as she spoke that she was being unfair. He hadn't done anything against her will.

He didn't flinch. "You know what I mean."

She looked down at herself, as though expecting some sign that she was different inside her clothes. But all was the same.

"You didn't break anything, Cord. Not exactly, but I don't think either of us wants to get into those particulars. You don't have to take care of me. That's ridiculous. I can take care of myself."

"What if there's a child?"

It was an idea that hadn't occurred to her. It hit her hard, and she took a step away from him.

"I don't think a baby's possible after just one time. And I promise you, there won't be another."

She didn't know which part of her statement brought the tight lines between his eyes. The lines gave the only hint that he was upset.

"You're wrong, Kate."

She held her breath. Was he about to declare he couldn't live without possessing her again?

"One time is all it takes."

She turned brittle. "We'll see which one of us is right, won't we?"

With that, she fairly ran the rest of the distance to the inn. Along the way she picked up her discarded coat and hat, and the saddlebags she had filled with supplies from her father's suddenly favorite mercantile store.

From her hitching post, Moonstar greeted her with a pair of rounded, curious eyes, as if she knew something had happened to her mistress, something bad. Kate hoped the loss of her maidenhood wouldn't be so obvious to humans. Having a smart horse was difficult enough.

She tied down the saddlebags behind the saddle and stroked underneath the mare's forelock. "I won't be long, girl. Then we can go home."

She meant, of course, the ranch. Not town, never town, when she was speaking of home. The stop in town would be for overnight, and only because she could get rid of her escort faster there.

T. J. had requested her visit, but he was just showing off for the Netherbys, proving what a devoted father he was.

Cord walked up behind her.

"Do you feel like riding so soon?"

It seemed both a caring and an insensitive question. She pasted on a smile. "Now that you mention it, I probably need to rest. Why don't you ride on ahead? I'll be fine. I've done this many times."

He leaned back against the post where his own horse was tied. "I'll wait."

Arguing would be a waste of time. She started for the door to the inn. He was right beside her.

She felt a return of the panic she had first felt when she saw him standing by the bar, a glass of rotgut whiskey in his hand. She could use a shot of that whiskey right now.

Going inside like this was probably a mistake. But she couldn't bring herself to leave so suddenly.

"I'll use one of the back rooms," she said as she hurried through the front door. "You absolutely cannot go in there."

She expected an argument, but she didn't get it. The smoke-filled room looked no different from when she had left it; the difference rested with her. She nodded to both the bartender and the musician, who had given up the concertina for the moment. The card players, however, kept playing.

She knew several of the men from past visits, but none ever gave her trouble. That had been established the first time she walked inside the inn. Occasionally a stranger came in, like the one Cord had seen approach her when she came out of the room, but all strangers got educated fast.

She gave the bartender a questioning look. He nodded. With Cord watching, she walked past the tables and opened the door to the room where she had been before. Slipping inside, she closed it fast and took a deep breath.

The room was as unlike the rest of the inn as it could possibly be. Swatches of needlework-covered cloth had been nailed in haphazard order to the walls in every conceivable place, concealing the drab adobe and wooden framework almost completely, and a rag rug covered the dirt floor.

A woman sat on a quilted bedcover at the side of the bed. She was wearing a loose-necked blouse and an embroidered skirt, as brightly colored as everything else in the room. She looked very much like Kate, except for her dark hair and unhealthy pallor, and the haunted look in her deep-set eyes.

"Hello, Jess," Kate said, and then added unnecessarily, "I'm back."

Jessica Anne Calloway managed a smile. "When you left, I didn't think I'd see you again for weeks." The smile died. "What's wrong? Did one of the men hurt you? I'll kill him if he did."

Kate threw her coat and hat on the bed. Sitting beside her sister, she took her hand.

"Nothing like that."

But she couldn't keep her secret, not from Jess. They had never shared confidences as children, but they shared them now. Jess was four years younger, but in many ways she was far older than Kate would ever be.

Experience aged a woman, as Kate was learning fast.

Dear, precious, fragile Jess. The story about her, the one believed by the world, was true up to a point. She had been betrayed by the man her father selected as her betrothed. A dozen onlookers witnessed the gunfight between the two men, and others had seen Jess flee. Reports of her subsequent rape, near the very place where she now lived, had been, if anything, softened. She had been brutalized.

But she had also survived and taken refuge here, where kinder men hid her, and when her body healed, she had earned her keep the only way she knew how. Kate had fought her plan and lost. The grave had been dug, the tombstone ordered, the lie sworn to until all doubt was crushed.

The easiest part of the ruse had been keeping T. J. away.

Since that time two years ago, she had searched her sister's eyes a thousand times for a sign of the fun-loving, optimistic young woman who used to be. But she was no more, the last remnants evident only in her artful endeavors with needle and thread. Jess saw difficulties as proof life held no hope; Kate kept thinking that if she tried hard enough, the problems in her life would end.

At the moment, still feeling her lover's hands on her body, Kate was thinking Jess might have the right approach.

"Cord followed me."

Jess drew in a sharp breath. "The one you were telling me about? He's out there now?"

"He followed me. I don't know why I didn't see him."

"He knows."

"When I left before, he was out there waiting for me. He followed me from town. He doesn't know about you. I showed him the grave, and that satisfied him as to why I'm here. I promise. Our secret's safe."

But Jess kept staring at the door, as though the world were going to burst through at any minute.

"Don't worry. He won't come in here."

"Lots of men come in here. They think they have the right."

She reached for one of the tightly wrapped cigarillos she had begun to smoke. Lighting it from the lantern by her bed, she blew the smoke away from Kate.

"Of course," she added, "most of them do have the right. If they've got enough coins."

It was a side of Jess's life that Kate could barely think about.

"Come back with me, please. Now."

It was an often repeated request, this time made more desperate by all that had taken place this afternoon.

"You don't give up easily, do you, sister?"

"In this, I'll never give up. Eventually, I'll get my way."

Jess laughed softly. "What exactly would I come back to? I wouldn't be like someone holy risen from the grave, and you know it."

"You have a skill. You've created great beauty in here, with only the few supplies I've been able to bring you. This room throbs with color. People will pay good money for work like this."

"Not when they find out who created it."

Kate could have told her they already did, in one of the fanciest shops in San Antonio. The occasional pieces of work Jess gave her went directly there. Kate was saving the money for her, anticipating the day when she decided to return to the world.

"I can't deny there would be talk," she said. "For a while. You know talk means nothing to me."

"Nor to me. But I don't belong in the life I once led. I probably didn't ever belong, but I didn't realize it. T. J.—"

She broke off and studied the ash on the tip of the cigarillo. At last she looked up at Kate.

"If I saw him again, I would kill him. And then I would be thrown into jail, maybe even hanged." She glanced around the small room.

"If I have to have a prison, this one is my choice."

Jess said nothing Kate hadn't heard before, but she still did not understand the abiding hatred her sister held for her father. She had always been the favorite, the beloved daughter. When she had run from the scandal of her broken betrothal, T. J. had let her go. For that, he should be harshly criticized. But never forgiven? He couldn't have known what would happen to her with the bandidos. Neither could he have saved her from the attack.

"Right now I'm not exactly fond of our father either. But I'm not ready to shoot him. And neither are you."

But she really wasn't sure about her sister. She had not been in a long, long while.

She was searching for a stronger argument when someone knocked at the door. She didn't have to ask who it was.

"I'll be right out, Cord." Hastily she crammed her hair up under her hat and slipped on her coat.

"You haven't eaten," she whispered, gesturing to the table where the food she had brought lay unwrapped.

"I'll get hungry later."

"You'll come back with me one of these days. I promise."

"Maybe." Jess studied her face. "Are you sure you're all right?"

"I'm sure," she said with more conviction than she felt.

She sighed in resignation. There was nothing

271

she could do but kiss her sister on the cheek and give her a quick hug before easing through the barely opened door and hurrying outside, drawing Cord away from the room, away from the inn, back into town.

It was probably best that she hadn't been given more time to talk. In another minute, she would have been telling Jess how much alike they really were, how she, too, had a lover who would bring her nothing but harm.

As feisty as her sister could be, she just might have come out of the back room and shot him between the eyes.

Chapter Twenty-five

Over the next few weeks, moving through the first half of a cold November, Cord threw himself into work at the ranch, seeding the tilled fields and helping with the construction of two adobe huts, one close to the main house, another—a rougher, dirt-floor *jacal*—out where cattle would eventually graze.

With the aid of two neighboring farmers, the barn had been framed. It, too, would be adobe, and sufficient to accommodate only a couple of horses and a milk cow, but he wasn't in the empire-building business.

Still, he worked hard. He liked what he did, and it kept him from thinking too much.

Thinking took him back to another stretch of countryside, to a hilltop cemetery, to an out-of-the-way cantina and whorehouse that called itself an inn. Mostly, thinking took him back to the bank of a creek where he had gone crazy and done the one thing that in all this undertaking he would regret for the rest of his life.

There was only one way to put it: he had ruined Kate Calloway. She didn't know it, but that was what it had amounted to. Worse, given the opportunity, he wasn't sure he wouldn't do it again.

The return to Texas had been in the pursuit of lost honor and of justice too long delayed. But he had ruined her without a thought to honor or justice. It mattered not that he had been misled into thinking her other than she was, or that she, lied to by her father, had purposely done the misleading.

And how had he behaved afterward? Had he cosseted her, assured her he would take care of her if she wanted, expressed regret for what had happened even though at the time it would have been a lie?

Nothing like that. In almost complete silence he had escorted her into town, and when she was inside her father's house—neither of them suggested he accompany her past her front door—he had ridden hard for the Lone Star, putting distance between them. He had not seen her since, nor had he heard from her. By now, she must have decided he was a thorough scoundrel. If she had a man around honorable and caring enough to defend her, he ought to be gunning for her debaucher.

But Cord was safe. Kate had only one person she could depend upon—herself. Should the worst come to pass and she found herself carrying his child, he feared her strength would be insufficient to protect her.

Kate's problem lay in the fact that she was two people, separate and distinct, and he never knew which one he was going to face.

The Kate he had first met—on a hill not far away, where he was contemplating killing her father—that Kate would be coming after him with her shotgun, and it wouldn't be to force him into marriage. Her target would be between his legs. This time she would shoot.

But the Kate who had lain with him by the creek was a woman meant for loving, not violence. She was the woman he had hurt.

Worse, he would hurt her again. Through her father. On a recent trip into town, Lucky had picked up a report from the young, idealistic lawyer he had hired weeks ago. The investigation he had authorized was moving along, tedious and slow, but still moving along. He felt like a bastard not letting Kate know. He had told Lucky, but he hadn't told her. He wouldn't stop what was already in motion, but still, he ought to tell her what was going on.

On a cold, misty morning shortly before the official start of winter, he was drawing water from the well, thinking about Kate despite his best efforts to keep his mind on work, when a familiar voice broke into the stillness.

"You want to talk about it?"

He glanced over his shoulder at Lucky. Like Cord, he was wearing a fleece-lined wool coat, but his hair was wrapped with a thong at the back of his neck, and his hat sat low over a pair of bark brown, always watchful eyes. With mist still hanging low, he seemed to rise out of the ground. Cord hadn't heard him approach. He seldom did.

"Talk about what?"

"Whatever's on your mind," Lucky said. "For a couple of weeks now I've been waiting for it to pass, but it doesn't look like it's going to. I know it's not the business with the lawyer. It's something more personal."

The fact that Lucky was talking like this, when neither man was given to intruding on the other's privacy, told Cord how far gone he had been in his musings. Like the morning chill, Kate's unspoken name hung in the air between them. But there were confidences no man could reveal to another—no decent man, and he still considered himself decent.

He hefted a bucket of water to the ground. "It's nothing that needs discussing."

Lucky shrugged. "If you change your mind, I'll be here."

He started to leave, then hesitated, taking in the adobe hut, which had been built beyond the cistern, fifty yards from the stone house, and the framework of the barn farther to the east, and then straight ahead, the hill beyond which lay the field where crops would appear in the spring. He saw it all without moving his head, just shifting the eyes, which was his habit.

"I've been doing some thinking, too. Joaquin and his wife moved in yesterday. We've got Domingo and Salinas in the *jacal*, and you and me bunking down in the house. You keep this up, and we're liable to have ourselves an empire."

"Is that what you want?" Cord asked.

"I'm here to partner you. I thought to point all this out in case you hadn't noticed. What with so much on your mind and all."

Lucky spoke with an innocent air that wouldn't have fooled a child. If he couldn't get at what was bothering Cord in one way, he would try another.

"I'm not after an empire. I'm moving on as soon as my business is taken care of."

"Ruining T. J. Calloway."

"I need more than one way to go about it. Call it insurance. The business with the lawyer may not work out the way I hope. I want a base of power, enough to strip Calloway of his authority. For that, I need authority of my own."

He wasn't saying anything Lucky didn't already know, but he needed to hear it again himself. Sometimes lately he had lost his focus. In Texas, still in its raw youth, ancestry didn't matter, unlike the way it had been in Spain, or even in New Orleans. Here, money was the one thing that talked louder than blood or guns.

Money and cattle. In this part of the world, the two went together.

With that thought in mind, after Lucky had gone on his way, Cord spent much of the day packing in supplies. The next morning he rode out with Domingo and Salinas, his newest worker from the Calloway Ranch, to round up a herd of cows from the bands of wild Longhorns roaming the South Texas brush country. Lucky stayed behind with the two other recruits from the Calloway, Joaquin and his wife Teresa, to start work on bricking in the barn.

They stayed away a week, returning with a herd of fifty feisty cows bawling to announce their displeasure at the capture, and even more the indignity of the branding that began right away. In Cord's absence, the barn had come close to completion.

He spent another two weeks working at building up a remuda, his stock of horses, supplementing the dozen wild mustangs he caught with some cow ponies bought from a wealthy Tejano at a ranchero farther south. The ponies were tame enough to put out to graze; the mustangs he kept penned in a newly constructed corral.

While he was adding on, he bought a boar for breeding to the sow he'd acquired weeks before, and a bull, too, to service the cows. Both the boar and the bull required separate pens. Neither the cows nor the sow gave any sign they were impressed.

Together with the rooster added to his collection of hens, he was ready for his stock to reproduce; the subject of reproduction was one that never completely left his mind.

On a blustery afternoon in early December, Lucky returned from town with a wagonload of supplies. Cord felt right away a tension in his partner. Nothing was said concerning its cause until the wagon was unloaded and the horse brushed and fed and secured in the barn.

Inside the house, with the fire crackling and the wind rattling the windows, Cord poured them each a cup of coffee. Lucky tossed another letter from the lawyer onto the table, which Cord ignored.

"What's happened?" he asked without ceremony.

Lucky did not pretend to misunderstand. "It's Kate."

Cord took a deep swallow of coffee, but he barely felt the heat that burned his tongue and throat.

"She's getting married," Lucky added.

"Good for her," Cord said right away, but it wasn't what he was thinking.

He glanced at the small bed where a lifetime ago she had slept while her ankle healed. An image flashed before his eyes, of a deserted part of a forest and of Kate lying beneath him, her hair a mass of gold-streaked red against pale green grass. Over the noise of the fire and of the wind, he heard the soft sighs and whimpering sounds that came from her as they made love. He had held her close, trying to protect her from the cold ground. And she had held him, too, her arms strong around him, her legs—

He broke off the image. In the past weeks, since leaving her in town, he had frequently fought specific memories, but they had never been as sharply distinct as now.

He felt Lucky's eyes on him. His cup shook, and he set it on the table.

"If you see her, pass on my congratulations. I hope she's found herself a better man than her mother managed."

"The fortunate bridegroom is a lawyer by the name of Joseph Wharton."

Impossible. Cord's lips twitched, the lone sign of his surprise. Wharton had to be thirty years older than Kate, a thinner, paler version of Calloway, a man of suspect politics who started salivating whenever he looked at the woman who was now his bride-to-be.

Kate vibrated with life, with spirit, with heart. He knew all too well her capacity for passion. The mourning for her sister proved she also had a great capacity for love. What reason could she possibly have for shackling herself to a man more than twice her age and half as alive?

He could think of only one reason. It came to him fast and sharp and with absolute clarity, the one explanation that he could accept. She had a reason, all right. For a woman, it was one of the best.

Fury exploded within him. He had been worrying about her, making himself sick, but at the moment all he could think of was getting his hands around her throat.

He checked his pistol and rifle resting by the front door and strapped on his holster. He was shrugging into his coat when Lucky spoke.

"Do you plan to shoot her?"

Lucky was standing by the fire as he spoke, cradling his cup in two hands, his eyes showing only innocence.

Cord took the leather packet from inside his coat and tossed it on the table. "Not unless she gives me trouble."

"Silver-tongued and friendly as you are, why would any woman want to do that?"

Cord let the closing of the door behind him

serve as his response. He was in the barn saddling Sunset when Lucky came in.

"I take it you're going to discuss wedding plans with her."

Cord tightened the cinch and slipped the rifle into its scabbard. "You might say that."

"She's a good woman."

Cord stopped. As successful as Lucky was at getting women, he had never heard him say a kind word about any of them, nor anything cruel, either. In fact, he never said much of anything about anything, instead taking life as it came.

Until lately. On a few occasions he had become a veritable magpie.

Somehow Lucky had guessed what had happened in the country. He had probably figured out what was going through Cord's mind right now. And he was coming to Kate's defense.

Cord looked at his long-time friend. "Kate's got her flaws." He did not bother to elaborate.

Lucky looked as if he wanted to argue, but he held back.

Cord flipped the reins over Sunset's head. "I'll spend the night in town."

"She's not there."

"But you said—"

"The marriage was being talked about. She wasn't around to do the talking."

"The ranch, then."

"That was some of the talk, how she was in the country when her betrothal was announced."

"How did you hear all this?"

"I buy the supplies, remember? Women don't seem to mind my listening to their gossip. They were the ones critical of her being where she was. The men didn't seem to care, mostly being of a mind to wonder how Wharton had come into such good fortune."

By the time he was done, Cord was only half listening to his partner's chatter. So Kate couldn't face people, could she? More than ever, he was convinced he was right about her purpose. She was ashamed, both of her condition and of the way she was dealing with it. All of this stank of T. J. Calloway. But she didn't have to go along with him, not in a matter as serious as this.

Cord was astride Sunset and out of the barn before Lucky could say anything more. Joaquin came out of his new home to watch him, but Cord was thinking too much about Kate to acknowledge him.

From the beginning he had known she would be a complication, but he'd had no idea how serious. He cursed himself for being a fool, more than he cursed her or even T. J. There were problems here he would have to work out, but he could see only one way to begin. And that was with Kate.

He rode hard, shifting his course when the terrain made it necessary, but mostly moving straight north. He had never been to the Calloway ranch house, but he had a good idea where it was. Kate had told him once he was not to come on Calloway property, but it would take an army of Texas Rangers to keep him off now.

He covered the distance between the two ranch houses in little more than an hour. Dusk was settling over the land, and there was a chill in the air that promised a frost, early for this time of year so far south in the state.

In the creeping darkness he could see a ribbon of smoke that drew him on. The house sat atop a hill where it could catch whatever summer breeze came its way. Too, the site provided a good view of anyone who might approach. From the base of the hill came the rippling sound of water over rock. Its hilltop perch also made the house safe from the occasional floods that struck after a heavy rain.

She was protected from just about everything. Except him.

The barn and a couple of smaller buildings were at the base of the hill. Cord reined Sunset to a walk as he rode past them. Tug Rafferty came out from the barn, accompanied by a pair of men Cord did not recognize.

"Hey, where're you heading?" Tug yelled out, but Cord kept on riding. He did not stop until he was at the front door. Dismounting, he glanced at Tug, who had come running up the hill after him.

"Take care of my horse," he said. "Miss Kate and I have business. We do not wish to be disturbed."

Tug grunted but did not protest.

Cord hurried up the front step and barged inside, dispensing with the formality of knocking and awaiting permission to enter. The door opened onto a big room filled with overstuffed furniture, none of it fancy, all of it comfortable in appearance. Kate stood at the side, poking at a fire that burned in an oversized stone fireplace. She was wearing the green dress her father had sent to the Lone Star, and her hair was loose, falling in red-gold waves against her shoulders.

When she looked at him with her thick-lashed blue eyes, he lost the edge of his anger. For all his thinking about her, he had forgotten how tiny she was, and how pretty.

Straightening, she kept a grip on the poker, and he remembered the way she held a gun. But she didn't speak, she just stared at him, and for a moment their eyes locked.

Shaken, he had to force himself to look down past the line of her neck and throat, past the swell of her breasts, to the waist still small enough for him to span with his hands.

"The baby you're carrying is mine," he said. "Forget Joseph Wharton. If you're contemplating marriage to anyone, it will be to me."

Chapter Twenty-six

The poker fell to the hearth with a clatter, and Kate stared in disbelief at Cord.

"Would you mind repeating that?"

"I said the baby—"

She held up a hand, but it was shaking so much she dropped it right away.

"I heard you the first time. I just couldn't believe it."

What baby? she wanted to scream, and even louder, *What marriage?* The two concepts shook her so much, the name of Joseph Wharton barely registered.

She hugged herself. Cord was probably thinking she was protecting their unborn child. A child that didn't exist. He had truly lost his mind.

A knock sounded at the door, and Tug

stepped inside. He looked at Cord, at her, and back at Cord.

"Sorry, Miss Kate. He was in here so fast I didn't have a chance to stop him."

She gave him what she hoped was a reassuring smile. "It's all right. I'm fine. If I need help, I will let you know."

Her needing help with Cord was definitely a possibility, but there was no one on the face of the earth who could provide that help except herself.

Once she figured out what was going on.

Tug muttered something she was glad she didn't hear, then went back outside, leaving her alone with Cord. A very grim Cord in his heavy winter coat and black trousers and the ever-present black hat pulled low over his eyes. He filled the room, and it wasn't with affection and good will.

Over the past weeks she had been telling herself she didn't really love him, that what she felt was loneliness mixed with awakening desire, or some such nonsense. It had sounded good to her in the silence of her room, when she tossed about in the night and tried to sleep.

When the monthly inconvenience came to call, she had told herself she was glad, joyous, deliriously ecstatic, and she had almost believed it.

Right now she realized how absurd all those arguments with herself had been. When he first strode into the room, she had almost leaped across the twenty feet separating them and thrown herself into his arms.

He looked so good, coming out of the night

like a dark angel, in a place he was forbidden to visit, striding inside in that commanding way of his, those incredible eyes searching only for her. For a far too brief moment, she had thought he was there because he simply couldn't stay away any longer.

But then he had made a terrible mistake. He had spoken. Harshly. Cruelly. And she had taken a better look at him.

Before this moment, she would not have supposed a proposal of marriage coming from him would hurt. In this, as in so many other things, she had been wrong.

No longer did she want to throw herself in his arms. At the moment, all she could think of was sitting down. She went for the nearest chair. He came across the room to help her, but she moved too fast for him. As she sank into the cushions, he hovered over her.

But of course he would. He thought she was with child, which naturally rendered her incapable of even the simplest exertion. Worse, he thought she was marrying Joseph Wharton to cover up their misbegotten tryst. It had taken a moment to work out all he had said, but finally it was seared into her mind.

Right now Cord seemed not in a mood to listen to a word about his being wrong on every count. Which was fine, since she was not in a mood to tell him.

She drew in a slow, deep breath, and then another, until she was satisfied that her mind was sufficiently clear. The next few moments would be all-important to the rest of her life. She wanted to call Cord a blockhead, and an insensitive one at that, but she chose a more subtle approach. She was, after all, the daughter of an attorney, and both her mother and Jess had taught her a thing or two about dealing with men. Mostly they had stressed the importance of not always telling the truth.

She stared at her hands. "How did you hear?"

"Lucky found out about the betrothal in town. I figured out the rest on my own."

"How clever of you."

She sounded weak. Cord would think it was because of the baby. In truth, most of her energies went into figuring everything out. T. J. must have announced she was marrying his friend and fellow lawyer, a man of considerable if not wealthy means, and a political crony with similarly misguided opinions.

When Cord had taken her back into town after—well, after everything—her father had found out they had been together for the afternoon. Though he hadn't known what had taken place, he was furious, a condition he stayed in lately whenever she was around. When she told him she would be staying in the country at least until the first of the year, skipping all the end-of-year festivities, he had exploded.

"What will people say if we're not together at Christmas?" was the essence of his argument.

"You can come out to the ranch. That way it will be just family."

It was a ridiculous suggestion, she knew, asking him to isolate himself with the only daughter he knew he had, but still, she had wanted to try.

And now this news of her engagement, which she was sure he planned to celebrate with more than one gathering of potential supporters, gatherings she could scarcely avoid.

Accustomed as she was to his anger over her behavior, she had never thought he would react like this.

And now Cord was accusing her of foisting their child off on an unsuspecting fiancé. Clearly, he didn't think much of her, any more than T. J. did.

As usual, when he upset her so much, she didn't want to cry. She wanted to scream.

The one thing she did not want to do was assure him he was wrong. That would put his mind at ease and send him on his way with the feeling that he had been noble and had tried to do the right thing.

If you're contemplating marriage to anyone, it will be to me.

How could he be so cruel? He might as well have plunged a knife into her heart.

Shrugging out of his coat, he tossed it, along with his hat, onto a nearby chair. The holster and gun soon followed. At least he didn't plan to shoot her should she disagree with his less-than-romantic proposal.

She forced herself to look up at him. "You have no business telling me what I will or will not do."

He kneeled in front of her. She shoved at him, and he sat back—awkwardly, she was glad to notice.

"You're stronger than you look," he said.

"Meaner, too."

She got up, stepped around him, and returned to her place by the fire.

"The more I think about it," she said, picking up the poker and returning it to its holder, "the more marriage to Joseph seems like a good idea. He'll be a good father. I'll admit when I first heard the idea"—five minutes ago—"I didn't like it at all, but it's growing on me."

She didn't know where the words were coming from, or the strength to deliver them so casually. But she liked the sound of them and she liked the tension lines between Cord's eyes.

"As soon as possible," she continued, "I will marry Joseph. Excuse me, Joey. He likes for me to call him that when we're alone."

With a growl, Cord came off the floor after her. Taking her by the shoulders, he turned her to face him.

"No, Kate. You won't marry him."

His fingers pressed into her flesh. In the many ways she had imagined him touching her again, she had never thought of anything like this.

"Take your hands off me, Cordoba Hardin. It's not seemly. After all, I am a woman who is spoken for."

His lips twitched. "I'm the one doing the speaking. Do you really think I would let another man raise my child?"

Kate hadn't thought she could shrivel more inside, but again she had been wrong. Cord wasn't thinking of her and what she was going through; he was thinking of his baby and himself.

"There is no way you can get me to marry you.

If you persist in this ridiculous cause, I will make sure right away that Joseph believes the child could very easily be his. If you don't know what I mean, let me explain it. Slowly, in terms you can understand. I will lie beneath him, much as I did with you. I do not think he will object."

At last he let her go. She turned and headed for the hallway and the privacy of her room, pausing only once to say, "Close the door after you, please. The house is warm and I would like to keep it that way."

As usual, he did not obey. He caught her in her bedroom, standing beside the bed, thinking how foolish she must look in the green dress that she had once scorned. But after she and Cord had been together, she felt a need to be feminine and pretty and as different on the outside as she was in her heart.

She dressed up like this only at night, when she sat down to a solitary meal. At the moment, feeling as though he'd caught her doing something obscene, she wanted to pitch all the new dresses into the fire.

Fortifying herself with a deep breath, she faced the man she loved.

"You won't leave me alone, will you?"

"No."

"You must not have gotten enough the first time we were . . . together. Or maybe it was more than you wanted. Which is it, Cord, too much or not enough?"

It was a definite growl she heard coming from his throat.

"You'll have to speak up," she said. "I don't interpret animal sounds too well."

In an instant he was across the room and taking her into his arms. "Interpret this."

He kissed her. Not roughly, not meanly, but with a restraint that took her by surprise and was her undoing. She could feel the emotions trembling in him, but he simply kissed her, his lips on hers, arousing feelings within her she had told herself she must not feel again.

She rested her hands against his chest, but not, God help her, to push him away. She simply wanted to touch him, to welcome a moment of tenderness.

And then she remembered all he had said, and she interpreted the kiss. He was wooing her to his way of thinking, gently, when demands had failed.

She broke the kiss and stepped away.

"Get out."

There was nothing gentle in the look in his eyes or the set of his lips.

"Not until we've settled what is between us," he said.

"It's already settled. I'm not marrying you, no matter what you say. We don't love each other."

She spoke only half the truth, but she didn't think he would catch the quaver in her voice.

"Are you in love with Wharton?"

"He has my best interests at heart. He will never be unkind."

"Is that what you think I will be? Unkind?"

She could tell him he wouldn't mean to be, but his civility, his care of her, would be far more heartless than outright abuse.

She didn't want him civil right now, or concerned for what he supposed was her condition, or anything that approached an act of kindness. He was looking upon her as his own personal charity and opportunity for sacrifice. The knowledge sent a shudder to her soul.

There was one way to bring out the beast in him. It was a lessen she had learned from Jess.

She began to unbutton her gown. "I'm going to bed. It's been a long day."

She shifted to pull back the cover and to fluff the pillow, and then she continued with the buttons, exposing the lace chemise she wore underneath. The light from a bedside lamp flickered across her skin. He watched as she stepped out of the gown and tossed it aside, leaving her in the chemise and a long white petticoat, and a pair of underdrawers that he couldn't see. Sitting at the side of the bed, she eased out of the slippers and rolled down the flesh-toned stockings, one at a time, before dropping them on top of her gown.

When she reached for the ties that held her chemise together, her fingers froze. She couldn't go on. This exhibition wasn't anything that the woman she knew herself to be could continue.

When she stood and started toward him, his intake of breath was as sharp as a log snapping in fire. When she raised her hands, she could feel the anticipation in him, and the heat.

When she shoved against his chest, she caught him by surprise, as she had intended, and he took a step backward. She continued to shove him until he was standing in the hallway outside her room.

"Go away," she said, not daring to look higher than the hollow of his throat.

Putting distance between them, she slammed the door, staring at the panel of wood that separated them, half expecting him to barge in again. But he didn't. Neither did she hear his footsteps walking away. She could sense his presence through the door. She could picture the look in his eyes and the tight pull of his lips.

Worst of all, she could still taste him on her lips.

She counted to ten in English and then in Spanish. Who was she trying to fool? Certainly not herself. And probably not Cord. She reached for the door to open it. If he was still there in the hallway, the night would go one way; if not, another. Either way would not be good.

He was there right where she had left him, the glitter in his eyes and the tightness of his mouth exactly as she had pictured them.

"What took you so long?" he asked.

What, indeed.

"As long as I'm already with child," she said with a shrug that belied the pounding of her heart, "you may as well come in."

This time when the bedroom door closed, they were both in the room. And she knew neither of them would be leaving for a long, long time.

Chapter Twenty-seven

Kate stepped deeper into the room, and Cord followed. She was not going to get away from him. Not tonight. Dressed in nothing but a white camisole and petticoat, her hair gloriously free, she looked pure and provocative at the same time. Mostly she looked provocative.

"You're sure of yourself, aren't you?" she said.

Right now he wasn't sure of anything except what the next hour held. All the tight reserve, the inner armor he had built up over the years, began to crack. It was as if he walked on land that shifted under him. Kate frequently had that effect on him.

She was Calloway's daughter, but he did not care. Tonight she was simply Kate. As if Kate could ever be called simple.

Her hand fluttered to her hair and then

dropped. He reached out and took it, pulling her close to him. She didn't resist.

Neither was she quiet. "This doesn't settle anything between us," she said.

"That's not why we're doing it."

"Then why?"

He cupped her breast, and through the thin cotton chemise he stroked her nipple with his thumb. She closed her eyes and took in a sharp breath. He pulled at the ties that held the undergarment closed. The lacing loosened and the white cotton parted, revealing the gentle swell of her breasts. Cord forgot honor, forgot retribution, forgot everything but the woman's body under his hands, and the strong heart that beat within her.

"Is this reason enough?" he asked.

Her answer was a quick, small nod, and then, as if the nod were not enough, she covered his hand with her own, holding him in place against her breast.

He remembered the way she had prepared for bed, as if she didn't know what her undressing was doing to him. He remembered, too, how she had regretted her actions, if only for a moment, and shoved him from the room, not trusting him to leave on his own.

Only Kate could ease out of her clothes and then turn coy, making him believe both the boldness and the shyness as part of her nature. It was a powerful combination. If she hadn't opened her bedroom door to him, he would have kicked it down.

A flood of passion rushed through him. Tonight they would both be bold.

His hands were sure as he finished undressing her. Hers were more tentative as she fumbled with the clasps and buckles and buttons that were part of what he wore. For Kate, he needed simpler clothing. For her, he needed no clothing at all.

When they fell upon the bed, both naked, he covered her body with his and kissed her, easing back to let his hands stroke her smooth, tender flesh. Before, the sex between them had been furtive, hurried, hidden in the shadows of the woods. Tonight he had to let her know she was his, and no one else's. For that, he must be deliberate, and thorough. He especially needed to be thorough.

Almost too late he remembered the child she carried, and he tried to pull away.

She caught his shoulders and pulled him close. He looked down at her fine features, at the sprinkling of freckles across her nose and cheeks, at the parted lips, and, last, at the heat burning in her eyes.

"I need to be gentle," he said.

"No, you don't."

She spoke sharply, insistently, and Cord decided to believe her. The only thing he really needed to do was make love to her right, bringing them both release.

He didn't do it quickly. Touching and stroking and exploring, he listened for the small, quick breaths, the barely heard moans that told him she liked what he did. He heard them often—she seemed to like everything—and he gave the moans back to her, letting her touch and stroke and explore his body in a way she had not done before. She was studying all of him with her hands and, sometimes, with her tongue and lips.

He had thought he knew the ritual of sex, but in her eager inexperience she taught him new pleasures. It was as if she were opening new doors for them both. He didn't know what to make of all that happened except to fall a little deeper under her spell.

Bringing her rapture became as important as satisfying himself, and after a while it became all that he could think of. Her sighs, her cries drove him wild. Her spirit, her eagerness, her excitement were as erotic as the silkiness of her flesh. Her body held a thousand secrets and she was revealing them all to him.

When their bodies joined, she climaxed almost immediately, and it was up to him to ride her hard, playing catch-up as he so often did where she was concerned. All he knew was the pounding of his blood, the surge of pleasure, the wild shout that filled the room, a shout he realized belatedly had come from him.

He stayed inside her a long while, unwilling to break the spell that enveloped them. The spell couldn't last—it never did—but then, never before had it been so powerful. She clung to him with more strength than he had known she possessed. Even on this cold night, their bodies were slick with sweat, and it was a long time before his breathing slowed and his pulse steadied to a hard, even beat.

When he eased away to lie beside her, she kept her hands on him and her eyes closed.

This had been a new experience for her, this coming to the height of pleasure. For him, it was also new. Never before had he been the first to show a woman what lovemaking could be, his preference being for experienced partners who knew what to expect, women who did not let themselves become involved beyond a momentary intimacy.

From the beginning, bedding Kate had been wrong, against all he had planned for himself, but he saw now that it was right, too. He felt warm inside, and joyous, as if someone were gently stroking his heart.

The only thing missing was talk from Kate, a reaction to what they had done, to what had happened to her. She lay beside him in absolute quiet, eyes closed, her hand pressed against his chest.

The silence got to him. He missed the sound of her voice.

"Are you all right?" he asked.

She nodded.

"It's harder than I thought to be gentle," he said. When she held her silence, he stroked her breast and down across her abdomen, adding, "I've never made love before to a woman carrying a child."

That opened her eyes. She also dropped her hand, quickly, as if his skin seared her palm.

"You're forgetting Diana," she said.

She spoke flatly. When he looked down at her, she averted her eyes. She was right. He had forgotten Diana, but not in any way she could ever imagine. Diana had never been with him like this. They had never made love. That pleasure had fallen to a bastard twice her age, a man without conscience, a man of evil appetites.

Kate's father.

Now was the time to tell her so, and more, exactly what he was doing about it. Which did not include bedding the bastard's daughter. Never that.

"Kate—" he began.

"I'm sorry," she said. "That was cruel of me. I don't know what made me say it."

She reached down for the cover, pulling it over her nakedness, all the way to her chin. When she looked up at him with wide, damp eyes, a smile flickered across her lips. It was as if she couldn't decide what emotions she was supposed to be feeling, or how she should behave.

"I should have told you how much I enjoyed what we did," she said. "But then, I was expecting you to say something like that, too."

She had a way about her that made him feel guilty; more often than not, he had no idea why.

This time he knew.

"I enjoyed what we did," he said. As soon as the words were out, he knew they were too little and too late.

"Good," she said. A brittleness had crept into her voice. She edged farther away from him, to the far side of the bed. "At least this time there were no ants."

"You mean the first time? I don't remember ants."

"That's because you weren't lying in the

grass. I didn't feel them either, not until afterward, when the bites started to itch."

"Why are you being so casual about what's happening between us?" he asked.

"I'm not casual. It's just that we both need to put this into perspective. We're sharing an intimate moment. I guess that's the way to put it. But that's all it is."

"So why are you gripping that cover so tightly? I'd have to cut it to get it out of your hands."

"I thought the intimacy was over."

"Not necessarily. Unless you want it to be."

"Oh." She gave every appearance of reconsidering the situation. "I guess I don't."

Cord was ready to follow her across the bed when he heard what sounded like footsteps in the hallway outside her bedroom door.

"Aren't we alone?" he asked.

"One of the women has been helping me inside the house. She must have returned for something."

Cord eased from the bed and walked silently to the door, jerked it open, and peered out into an empty hall. Remembering his nudity, he closed it fast and turned back to find a very interested woman staring at him from under the cover. She looked away as if she had done something wrong.

He came around to her side of the bed.

"It's all right to look, Kate," he said, "if that's what you want to do. I'd far rather look at you."

She sat up in the bed, letting the cover fall to her waist.

His body hardened. She didn't try to hide the interest in her eyes.

"Touching's all right, too," he said.

That was exactly what she did, but not in the way he had imagined. She touched him with her tongue, just the tip of his erection, and only for a second, but the shock and the pleasure of it sent him to his knees beside her.

With a cry, she pulled him into the bed, her hands and lips working him over, cracking the last of his reserve.

"This doesn't settle anything between us," she said, hoarsely, almost desperately. "Turn down the lamp, all the way."

In the darkness she grew more bold, something he had not believed possible. Her energy was boundless as she explored him with her hands and then with her breasts, rubbing the taut peaks against his chest and down lower, through the dark hairs that surrounded his erection, and even his sex itself.

When he could stand it no longer, he pulled her to him, ready to turn her to her back and finish what she had so admirably begun. But Kate had other plans. Smoothly, swiftly, she straddled him, whispering, "Can we do it this way?" Then she settled herself on top of him, finding the answer for herself.

This time the swirls of passion rose in harmony, and their peak moment of pleasure came at the same time, each swallowing the other's cries. He held her tight, through the fog of satisfaction, wondering how she would view all that she had done. She was not a woman who went easy on herself.

Eventually, after a long while of holding and stroking and kissing, she proved him right.

"You must think I'm terrible," she said.

"No, Kate. Never."

He tried to pull away from her embrace and relight the lamp.

"No," she said. "I don't want you to look at me."

It seemed a little late for modesty, but he doubted she would appreciate his pointing out that fact.

"You'll have to tell me why not," he said. "I hope it's not because you have regrets."

"No regrets. Just embarrassment."

"You've done nothing to be embarrassed about."

"I did some strange things."

"Nothing we did was strange. Unexpected, yes. But very fine. And very natural."

"I guess I don't know what's natural and what's not."

"I've got years to teach you, Kate. And you've got years to teach me."

She grew still and quiet. In the dark, he listened to her breathe.

"You are my responsibility," he said when he could stand the silence no longer. "Not T. J.'s. And certainly not Joseph Wharton's. You're mine. And mine alone. After tonight, you have no choice but to marry me."

"No," she said, softly at first, and then louder, "No," and louder still, "No, no, no."

She was out of the bed before he could reach for her, relighting the lamp, picking up her undergarments from the floor so that she could hold them over her nakedness.

Her hair was wild, her lips swollen, her skin reddened from the brush of his bristled cheeks. Mostly, he saw her eyes, darkly wounded as if she had suffered a great loss.

"You're so sure my betrothal is because I'm with child. Maybe I'm pregnant and maybe I'm not."

"Are you?"

"It doesn't matter. Whatever the case, I'm not marrying anyone. I've just decided for sure. Not Joseph and certainly not you."

"You have no choice."

"About many things, no. About this, yes."

"Trust me, Kate. We can make this work."

"That's not exactly a sentimental declaration, is it? Tell me the truth. You hadn't planned to settle here, not for the rest of your life. Whatever the reason for your starting a ranch, it's not to make a home."

"What makes you say that?"

"It's something I've felt from the moment I met you. I know more than ever I was right."

"So we'll leave. It's better that we both get away."

"You will leave. Not me. I apologized for mentioning Diana, but I'm not apologizing now. She was young and confused. I am neither. Should I bear either a son or a daughter, I can raise the child in the country. T. J. won't like it, but at least he'll stop ordering me into town. He might even write me off the way he did Jess."

He could hear the hysteria rising in her

voice, but he also heard the determination and the stubbornness.

"I won't let you do this, Kate. There are things you don't know."

"There always are. Believe me, Cord, you have no choice. Don't treat me like a charity case. This is not a repeat of the past."

Of course it wasn't. He should have told her he was not the father of Diana's child. He should have told her the truth. But then, he also should have kept his hands off her. There were some things he was not strong enough to do.

"There's a place in the barn where you can sleep. It's warm enough. I've spent many a night there awaiting the birth of a foal. I would very much appreciate your being gone by dawn."

The finality of her words gave him little choice, and he dressed quickly, while Kate stared into the night outside her bedroom window. He saw only one solution to the problem, the only way he could truly find peace and at the same time be honest with her. Calloway must confess his guilt. Once the truth was known, they could get on with their lives.

He went into the parlor and put on his coat and hat, feeling by habit for the leather packet in the coat pocket, the one with Diana's letter inside. But he had left it behind. It was the right thing to do, considering his purpose tonight. But the beautiful, doomed young woman still must be avenged.

He was settling his hat low on his forehead when he remembered one last thing. Returning to the bedroom, he found Kate still staring into the night. When she glanced at him, she didn't look surprised that he had returned.

He crossed the room in three long strides and took her into his arms.

"I've never been with a woman who brought me more pleasure, Kathleen Calloway. No one has ever come close."

He kissed her thoroughly, deeply.

And then he went to the barn.

Chapter Twenty-eight

Kate dreamed she was sinking in sand. The grit came to her neck, then into her mouth and eyes, suffocating her, blinding her, driving her to the edge of despair.

She awoke with a cry, sat up, then fell back in the bed and waited for her pounding heart to slow.

She didn't know if the sand was of Cord's making or of hers. But she was drowning in it, asleep or awake.

When she finally dragged herself from the bed, she felt as tired as when she'd tried to fall asleep sometime after midnight. Without looking at the clock on the mantel over the fireplace, she knew the hour was late, long after dawn. Cord must have left; otherwise, he would be here, tormenting her.

Stumbling through her morning ablutions,

she managed to get dressed, putting on a warm wool shirt along with the leather skirt and vest and the plain brown boots that formed her daytime uniform. Hanging the green dress in the wardrobe, tossing in the chemise and petticoat after it, she wondered if she would ever wear them again.

Biscuits and bacon awaited her in the kitchen. They were piled on a cloth-covered plate at the back of the stove. Dolores, the woman who had been serving as her housekeeper and cook, had returned to her own husband and children in the *jacal* not far from the ranch house. The laughter of the children came through the back kitchen door.

Kate forced down breakfast and two cups of coffee. She would need all the fortification she could get to do what she had to do.

Hastily she cleaned her dishes. Twisting her hair beneath the floppy hat, she pulled on her leather coat and heavy gloves, then went outside to the barn. The milk cow in the back stall cast her a baleful glance, then returned to munching hay. Otherwise, the barn was empty.

The bedroll Cord should have used for the night looked undisturbed. Either he had ridden out after leaving her, unheedful of the dark, or he'd straightened up after himself this morning, being very neat. She didn't know him well enough to guess which was true.

Fighting off depression, she whistled for Moonstar. When she was done saddling her, checking the shotgun in its scabbard, and packing the leftover biscuits and bacon for the trail, she went on a search for Tug. He was nowhere to be found.

She found Pete, Dolores's husband, in the corral rounding up the Calloway ponies that needed shoeing.

"I'm going into San Antonio," she said. "If you see Tug, tell him I don't know when I'll be back."

Pete nodded, then went back to work. He didn't stare at her or give any sign that she looked different from the way she looked every morning. Maybe he didn't know what had happened in the ranch house last night. Maybe the whole world was ignorant. Maybe her secret was safe.

She had been so certain she was the subject of gossip today, certain her shame was known to everyone. Surely Cord had marked her in some way.

Was it possible no one cared?

A loneliness as vast and dark as midnight swept over her. She tried to shake it off, but it wasn't the kind of feeling that would leave right away. Maybe in a day, or a year, but not right away.

She didn't allow herself to truly think of Cord until she was well on the trail into town. She wondered if this time she was carrying his child. She wondered how she would keep him from finding out. In her own misery, Jess had chosen to run and hide. But that wasn't Kate's way. Unless she was given no choice.

You are my responsibility.

Cord was being honorable again.

I've never been with a woman who brought me more pleasure.

She would like to think it was Cord being honest. She couldn't imagine there being in all the world a pleasure greater than what they had shared last night. Unless, of course, that pleasure was given and received in love. By both participants. That would be the best thing any woman could experience.

Such was not the case here.

She rode hard, forcing herself to stop and rest Moonstar. By late afternoon she was in San Antonio. Swallowing a fear that her father would be in consultation with her fiancé, she barged into his office.

He was with someone all right, but it wasn't Joseph Wharton. She caught him embracing a very flustered young woman she recognized as Rebecca Netherby. The girl's bonnet was askew, and her yellow hair was pulling free from its complicated twist at the back of her neck. Jumping away from T. J., she chewed at her full lower lip and studied her hands.

"Kate, have you no manners?" T. J. barked. "I've taught you to knock at closed doors."

He was embarrassed, as he had every right to be, but she sensed a simmering fury beneath the embarrassment. It was a common reaction lately whenever she came near.

"I can come back," she said, "when you two are done."

"Nonsense, Kate." He looked her over, giving special attention to her shapeless hat. His lips pursed in the middle of his beard and moustache, but she saw far more than simple disapproval in the expression. "We need to talk now," he added.

Kate doubted he had a real conversation in mind. *I need to tell you a few things* was what he meant.

Rebecca Netherby simpered, and T. J. looked at her as if he had momentarily forgotten she was in the room.

"This poor young woman has suffered a terrible loss, and I was comforting her." He patted the girl's arm. "She does not need the added shock of a witness to her distress."

From the wondering look in the girl's round brown eyes, Kate guessed she didn't know what in the world T. J. was talking about.

"I'm so sorry," Kate said. "What was the loss? A parent?" In case such were true, she had a father she would gladly donate in the dear departed's place.

"A kitten," T. J. said. "A beloved kitten she was kind enough to name Thomas."

Kate had to give her father credit. Despite his distress, he could think fast and make lies sound like the truth. Which was why he would make a successful politician.

"A kitten," she said. "I never would have guessed." And to Rebecca, "You must be devastated."

The girl's eyes narrowed slightly. She was not, it appeared, the overripe simpleton Kate had assumed.

"Mr. Calloway gave little Tommy to me as a gift. So naturally, I came to him when the poor creature was crushed beneath the wheel of my carriage this morning."

It would seem the fair young woman also had a flair for the macabre.

"I'll be sure to pass on my condolences to your parents when I see them."

"That won't be necessary, Kate," T. J. said.

"No, it won't," Rebecca said. "Papa didn't know about him. He's never cared for cats, and I hadn't decided just how to tell him about Thomas."

"The kitten," Kate said.

"Right," Rebecca said.

Kate knew she ought to pursue the situation further. Her father could get in serious trouble dallying with Miss Netherby, but she was in too much serious trouble herself to worry about anyone else at the moment.

"If you don't mind grieving elsewhere, I would very much like to talk to my father alone."

Rebecca looked at T. J.

"Please, my dear, we will confer later."

With a shrug, Rebecca made quick work of straightening her hair and bonnet, giving the impression that she had done so several times before. With a nod to T. J., she left. Kate didn't bother with preliminaries before launching her attack. She needed to be fast, before her father started in with whatever had angered him.

"I am not marrying Joseph Wharton. Not now. Not ever."

She expected an explosion. What she got was a very calm, "Oh?"

She stirred nervously, determined, yet fearful of what was to come. There was no way T. J. could change her mind. But that didn't mean he couldn't find devious ways to try. Otherwise, he never would have announced the upcoming nuptials so openly.

He tugged at his vest, then poured himself a glass of brandy. Settling in the leather chair behind his desk, he drank it down, then set the glass aside, each action completed slowly, methodically.

"So you heard about the betrothal," he said. "How?"

"Never mind how. You shouldn't have made the announcement without discussing it with me."

"I knew what you would say." Still calm, still tightly controlled.

"I'm saying no."

He slammed his fist on the desk. She jumped, and the brandy glass bounced and rolled on its side.

"You will not say no to me," he said, straightening the glass. "Not in this matter. Not now."

Everything about him remained calm, except for the slamming of his fist, but she knew he was raging inside. Never before had she seen him like this. Another time, in a less important matter, she might have tried cajolery, or a postponement of their argument. But not now. What he had done was too unthinkable.

"You had no right to commit me to marriage," she said.

His smile was small and chilling. "I had every right. Joseph has long been an admirer of yours, which you cannot deny. All of San Antonio is aware of how he feels. When I heard about that scoundrel escorting you back from the cemetery, I knew it was time to accept my fatherly responsibilities. You are betrothed to a man who can provide for you and, I should think, give you children. That is what you want, is it not? All women want children, though God alone knows why."

Kate would have been hurt, but her capacity for pain had been used up by Cord.

"I'm not marrying him. You can't make me."

"Perhaps I won't have to." He twirled the glass. She stared at it, as if caught in a trance, stiffening her resolve for what would come next. "Have you thought about what you will do if you're already with child?"

He said it so casually, so softly, not at all in his usual bombastic style, that it took a moment for the words to sink in.

And he was not done. "It's most important you marry Joseph before he learns what a tramp you have become."

Kate made a little sound in her throat. A moment passed before she could breathe.

"A tramp?" She felt bloodless, empty. "What are you talking about?"

But she knew. In that one word, he had summed up all she'd been thinking about herself. The worst thing was she hadn't realized it until now.

"I'm not condemning you, Kate, but God in heaven, did you have to pick someone like Cordoba Hardin? Last night. In your own bed. Have you no sense of shame?"

She remembered the footsteps in the hall. He had a spy. She didn't need long to guess the spy was her foreman, Tug Rafferty. He must have ridden into town early this morning, before she was even awake. For a terrible moment, she wondered if Tug knew about Jess. But he couldn't. Otherwise, T. J. would know.

"I'm not trying to hurt you, Kate, though it must look like that to you. Joseph believes you are an innocent maiden, a virgin, to put it bluntly. I'm sure you agree that there is no reason you and I can't be blunt with one another now. He has waited a long while to take himself a wife. He wants her perfect. In most ways, you are."

"Why are you doing this to me?" she whispered, but not so low he couldn't hear.

"I'm simply trying to avoid a potentially scandalous situation. Of course, you are my biggest concern. But you should also realize the scandal would hurt me equally." He rubbed at a spot over his right eye. "I know you are not so selfish as to destroy my deepest wish for political success, and all because of a matter that, if handled properly, will help you as well as me."

He spoke so reasonably that anyone else listening might consider him the wronged one. He almost made her believe it herself.

She collapsed in the chair facing the desk. Here was the smothering sand of her dream, the wheedling words of her father, proving what she had always known: reality was far worse than anything her mind could conceive.

Tragedy did not have to come in death or violent clashes. It could creep in with the voice of common sense. But common sense seldom had anything to do with matters of the heart.

"Now, I'm not blaming you for giving in to

nature's urgings," he said. "I was beginning to think you didn't know such feelings existed. Your mother didn't, not after a while. But still, you can't expect Hardin to do the honorable thing."

"The way you would with Rebecca Netherby." It was a feeble defense, and he had to know it.

"Come, come, Kate, that was uncalled for. I told you I was consoling her."

"I forgot the dead kitten."

She could hear the words coming out of her mouth, but they seemed to have no reality, the way nothing that had happened in the past twenty-four hours seemed real.

"Cord never called me anything like a whore, did he? You're the one who came up with that."

"I admit to exaggeration," T. J. said, "but he was most certainly crude and rude. I'm simply trying to take care of you, then and now. Joseph is a good man. He won't question your pregnancy, not if the wedding is within the month. By Christmas. It is my fondest wish."

He spoke almost affectionately, something he never did without witnesses. For the first time in her life, her father frightened her.

It took the last reserves of her strength to stand.

"Whatever I am, Papa, whatever I've done, I'll take care of myself."

Papa sounded strange on her lips. She hadn't called him that since she was a little girl and he had ordered her to call him by his name.

"You can tell Joseph the betrothal is off, or I can write him a letter. He's your friend. He de-

serves the truth. I'll stay in town tonight. Tomorrow I'll ride south for a day or two. When I
return, let me know what you have decided."

"Think again, Kate."

"That's not necessary. I've considered everything carefully."

"Perhaps not everything. If Hardin has truly
wronged you, it is my obligation and my responsibility to see that he is made to pay. Marriage, of course, is unthinkable. The man hates
me—why I have no idea. I have considered the
matter carefully and decided it is my politics
that aroused him to such anger."

"Made to pay? How?"

"I do not know. But I am reminded of what
happened to the man who wronged your sister."

"You would kill him?"

"I would do what I could to drive him from
the county. He is not the sort we want in Texas.
If he proves a violent man, that is his choice.
And if Hardin's safety is not enough for you to
change your mind, remember what happened
to Jess."

Here was what he had been leading up to all
the while, the final argument he knew she
could not fight. It was not an issue of obeying
or not obeying him, but a matter of protecting
Cord's life.

And he spoke of it with calm and reason.

"You wouldn't."

"I pray violence will not be necessary. Which
it will not, of course, if you wed Joseph as I
have arranged."

Kate felt as though all her blood had drained
away. The world would agree with T. J.'s as-

sessment of her troubles, and with his solution, too. But it shattered her heart.

She nodded at him woodenly, unable to agree or to argue. Hurrying from the room, she threw herself onto Moonstar, wanting to ride forever, away from everything she knew and everyone she loved. Instead, she rode to the house with the white picket fence and went upstairs. T. J. wouldn't bother her tonight. He had given her much to think over. In his mind, she could come to only one decision. The wedding would be held before the year was out.

That night Caprice served her supper in her room. She asked no questions, just clucked and pampered and cosseted, and later took away the tray of untouched food.

Early the next morning Kate tried to write a letter to Joseph Wharton. She made several starts, not knowing what it was she wanted to say. In a perfect world, she could have written the complete truth. But then, in a perfect world Cord would have fallen wildly in love with her and carried her away from any kind of harm.

Since this wasn't such a world, she couldn't write what she wanted. And she wasn't wildly loved.

Leaving before her father was out of bed, she made the ride to the inn in record time. Jess had a customer, and she was forced to wait at one of the tables until he came out of the back room. She didn't look at him. She didn't want to know who he was. If she didn't look at him, she couldn't hate him, not specifically. It was easier to deal with Jess's men if they were faceless. Her sister swore she never accepted the offers of men who were unkind.

How she could tell their characters, Kate didn't know. Sometimes a man could be especially cruel when the opposite was his intent.

You are my responsibility.

Cord had meant it in the kindest way.

You are my biggest concern.

T. J. had lied, to her if not to himself.

She waited a few minutes, then knocked at the door and went inside. As always, the room vibrated with color, with life. Not so Jess. Her sister wore a white robe, and her dark hair fell about her too-thin shoulders, long and lustrous. She looked almost virginal, until Kate looked into her eyes. They were the eyes of a woman long dead.

"Did that man hurt you?" she asked.

"Of course not. I told you they never do."

"They can hurt you without meaning to."

A spark of life came into her sister's eyes. "What are you talking about? Something's happened. What is it?"

She half rose off the bed, for once the protectress instead of the protected.

Kate hadn't known she was about to cry. In all that had happened over the past years, her sister had never seen her tears. She saw them now. It was Jess's turn to be the comforting one, to take Kate in her arms and let her unburden her soul.

"It's Cord," she said.

"What did he do to you?" Jess snapped.

Of course Jess would assume he had inflicted hurt. He was a man.

Kate would tell her about him, everything, what they had done, his offer, her unrequited love. But somehow she couldn't bring herself to mention their father, not the betrothal, not the threats. There was too much hurt between Jess and T. J. already. It was not her purpose to be the cause of any more.

Chapter Twenty-nine

Cord was at the Lone Star, saddling Sunset outside the barn, preparing for an early journey into San Antonio for his confrontation with T. J. Calloway, when Domingo came riding up hard.

"Comanches," Domingo gasped as he dropped to the ground.

Cord's blood ran cold.

Lucky appeared mysteriously at his side. "Where?" he asked.

"*Quién sabe*? Everywhere, señor."

"Any sign of them to the north?" Cord asked.

"I know nothing of Miss Kate or her people." Domingo wiped at his forehead. "Not far to the west they have burned out a family. Two days past. All are dead." He made the sign of the cross. "*Madre de Dios*, such attacks have not happened in a long while."

"And now?" Lucky asked.

"They move about the country. This is all I know. The rider who spreads the word did not tell more."

"Any idea what got them riled?" Cord asked.

"The settler was foolish. He put out a barrel of poisoned sugar, as if he would help the Comanches. Many ate from the barrel, women and children, too. It is also true that before the sugar, the old chief Soaring Eagle died."

Cord let out a long, slow breath and muttered, "Good God."

Lucky glanced at him quizzically.

"The chief was a friend of Kate's. I know. It sounds crazy. I wouldn't believe it myself if I hadn't seen them together." He stared in the direction of the Calloway Ranch. "She may not know he's dead. She needs to be told."

"I'm riding with you," Lucky said.

Cord nodded, and to Domingo he said, "Make sure everybody's inside the stone house, Salinas, everybody. There's enough food in there to keep you several days."

"But the horses and the cattle—"

"They'll leave the cattle alone. And as for the horses, they're welcome to them. Just keep yourselves alive."

He was on the trail fast, Lucky at his side, covering the same ground that had taken him to Kate only two days before. He didn't want to think about that last visit, what they had said to one another and what they had done. Thinking might slow him down.

Besides, he had done little but think about her since leaving her bed.

Tug Rafferty was standing at the front of the house when Cord and Lucky rode up, horses lathered. He looked calm enough, and safe. But that didn't mean Kate was the same.

The foreman couldn't hold his calm for long. He glanced nervously at Lucky but held his ground, bowing his neck and flexing his arms, as if he would pump all the blood he could into his bulging muscles.

"I don't want no trouble from you two," he said. "Nobody's gonna sneak up on me today."

Lucky stared at him in silence. Tug shifted his weight to the back of his heels.

"Where's Miss Kate?" Cord asked.

"Not where you can talk to her."

Lucky dismounted and took a step toward the foreman, his arms hanging loose. His only weapon was the pistol strapped to his hip, but he made no move for it. Tug wasn't looking at the pistol, anyway; he was looking into Lucky's eyes.

"I said I don't want no trouble," Tug said hastily. "She ain't here."

Cord wasn't as subtle as his friend. Drawing his gun, he aimed it at a spot between the foreman's eyes. "Where is she? In town?"

Tug shook his head. Sweat beaded across his forehead.

Cord cocked the hammer.

"She was in town," Tug said hastily, "but she's gone down to where her sister's buried."

A cold wind swept across Cord, rustling the leaves that had fallen on the front yard, and he lowered his weapon. "Does she know about the Indians? They're raiding again."

323

Tug's eyes widened with fear, but only for an instant.

"Maybe she does, maybe she don't." He shrugged his massive shoulders. "It don't matter. Those Injuns don't worry Kate none."

Lucky moved fast on catlike feet and sank a fist into Tug's sneering mouth. For all his superior bulk, Tug stumbled backward and sat hard on the ground, blinking up at his assailant.

Lucky stepped back and caught Cord's eye. "He wasn't taking us seriously."

"If you're lying about where she is, Rafferty, I will kill you," Cord said.

"I ain't lying." He wiped at the blood dribbling from a cut on his lip, smearing a stain across his chin. "She rode there early this morning. It's what she told Calloway she was going to do."

Cord took a slower look around him, at the house, the barn, the trees. Everything looked neat, efficient, pleasing in a quiet way. Like the mistress who ran it. He hadn't noticed many details about the place when he rode up two nights ago. It seemed important to notice everything now.

"Watch out for your people," he said. "Soaring Eagle isn't around any longer to protect them."

"What—" Tug began.

But Cord was already reining away, with Lucky bounding into the saddle to ride beside him. Silently, he cursed. They had lost an hour going in the wrong direction. More than half the day would be gone before they could reach the cantina. A great deal could happen in that time, all of it bad.

Neither man spoke, Lucky letting Cord lead the way, taking the position of lookout in case they crossed the path of the Comanche band. Cord rode all-out, daring the Indians to spot him and attack. The cold that had blown across him at the Calloway Ranch settled inside him, chilling whatever fear he might have felt.

He thought about the trembles that had assailed him for so many years. He hadn't suffered them in a long while. Any that might come upon him today would be because of Kate.

Instead of Comanches, they spotted a herd of deer and several flocks of wild turkeys. Galloping hard over the breadth of a grass-covered valley, they disturbed a covey of quail. At the sudden fluttering, Cord's heart jumped in his throat.

The route took them across the Hondo and up a steep embankment, over a pair of high, wide, brush-thick hills, and then onto the flatter land that led eventually to the coastal waters and to Mexico. Cord had to blaze a trail through the untracked land, moving unerringly south-southeast, as if a magnet were drawing him to the woebegone cantina where Kate thought she could find refuge.

A thousand emotions roiled within him, but one thought drove him on: he would strangle her, once he made sure she was safe.

He estimated that they were close to their destination, within a half hour, when he sensed the presence of the enemy. He and Lucky were riding in a stand of trees beside the banks of a shallow creek. He wondered if it was an upstream section of the same creek where Kate had first given herself to him.

Reining back, he motioned to Lucky, who had already slowed his horse to a walk. When they broke through the trees into a small clearing, both men halted and stared at the burned-out shell of what had been a small frame house. Smoke curled from the blackened embers. There was no sign of life; whoever lived here had either escaped or died in the fire.

Small gray-and-white feathers clung to the branches of the trees in front of the house, and more feathers were strewn across the ground, giving silent testimony to the riders who had been here before them. The Indians had use for the cloth that covered feather mattresses; the feathers themselves were expendable, like the people who slept and made love in the bed.

Everywhere around them were the tracks of unshod horses. The Comanches had been here, all right, and from the heat rising above the house, not long ago.

It was time to be smart.

Cord checked his pistol, then unsheathed his rifle and held it at the ready in his hand. Lucky did the same. Both men followed the tracks of the Indian ponies, the way they had tracked the opposing army down in Mexico and, sometimes, the Apaches, who had proven a far more formidable foe. Any apprehension Cord might have felt eased from him, the way it had during the war. He was doing what he had to do.

Years before, after he left his brother's Crown of Glory Ranch to strike out on his own, he had tracked Comanches this way, too. Never, not in Mexico nor in Texas, had the stakes been so high.

As they neared the cantina, they heard the whoops of the Indians before they saw them, and they heard the pounding of hooves. As if they had conferred, each man slipped from the saddle and slapped his mount away, then crept toward the chilling sounds, their footsteps quieter than the soft breeze in the trees. In the December afternoon, with twilight approaching, they were screened by shadows. Whatever noise they might make was masked by the ululating Comanche cries, their scent lost in the unmistakable stench of death.

When they could see the blur of ponies through the trees, they came to a halt. Lucky shouldered his rifle; Cord did the same. Another step, another, and they could make out a half-dozen riders, naked except for their narrow loincloths and calf-high leggings. Each brave waved a rifle overhead as he rode by the front of the cantina, firing through the open windows while on the move. Answering gunfire caught one of the Indians. He slumped across the neck of his pony and rode on.

Beyond the cantina, flames licked the air. It was the stable, set afire. Sparks landed on the cantina's ancient shingle roof. Cord remembered the wooden frame of the adobe building, and the straw scattered across the hard dirt floor. Once the sparks caught, the place would burn fast.

One of the braves had dismounted and was crouched over a man's body at the edge of the trees a half-dozen feet away. The Indian raised a knife. Lucky shot him in the chest. At the same time, Cord fired at one of the riders. The Indian stiffened and fell, and his pony galloped into the woods on the far side of the cantina.

After that, everything happened fast. The Indians turned their mounts in the direction of the unexpected gunfire. Cord scrambled crablike to the left, Lucky to the right, both firing their repeating rifles, making each bullet count.

Smoke and the choking smell of gunpowder filled the air; the gunfire was so fast, so furious, it sounded like a single shattering explosion. The shots came from the Indians, from Cord and Lucky, from the narrow windows of the cantina. When his rifle clicked empty, Cord reached for the ammunition he carried in his coat. He sensed the Comanche behind him more than he heard him. Whirling, he pulled his pistol and fired.

The brave jerked upright and stared down at the wound in his chest. His eyes locked into a stare of disbelief and he dropped his knife, then fell to the ground. He did not move again.

Using his left hand, Cord reloaded the rifle, never losing control of the pistol. It was a skill he had learned in Mexico.

Continuing to fire, he saw one Indian fall, and then two more. They seemed to come in an endless parade, their numbers increasing. Then, as suddenly as they had first appeared, they were all down, dead or wounded, their riderless horses galloping into the trees that surrounded the small adobe cantina.

The silence was as deafening as the reports of the guns. Minutes crept by. Slowly Cord stood and moved forward to the clearing, where he viewed the carnage. Eight Comanches down, three whites who must have been caught outside the cantina, the Indian he had killed in the brush. He counted an even dozen dead.

But no sign of a woman. Lucky came up to join him; neither man spoke.

The door to the cantina creaked open. Out stepped the old *paisano* who wore the faded serape. On this day he held no concertina in his hand. After him came the bartender, and then another man and another, all of them somber, the threat of death still burning in their eyes.

One stared around him, looked at Cord, and settled his wide, dark eyes on Lucky.

"God smiled upon us today," he said in Spanish, "or perhaps it was the Devil. Whoever sent him, I give thanks to the man with the yellow hair. Never have I seen such shooting. They came at the back door. You, señor, stopped them. Five braves, all down, before they could fire a shot."

Lucky stared back at the man and nodded, but he did not speak.

Suddenly Kate was there, bursting through the crowd of men, running past them, ignoring the bodies on the ground. She threw herself into Cord's arms, looked up and covered his face with kisses, then buried her head in the folds of his coat, clinging to him while she drew in great gasps of breath.

Beyond her, Lucky watched. With something approaching a smile, he looked away.

Cord forgot him and the almost-smile. Kate absorbed his attention, and he held her just as tightly as she was holding him, feeling her warmth, sensing the pounding of her heart. He didn't let her go for a long, long while.

Chapter Thirty

When she finally caught her breath, Kate forced herself to move away from Cord. She had made a fool of herself running out to him that way, kissing him before the world as if she had the right. But maybe it was not so bad to be foolish in the cold twilight when they were both surrounded by death.

She looked around her, looked especially hard at the fallen Comanches. Her eyes blurred. "Are they all dead?"

"Some might have got away," Cord said.

Lucky shook his head.

"Lucky says no. That means we got them all."

Hesitant, each step forced and slow, she walked to one fallen body, and then another, knowing all the men watched, maybe wondering whether she was a ghoul who enjoyed the evidence of a massacre. But she felt no joy, only a deep, dark sadness at what lay before her.

There was Night Stalker, his blunt features still twisted into a grimace, even in death, and there was Broken Hand, the gentler brave who saw into the future. Had he foretold his fate today? She saw others, too, some she could identify by name. But she did not see the body of the man who had taught her who they were. She did not see their chief.

"Soaring Eagle is not here," Cord said. "He died. I don't know when."

As always, he read her mind.

"That's why they attacked," she said. "His was the voice of peace."

Cord looked as if he would say more, but he kept his silence.

Drawing her eyes from him, she looked, too, at the fallen men who had been caught as they approached the inn. One of them she recognized as a frequent visitor, but the other two were strangers to her.

A great sadness for them all settled on her. Such waste. It was a cause for tears. She brushed them from her cheeks and looked at Cord.

"You came here. Why?"

"I heard about Soaring Eagle. And it was worse. Someone gave the tribe poisoned sugar. They were after retribution, and I knew you wouldn't have sense enough to take care of yourself."

The longer he spoke, the angrier he sounded.

She lifted her chin. "I was firing from inside.

I'm not completely helpless. Nor so stupid I don't know when to shoot."

She glanced at Lucky, who stood at the edge of the woods, apart from the others.

"You came, too," she said. "Thank you. It seems inadequate for what you did, but thank you."

Looking over her shoulder, she expected to see Jess walk out, but she knew her sister was avoiding Cord. For some reason, she had decided he was her enemy as much as T. J., that somehow word of her existence would get back to town if Cord knew she lived. She had fought alongside Kate and the men, loading guns, passing them along, but when the shooting stopped, she had retreated to her room.

A few of the men had gone around to fight the stable fire and to put out the sparks blowing in the wind. The inn was no longer in danger. But that didn't make it the refuge that Jess so desperately sought.

Cord wasn't an enemy. Kate was not sure exactly what to call him, except her lover and the man she loved. She wondered if maybe he wasn't beginning to care for her. But no matter how hard she wondered, she could not allow herself to hope.

Besides, even if it existed, his caring came too late. T. J. had made sure of that.

For now, Cord needed thanks, but not the words she had used with Lucky. She knew only one way to give it to him, one way to show him she had survived, and to celebrate the knowledge that he had as well. For that, they needed to be alone.

Taking his hand, she led him away from the terrible scene around them, led him into the trees, and deeper, toward the creek bank where they had first made love. Turning to face him, she took off his hat and tossed it aside. Hers had long been abandoned inside the inn.

"Are you sure about this, Kate?" he asked.

"I'm sure."

"It's cold."

"I'm hot. Besides, we won't take long."

By now, the heat she was feeling had shown up in his eyes. She kept her features solemn, but she felt a definite smile in the vicinity of her heart.

"The ants—" he began, a little halfheartedly, as if he was trying to come up with excuses, to hear what she would say.

"Take off your coat. We can lie on that. Anyway, I learned I don't have to be the one on the bottom."

She was trying to be very calm, downright impudent, but too much had happened for her to carry on with it a second longer.

"Oh, Cord, I was so afraid! Help me to know I'm truly alive."

Before she could blink twice, he shed his coat and tossed it onto the grass. In another blink, she was out of her vest and had her shirt half unbuttoned. She stopped rushing when he eased his hands inside the shirt and caressed her breasts.

She caught her breath.

"I'm feeling for your heart," he said.

"It's pounding in there somewhere."

"Here? How about here? Or there's always—"

Kate was close to swooning. "I can't stand much longer."

"You want me to stop?"

"I meant, I can't stand up much longer. You can keep doing what you're doing for a week."

She loved the glint in his eye, as much as she loved anything about him.

"You said we wouldn't be at this long."

"Since when did you ever listen to me?"

He leaned down to kiss her. She had thought never to kiss him again. She felt the brush of his lips against hers and then the probing of his tongue. Opening up to him, she wondered how some people could be so horribly cruel to one another and others be so exquisitely tender.

Unbuttoning his shirt, she pressed her breasts against his bare skin, wrapping her arms around his neck, standing on tiptoe so that she might hold him better and kiss him better and let him know that for this little while all was well with their world.

They sank to the ground at the same time, but he didn't break the kiss. He held onto her, cradling her to him as if she were something precious to him. It was easy to believe that she was.

For just a moment, the terror of the day came back to her, like a shot and a flash of fire. She couldn't keep from crying out. He broke the kiss and pressed his lips against her hair.

"You're all right, Kate," he whispered.

"What if they're around? What if they're still here and I brought you out to—"

"Hush. I'll tell you a secret. Lucky's taking care of us."

She almost broke away. "He's watching what we're doing?"

But Cord was holding on to her too firmly to let her go. "He's always watching. Always looking. But not at us. He's making sure we're all right."

"He didn't say anything when we left."

"He never does."

The fear began to fade, along with the ugly images in her mind.

"He's different, isn't he? He's someone very special."

"Do you want me to leave and call him for you?"

She tightened her hold on him. "You'd have a hard time getting away."

"I'm having a hard time staying."

Kate almost laughed, when only a short while ago she had thought never to smile again. Everything seemed so natural, the banter back and forth between them, the bawdy contest to see who could get in the last word.

This time she decided to let him win. And in the winning, she would have a victory all her own. Blood was pounding through her veins, heat building, and she learned something new about the erotic side of her being. Just by being near him, with only a few touches, she could bring herself to the peak of pleasure he had shown her in her bed.

Easing her arms from around his neck, she shoved him back on the coat. "Now," she said. She didn't have to tell him twice.

While he worked at the silver belt buckle, she slipped the leather skirt down over her boots and kicked it aside. Beneath it, she was wearing a pair of underdrawers that had been constructed with a very convenient opening. All she had to do was straddle him, make a quick adjustment in the cloth, and take him inside her.

He showed his appreciation by cooperating with everything she did. Keeping her knees bent beside his hips, she rested herself against him and pressed her lips against the hollow of his throat. Holding her in a tight embrace, he did what he did so well. His thrusts were quick and sure. In a whisper of heartbeats, the thrill of completion took over and she gave herself to the abandonment she found only with him, all restraints shattered, all worries burned to ash.

The power of what she felt shook her in a way that had not occurred before. He made love to her body, but she felt the impact in her heart and soul. If this were their last loving, she knew she would hold this hurried, incautious mating in her memory and relive it again and again.

The fact that she could think such thoughts, even as the waves of pleasure were sweetly receding, gave proof that she had not completely lost her sanity. She understood the way things were, and the way they could never be. But she would let the heartache come later. For now, she would love him and let him do to her anything he chose.

But he was far more sensible than she. He stirred beneath her, and she knew it was time for them to part. She would not, however, cling to him and mope. Instead, the parting would be clean and crisp. Later, when he thought of her, the memories just might bring a smile to his lips.

Though she would very much like to see that smile herself, she must believe that it would eventually come.

Sitting up, she eased herself off him. "Ants?" she asked.

He sat beside her. "That's not what I'm feeling." He looked as if he were going to elaborate, but she couldn't listen to what he had to say. It would probably be about marriage. He might even come up with something about how she touched his heart. What he didn't know was that she would be a very expensive wife. She might even cost him his life.

"I'm cold," she said, hugging herself. She spoke a lie. "Could we hurry?"

Tugging up his trousers, he pulled a bandanna from his back pocket. She recognized it as the one he had used to wrap her sprained ankle a lifetime ago.

"You might want to use this. Or let me."

She took it fast, before she could give in to the temptation that he offered. Drying herself, she dressed quickly, but all the time her mind was working. The idea that struck her was as insane as any idea she'd come up with since meeting him. But it felt right. And she was very much in favor of feeling right.

Standing before him, she listened for a moment to the sounds of the woods, the rustling in the trees, the shrill cry of a mockingbird, the ripple of water in the creek.

"Let's go see Jess," she said.

"The cemetery."

"No, Cord, not this time. I'm finally going to do something I should have done a long time ago."

Chapter Thirty-one

Cord followed Kate through the woods, watching as she chose her path. At each juncture where she had a choice of directions, he guessed wrong about which she would choose. For a small woman, she took long strides. He wondered if she were still feeling the effects of their lovemaking, the way he was.

Each time they were together, she seemed to get over it a hell of a lot faster than he did. Maybe women were more resilient. Back by the creek, she had seemed equally affected. He didn't think he was wrong about that.

Once she glanced over her shoulder at him. "I'm still here," he said.

She nodded and hurried on. Long before they arrived back at the cantina, he had figured out their destination. He also had a pretty good idea of what was going to happen once they got inside.

As surprising as the idea was, he must have been stupid not to have figured it out before.

They walked into the clearing where so many had died a short while before. All trace of the Indians had vanished. Someone had gone so far as to turn the dirt where their blood had spilled. The bodies of the slain whites had been tossed across their saddles. As if aware of their burden, the horses milled restlessly at the edge of the trees.

If Kate noticed the curious glances of the men who mingled out front, she gave no sign.

She picked out the bartender in the crowd of a dozen men.

"Where are the Comanches?"

"They have been taken for burial, Señorita Kate. In one grave."

She rubbed at a spot over her eye. "When?"

"Soon. The men look for a place where the dirt is soft and the grave can be deep." He glanced over the roof of the inn to where the smoke still rose from the burning stable. "There were those who wished to burn them. But the smell, Señorita Kate, the smell would be *muy malo*."

She looked at Cord. "They left women behind, and children, too. We can't forget them."

"We'll let the Rangers know what happened. And the Army. There are places that have been set aside for the families." He glanced around at the grim faces of those who had survived the attack. "It's the best we can do. Don't push it."

She sighed. "You're right, of course. It's just

that I owe it to Soaring Eagle to do what I can for them. For a long time he was my friend."

Cord knew the men were listening. But he also knew Kate did not care. If a man were to have only one friend in all the world, he could not do better than Kate.

But he wasn't looking at her in friendship. He was remembering what had just passed between them. She gave herself completely and then she pulled away, available one moment and elusive the second. She had no idea how special she was, and what she was doing to him.

At the moment, she was staring beyond him, at the bodies of the three slain white men lying across the horses.

"There's been so much hate, so much death. I think it all begins with lies." Her stare shifted to the front door of the cantina. "I'm as guilty of lying as anyone. It's time to stop."

He held his silence, knowing she had to tell him what she was thinking in her own way and in her own time.

Her eyes sought out and found Lucky, standing at the edge of the clearing, his hat pulled low over his watchful brown eyes. Despite all he had done for them today, none of the men approached him. He seemed to put out a silent signal that he wanted to be left alone, unless he was doing the approaching.

Cord was the only man who ever felt comfortable around him. Kate was not the only woman who talked to him. Her distinction lay in the fact that he liked her and considered her his friend.

"Lucky," she said, and gave him the smile that lit up her face. "You, too. Please."

Lucky looked at Cord, who shrugged. Both men followed without a word.

Much of the furniture in the cantina was either overturned or broken, as if the men had planned to use the pieces as clubs. On the board that served as a bar, both the bottles and the glasses were intact. Resting beside them was the small concertina from which the musician had coaxed beautiful melodies. Cord wondered how soon it would be before he brought them to life again.

Kate looked around quickly. Cord felt the momentary return of her fear as the memories of an hour ago made an assault. But she hurried past it all, came to the door of one of the back rooms, and knocked twice. There was no response that Cord heard, but she opened the door and went inside.

"I've got some people I want you to meet," she said.

"No." The woman's voice came through the doorway, loud and clear and certain.

"I'm the older sister. It's time you listened to me. If you won't come out to them, they will come in here to you."

Over her shoulder she nodded at Cord and Lucky, gesturing for them to join her. She gave every indication that she knew what she was doing, but Cord knew her well enough to see the worry lines between her eyes.

He went first, Lucky more slowly. He seemed to sense that for him, trouble waited in the small cantina room.

As they entered, the woman inside rose to stand beside the bed. She was wearing a white blouse that exposed her too-slender shoulders, and a brightly embroidered ankle-length skirt. She wore moccasins, the kind Cord had seen frequently in Mexico, but unlike most of the cantina women he had met, she wore no jewelry.

Her hair was dark and unruly, thick and long, and her dark eyes were sunken into a pale face. She was taller than Kate, and fuller breasted, but her arms were thin, her face and neck gaunt. He could see how beautiful she had once been, and was still, except that now it was in a spectral kind of way. A stranger would have sworn she was the older sister, not the young one Kate had tried so long to protect.

Around her was a splash of color, the likes of which he had not seen before, samplers written in both English and Spanish, scenes painted in thread, some abstract, others brutally lifelike, their predominant color a bloody crimson. It was as if she had created her own private museum of art, her own private world.

And yet she passed her days and nights in a public place, living both a public and a private kind of life, as only a woman could.

She studied Cord for a moment, gave Lucky a cursory glance, returned for another, then stared past them through the open door.

"You've seen me," she said flatly. "I'm alive. Now leave."

She turned and pulled a cigarillo from a small package resting on the bedside table. As if she had done so a thousand times before, she lit the tip from the bedside lantern. Standing tall, she blew the smoke in Lucky's direction.

"You're still here," she said. "I've closed up

business for the day." The hand holding the cigarillo fluttered. "Surely you understand."

Kate did not seem in the least shocked by what her sister said. "You're coming with us."

"Give up, Kate. My answer is the same as it's always been. No."

"I'm not giving up. Not this time."

Cord remained silent. This was Kate's show. Lucky stood behind them all, as quiet and still as the wall.

"Those Indians really scared you, didn't they?" Jess said.

"I'm not afraid of them. I'm afraid for you."

"I can take care of myself."

"No, you can't. Not the way you're doing."

The sisters spoke to one another as if they were the sole occupants of the room.

"You weren't killed by those bandits two years ago," Kate said. "You were assaulted. They did terrible things to you. But it's no worse that what you've been doing to yourself since the attack."

The cigarillo shook between Jess's long, thin fingers.

"You're not supposed to mention what happened. You promised."

"And I've kept that promise all this time. I let everyone believe you were dead because that's what you wanted. Today I figured out the truth. You've been trying to kill yourself while I've been working at keeping you alive. I was dumb. I went about it the wrong way."

"So now you want me to do something equally dumb. Like throw myself on the mercy of the loving and kind Thomas Jefferson Calloway, who will naturally rejoice that I am come back from the grave."

"I would never ask that of you." She lowered her voice to a whisper as she added, "Not anymore."

There was more in her words than Cord could begin to understand, a new kind of hurt she was keeping to herself. The betrothal . . . T. J.'s reaction to Kate's condition . . . the bastard had done something to hurt the one person in the world who loved him. The man was not only a villain; he was also a fool.

As he looked at Kate, he thought that maybe his long-time enemy was not the only fool.

Kate looked at Cord.

"Would you please escort us to our ranch? It's as much Jess's as it is mine, and it's time she lived there."

"No!" Jess's exclamation was as sharp as gunfire.

"It won't be for long," Kate said. "I promise. I have plans for you. Plans to keep you safe from harm. And I promise, on the grave of our beloved mother, that our father is not involved."

"I won't set foot in that ranch house. You know T. J. will find out I'm there. If he doesn't hear about it, he'll come out to parade around like he actually did some work there. And he'll see me. That will be worse." She puffed nervously at the cigarillo, drawing the fire close to her lips. "He wants me dead. In this, I want him to have his way."

"The inn is closed, Jess. Even if it opens again, there will be too many memories. And you'll smell death. That won't go away."

Even in situations as delicate as this, Kate was not one to mince words. He glanced at Lucky and could have sworn he saw admiration in the man's eyes.

Jess stared defiantly at her sister, dropping the cigarillo, grinding it out against the rug with the toe of her moccasin.

"I said—" she began.

"She'll come with me."

It was Lucky who spoke. All eyes turned to him.

"To the Lone Star," he said. He was looking straight at Jess. "She needs a bed and a roof over her head. We've got both."

Jess recovered first. "Why?" she asked. "Do you like what you see?"

Lucky shrugged, as always a man of few words. He had said what he planned to say. Interpretations would be left to his listeners.

Kate looked at Cord. It was his turn to shrug. "He owns half the ranch. What he suggests makes sense." It also surprised the hell out of him, but any questions he had for his friend and partner could wait.

He remembered how he had run to his brother's ranch a long time ago, when he was still a boy, looking for a place to feel at home. He had not been welcome, but then the woman his brother was to marry, the wonderful Ellie, had stepped in to embrace him. It was a debt he had never fully repaid. He could repay it now.

Jess would be safe at the Lone Star. No one would bother her. It was something he didn't have to point out to Kate.

"It won't be for long," she said. "I promise."

She spoke to him, not Lucky, and the warmth in her eyes said more than her words. For a moment he was aware of only her in the room and of the communication that passed between them.

"I can't leave here," Jess said. No longer did she sound defiant. She sounded afraid. "Do you really believe these two are going to be any better than the men that come in here? Especially that one," she said, flicking a sideways glare at Lucky.

"I know they're better. If I ask them not to tell T. J., they won't. Until I can put my plan together, you can hide out there as well as anywhere. It won't be long."

"What plan?" Jess asked.

It seemed like a reasonable question to Cord. He had wanted to ask it himself.

"We'll talk about it later." For the first time, edginess crept into Kate's voice. "But I promise I'll take care of you. Better than I've managed so far."

"You always were soft in the head," Jess said. "Like Mama."

"I'm not being soft now. I'm finally being tough. You've lost so much weight, I can wrestle you to the ground and tie you so you can't get away. There are three dead bodies outside tossed over their saddles. I'll toss you over Moonstar the same way and walk back to the Lone Star if I have to."

Cord kept thinking he ought to interfere, but there was no break-in point he could find. Besides, Kate was fascinating him, using her stubbornness on someone else for a change.

The irony that he was helping T. J.'s two daughters was not lost on him. He got an added jolt of satisfaction from knowing that the man would be furious if he knew. It wasn't anywhere near the retribution he was after, but it was a start.

Now all he had to do was tell Kate. She talked about wanting the truth. He hoped she meant the truth about everything.

As for what he would do with Jess when he actually got her to the Lone Star, he had not a clue. Having her there was Lucky's idea. He would have to assume responsibility for her. There was a great deal of pleasure in the thought.

But Jess was not so easily pleased.

"I'm a whore," she said. She looked from one man to the other, ending with Lucky, as if she would make one last desperate try at being left alone. "You look like men who know what whores are for. I don't think we've met, if you know what I mean, but there have been so many and I seldom look at faces. Now if you'd drop—"

"Jess, stop it."

Kate went to the bed, kneeled, and pulled out a small valise. She snapped it open. "Are all your clothes in here? I take it they are. Anything else you want to take?"

Jess looked around the room, spied the packet of cigarillos, and looked as if she wanted to pick it up.

"You may as well try to give them up now," Kate said. "Since you're determined to be miserable, you can be miserable about this, too."

As Jess watched her sister, her dark, sunken eyes began to show a sign of life. Grabbing up the packet, she tossed it into the valise. Cord could swear a smile tugged at Kate's lips. To her way of thinking, she had won.

What exactly she had won was another matter.

Kate swept the walls with her eyes. "Anything else? You've put so much work into all of this, it would be a shame to abandon it."

"I don't want anything here," Jess said, and without another look around her, walked out of the room.

Cord was the last to leave, making certain Kate didn't linger. The Lone Star was still hours away, and much could happen. They would have to camp out when darkness came, which wouldn't be long. There would be a hundred opportunities for Jess to bolt.

Lucky would have to be put on watch. But Cord didn't think he would need to point that out. He had never seen his partner look at a woman quite the way he had looked at Jess, not as if he wanted her but more as if he couldn't figure her out. And figuring her out was something he wanted to do.

The situation gave rise to speculations Cord would need a long time to think through.

Chapter Thirty-two

By the time Kate arrived at the Calloway ranch, it was late the next day and she was exhausted.

Jess and Lucky had been left at the Lone Star, but Cord had insisted on making sure she got home all right.

He was as much a cause of her exhaustion as anything that had happened. He wanted to talk. On the long ride, he kept trying to bring up subjects she couldn't think about.

"Later," had been her standard reply.

It still was her reply, even as she dismounted outside her front door.

"Give me two days," she said. "I could sleep a week, but I'll settle for two days. I truly, truly need to crawl into bed and pull the covers over my head. And I need to be there alone."

"That's not what I came here for," he said.

He sounded almost angry.

"I know. Believe me, I know."

But she also understood that if he came inside, she would eventually end up in his arms and he would talk her into decisions she would later regret.

He stepped close. "We need to talk."

How a man could smell so good when he'd been on a horse the better part of two days, Kate didn't know. But Cord managed it superbly. The olive skin across his cheeks was darkened further by bristles and there were shadows under his eyes, but he made all that look good, too.

Her last bit of strength went into standing straight and looking him in the eye, when what she wanted to do was lean against him and agree to all he had to say.

"That's the fifty-sixth time you've mentioned talking."

"Fifty-seventh," he shot back solemnly, and she fell in love with him a little more.

She gave up looking at him and stared at her hands. "I promise we will have as long a conversation as either of us can tolerate. Two days. That's all I ask. Nothing much will happen in two days."

She must be getting better at lying. He gave every indication he believed her.

But he wasn't quite so easily dismissed. Taking off her hat, he smoothed her hair and embraced her.

"Let's hope this doesn't keep you awake."

He kissed her, holding her tight, his lips warm in the cold air, and his tongue as sweet tasting as it had ever been. She could do nothing but kiss him back, knowing that this could be the last time she would touch him. If she held on a little too desperately and a little too long, he didn't seem to think it unusual. She had been holding on to him like this, in one form or another, ever since they met, even when she was trying to push him away.

The pushing had never been as hard as the holding, and he had to know it.

The ride had been long and the air blustery, but the toughest part of the day came when he let her go. Picking up her hat, he settled it on her head, tilting it one way and then another before being satisfied. "Did I ever tell you I like your hat?"

"No one else does."

"You surround yourself with the wrong people, Kate."

Not anymore.

It was a confession that would definitely lead to talk—and worse, to arguments. They would come soon enough, after her plans had been made.

She watched as he rode off, staring until the trail dust had settled and he was no longer in sight. One of the cowhands took Moonstar for her, and she walked slowly inside.

The need for sleep wasn't a lie; after he rode off, she barely managed to get out of her clothes before falling into bed. She didn't open her eyes for fourteen hours straight.

As soon as she awoke, she scrubbed herself, again and again, then dressed, wolfed down far more food that she would have imagined possible, and went out to saddle Moonstar.

Tug accosted her in the barn.

She was blunt with him. "It's not necessary to ride around me and tell T. J. I'm on the way. He'll find out soon enough."

Like Cord, the foreman believed her, even though she lied to him, too. She wasn't going to see her father. She had someone else she needed to visit first.

She found Joseph Wharton in his office. It was small and neat, with law books lining the walls, and it was attached to the house he owned a block north of the courthouse.

"Miss Calloway," he said, when she showed up at his door shortly after noon. He added a hasty, "My dear," to let them both know she was still his betrothed.

Tugging off the white cotton cloth he'd tucked behind his collar, he gestured for her to come inside. "Please pardon me. I was just finishing lunch. Won't you join me?"

Wharton looked thinner than she remembered him, taller, and his hair distinctly more gray. But he had the same eager look in his eyes that she knew too well.

"Could I have coffee instead?"

"Of course, of course."

He hustled her into the office, setting her jacket aside, and when she was seated, he picked up the tray of food on his desk and left. He returned shortly with another tray of coffee and small cakes.

His face looked drawn, as if he suspected the purpose of her visit. She served them both. He seemed to be grateful, as much for the courtesy as for the postponement of hearing what she'd come to say. While they ate and drank, he started talking about himself, something to do with his law business, but Kate barely listened and after a minute, he fell silent.

When they were done, he set the tray outside his office and returned to sit behind his desk, brushing at invisible crumbs on the desk blotter.

"Did you hear about the Comanches?" he asked. "Terrible tragedy. Terrible."

"For all concerned," she said.

"I shouldn't mention it to you, of course. It's not suitable talk for a lady."

When she closed her eyes for a moment, she heard the cries of the Comanches echoing in the room.

She took a deep breath. "I can't marry you, Mr. Wharton. I'm sorry, but I can't."

Wharton settled back in his chair and let out a long, slow breath. "I was afraid this was what you wanted to say."

Whatever reply she had anticipated, it wasn't the resigned reaction she got. T. J. would have blustered. Not so Joseph Wharton.

"I didn't know about the betrothal until it was announced," she said.

"I'm sorry. I had no idea. T. J. assured me you had agreed. Naturally, I was . . . quite happy. I have long been an admirer, as you doubtless know."

"My father lied. It's a habit of his when he wants to get his way."

She expected Wharton to defend his friend. Instead, he said, "I know. That is, I know it now." He attempted to smile. "Prevarication is not unknown to members of our profession, you understand. Or to those who would seek public office."

His eyes clouded, and he looked away from her. "I feel there is something I should tell you. He has not been himself lately. Some of the time I understand his rages, but on other occasions I am not sure. He has always seemed a reasonable man. Perhaps it is the headaches. Lately he has complained of them."

"Do you think he's ill?"

"Worry is probably the cause. There are rumors of an investigation into his law practice. Nothing certain. It could be a disgruntled client spreading rumors. Still, such talk can be vexatious."

Kate found herself concerned about T. J.; she didn't want to be, but she also knew he had a hold on her that would never go away. He was her father; until two months ago, he had been the most important man in her life.

She would have to go see him. She had no choice.

Wharton ran a hand through his graying hair, ruffling it out of place, and she felt an urge to smooth it for him. He was not a man who would like being ruffled.

For the first time she truly looked at him. He wasn't unhandsome. His eyes were a little close together and his nose a little narrow, but he was definitely not unpleasing. She had always been so fearful of being trapped by him in their earlier encounters that she hadn't really considered him as a man.

More, he was someone who cared very much

for someone who did not care for him. In a way, she and Joseph were two of a kind.

"Mr. Wharton—"

"You don't have to tell me why the marriage is off. I'm rather boring, and I know it. A young woman like you deserves more excitement in her life."

She blinked away her surprise. "If I have any more excitement in my life, I'll go completely insane."

"But I am boring. I talk about myself, and about politics. It's all I know. Women terrify me. You especially."

She almost laughed. "I've never terrified anybody in my life."

"Oh, but you do. I want to be around you, but when you get close, my mind ceases to function with any kind of cleverness. It is not a convenient habit for an attorney, you must admit."

"You don't know me. Not really."

A rueful smile tugged at his mouth. "I had hoped to change that."

"I'm not a good woman. Not the kind you deserve."

"Nonsense."

He looked impossible to convince. She took a deep breath and gave it another try. "I may be carrying another man's child. That's how unworthy I am."

At last she had managed to take him aback. He didn't speak for a moment, but simply stared at her as if he could not possibly have heard her right. Then he cleared his throat. "If he refuses to make an honest woman of you, I offer my services as your husband."

He said it stiffly, and she wasn't sure he meant it. Or, if he meant it at the moment, tomorrow or the day after he would be asking himself what he had done.

But he was a good man. A lump formed in her throat. Here she had two offers of marriage over a baby who probably didn't exist. Sadly, the one that carried the most affection came from the man least involved.

"My father said you insisted on a wife who was pure."

"Your father knows little of what I want."

Always they came back to T. J. "How did you two get to be friends?"

"Business and politics—and, of course, you. I am not a man who warms easily to others, but he did not seem to notice or to care."

"He sells houses with people still living in them. He kicks them out on the street. That must be the reason for the investigation."

"He has assured me he breaks no laws."

"And the politics. The American Party seems to me a party of hate."

"Not hate so much as fear. We're afraid of what this country might become."

He spoke more strongly about the Do-Nothings than he had spoken about her. It was not a high compliment, but she was glad. He wouldn't mourn the broken engagement for long.

"I'm not marrying anyone. I'm leaving town, and I would very much appreciate your advice."

This time he took a minute to answer.

"Any way I can help you, of course. That goes without mentioning. But I must say you are making a serious mistake." His protest had little force behind it; already, he sounded relieved.

"I have a friend who is wonderfully skilled at needlework. I've sold some of her pieces, and I know there's a demand for more. She and I would like to set up a small shop, but not here in San Antonio. Perhaps Houston, or Galveston."

"Why so far away?"

"I need to leave. You can understand why. I hoped you would help us set up the arrangements, or know someone who could, someone not associated with T. J. I have money to tide us over until we can establish the shop, but I know there are legalities to consider as well."

"You really ought to ask your father. Surely he could be of more help."

"I don't want him to know anything about it."

Wharton tapped his fingers on the desk. "This will undoubtedly cause him further stress."

"I'm sorry, of course, but his problems can't stop me from doing what I have to do."

"You'll leave the ranch?"

"Yes."

"This friend, the one who sews—"

"She prefers to remain anonymous."

He got up and began to pace behind his desk. "You've been honest with me. I feel it imperative that I be honest with you. But first you must tell me something. Is Cordoba Hardin the—father of your child? Forgive my boldness, but it is important that I know."

"Is it that obvious?"

"Not to everyone. But he is quite dashing,

dangerous looking, the sort a woman might find herself attracted to. And there is the matter of opportunity. But do not worry. Your secret is safe with me. The reason I ask is that there is something about him I feel you should know. He used to live here many years ago."

"He told me."

"Did he mention the terrible scene that occurred with your father?"

The blood drained from Kate's face, and a premonition of what was to come took hold. There was nothing she could do but shake her head.

"He claimed that T. J. had been the ruin of a young woman to whom he was pledged. It was obvious he was trying to assuage her father, especially after her tragic death. T. J. was forced to defend himself against the false charge. Hardin was badly beaten and left town in disgrace."

Kate remembered the day she first met Cord, when he stood on a hilltop aiming a gun at a distant rider.

"T. J. knows who he is?"

"I fear not. Your father has a convenient memory. When the terrible incident involving your late sister occurred, I was reminded of it, though I could not remember the young man's name. When I made reference to the early unpleasantness, T. J. did not know to what I referred."

"Cord's beating . . . did it take place on the street?"

"Before a crowd of witnesses. When he left, he swore vengeance upon your father."

Closing her eyes, she pictured the scene.

Proud Cord, humiliated, hurt, and bitter with hate. She tried not to think beyond the hurt.

Wharton was not done.

"Hardin was truly very young, very different in appearance from the way you see him today. When I saw him again, the night he brought you home after your injury, something stirred in the back of my mind. I think it was the rage he visited upon T. J. under his own roof. In the past week I have asked a few discreet questions. I found a family who knew the dead girl's father. They confirmed what I suspected, and were indeed surprised the villainous young man had dared to return."

"But you said nothing to T. J."

"I tried, but he would not listen. I have kept the knowledge to myself, but when you showed up today, I felt you had the right to know. Especially if he is the father—"

Wharton broke off and looked away, embarrassed.

Kate didn't have to ask what he was thinking. Cord had taken his vengeance out on her.

Maybe he had at first, taunting her, going so far as to kiss her, then mock her as he pulled away.

But not now. Surely not now. He had, after all, demanded that she marry him. The one thing that didn't make sense was why he would accuse another man of fathering Diana's child. Unless . . .

The door to Wharton's office slammed open, and the thought was broken. T. J. stood in the open doorway, his hair uncombed, his suit rumpled, his eyes crazed as they bored in on her.

"Bitch," he rasped. "Whore. It's all your fault."

She jumped to her feet, and he was upon her, grabbing her by the wrist, dragging her away from her chair. Wharton came around his desk to defend her, but T. J. shoved him away, and he stumbled and fell.

"I saw your horse outside." T. J.'s voice was calmer now, but just as frightening. "I knew you were here telling more lies."

"What lies?" she cried. "What do you think I have done?"

"I know they are after me. The lawyers . . . all of them." He looked across the desk at Wharton. "You, too. I have been betrayed." He looked at Kate, and the madness flamed in his eyes. "The two of you. You conspire against me."

She fought to pry his fingers from her wrist, but his grip was like iron. He dragged her through the door and onto the street.

"I will beat your bastard child out of you," he said, his voice rising. He seemed unmindful of who among the passersby might hear.

She stumbled after him. He came to a sudden halt, and she fell against him. His face grew rigid with fright, and pale, as if he were seeing a ghost.

In the street beyond him, Jess was standing, and behind her, Lucky and Cord.

"Hello, Papa," Jess said.

She was wearing Lucky's heavy coat, and beneath it her brightly sewn skirt; she had exchanged the moccasins for a pair of worn boots. Her face was pale and gaunt, and her hair wild from the ride. But there was no mistaking who she was.

She steadied her dark, sunken eyes on T. J.

"Surprise, Papa," she said. "I decided it was time to come back from the dead."

Chapter Thirty-three

"You're dead. Buried. Gone."

T. J.'s words came out in a hoarse whisper.

"No," Jess said. "I lived. I've been working in a cantina near the cemetery. You know the one—it's the burial ground you never saw. The one that holds my empty grave." She threw back her head, tossing her dark mane of hair. "You can guess what I've been doing these past two years."

She did not try to talk softly. Cord watched the crowd gather on the street and down the narrow walkway that led to the center of town. Mostly he watched the grip T. J. had on Kate's wrist. Had he been surer of his aim, he would have shot away the man's hand.

His heart hammered. "Let Kate go," he said.

T. J. gave no sign that he heard.

"I'm the one you want to hurt," Jess said. "Not Kate. She's the good sister."

"No," T. J. said, and then his voice became a roar. "You're whores. Both whores."

Joseph Wharton came up behind him. "See here, T. J., you can't say such things to your daughters. Let Kate go."

He put a hand on T. J.'s shoulder, but got an elbow in the ribs for his effort and a shake of the head from Kate. With a glance at Cord, Wharton backed away, but the distress did not leave his eyes.

Cord's fingers itched for the trigger of his gun. Instead, he reached inside his pocket and pulled out an envelope thick with papers.

He waved it in the air. "Let the women alone. You're finished, T. J. I have proof you've robbed and defrauded. I got the details today."

At last T. J. turned his demented eyes from Jess. As he stared at Cord, he drew in a raspy breath, as if the hate and rage had settled in his lungs.

"I've heard about those papers. You hired a fool to write them. They're lies. All lies."

"No," Cord said. "Everything is documented."

"You want to ruin me. You, a despoiler of women." He spat out the words. "But you can't. I'm too powerful. I have powerful friends. The governor has been in my home. One day I will take his place in the governor's mansion. No one can touch me there."

Whispers rippled through the crowd, but no one spoke. If Calloway had ever wanted a public audience, he had one now. And he held them all in thrall.

"What a hypocrite you are," Jess said loudly, breaking her father's spell. "You would know about lies, wouldn't you? You're not alone. I've been hiding behind Kate long enough. We both have. Did you ever tell her the truth about my betrothal? Or about why my lover was killed?"

"Shut up, whore."

For a moment he looked beyond her and saw the people. "She seeks to ruin me, too. She and Hardin are both jealous. They want the power that I possess."

"I can't shut up," Jess said. "Not now."

Again she spoke so all could hear. She looked at Kate, at Cord, her gaze lingering on Lucky before returning to her father.

"You owed him money, so much that you couldn't repay it. So you gave me to him. A present, a reward in lieu of cash. And when he was done, he gave me back."

T. J. stared at his younger daughter, and his world became just the two of them. But still he held his grip on Kate.

"He was supposed to keep you," he said. "Breaking the engagement was not part of the arrangement."

"The arrangement." Jess's laugh was more an exclamation of disgust. "The problem was, I didn't know about the debt, not for a while. I thought he wanted to marry me. I was very young. I wanted to marry him, too. I had never been in love before. And he was quite handsome."

Cord heard the catch in her voice. Behind him, Lucky gave a low growl.

"You didn't kill him to avenge my disgrace.

You shot him to keep from having to pay him. That was why I ran, not because of him, but because of you."

"Oh, Jess," Kate said. "You should have told me."

"I wanted to, but you defended him," Jess said. "I couldn't disillusion you. You had to exist in his world. And he hadn't done anything to you."

"But he had. When he hurt you, he hurt me, too."

T. J. dragged Kate in front of him and flung her in Jess's direction. She stumbled, but she did not fall.

"Aren't you two sweet and loving?" he snarled. "You disgust me. Where is your love for the man who gave you life? Where is the respect I am due?"

Cord moved toward Kate, but she shook him off and turned her wounded eyes to her father.

"I loved you. For a long time I yearned to be loved in return. And then when Cord came along, I feared you and what you might do to him. In all that time, I never really liked you. That's the saddest part of all. Everything I've done has been a waste."

T. J. raised his fist and with a roar came at her. Cord pulled his gun and fired over his head. There were shouts in the street and somewhere close a horse whinnied. T. J. retained enough sanity to stop and stare at the gun.

Cord aimed his weapon at T. J.'s heart. The air was cold, but sweat formed in the small of his back. Here was the moment for which he had long prepared.

"Touch her and you're dead," he said.

"No," said Kate with a sob. "No." She stepped in front of him, her back to her father, effectively blocking him from harm. "There's been enough killing. It has to stop."

She took a deep, steady breath, and Cord knew she saw only him in the street, thought of only him. With her looking at him the way she was, it was easy to forget everything else, too.

"I know about Diana and the baby," she said. "T. J. was the father of her unborn infant, wasn't he? To cover up his guilt, he beat you. He's the reason you left Spain and came back here. You wanted vengeance against him." Her eyes filled with tears. "But I got in the way."

Cord lowered the gun and held it loose at his side. "From the beginning, you were always there. I thought of you as a complication—"

A small cry escaped her lips.

"—but that was a long time ago. Things changed. You have a habit of changing them. You changed me."

For a moment he looked beyond her to her father, but the man no longer filled him with rage. Like Kate, he pitied him, but there was room for nothing stronger inside him. His heart was already full.

"I love you, Kathleen Calloway, and I want you to be my wife. It's not because of anything else. I'm not being noble. I simply need you more than I need air to breathe."

Kate brushed away a tear. "It took you a long time to tell me."

There was the familiar brashness in her voice, but there was a tremor, too, that tore him apart.

"Is that all you have to say?" he asked.

"One thing more. I love you, too. And yes, I very much want to be your wife."

She took a step forward.

But T. J. moved faster. Hurling himself at his daughters, he pulled a small black pistol from inside his coat.

"I'll kill you both—"

His cry was lost in a shattering gunshot. Blood darkened the front of his vest. Swaying backward, he looked down in surprise, as if someone had been uncouth enough to spatter mud on him. Staggering, he stared at Cord, and then beyond him to Lucky, who stood still, a smoking gun in his hand.

"Who—"

He fell before he could get out the rest of the question. By the time Cord got to him, he was dead.

Kate knelt on the ground beside him, her fingers probing against his neck for a pulse. Cord took her in his arms and eased her away.

"Your father's gone," he said.

He thought she would collapse. But, as was her habit, she surprised him. With a steady hand she stroked her father's cheek and closed his eyes. When she was done, she leaned into Cord and cried softly.

"So much waste," she whispered. "So much waste."

For all her sorrow, she was still Kate, still the older sister with responsibilities. Pulling away from him, she looked up at Jess.

"Are you all right?" she asked.

Jess nodded. "I didn't want him dead, you know. I just wanted him gone."

"I know," Kate said.

Around them, the crowd, frozen in place at the shot, began to stir. She turned her eyes to her fallen father.

"I'm all right, Cord. I promise. But I need to tell him good-bye."

He didn't try to stop her as she knelt over the body. Jess moved close, and at last she, too, knelt on the ground.

Cord backed away and waited in silence beside Lucky. The whispers of the women were too low to drift back to where they stood. Thomas Jefferson Calloway's death had come as he had imagined, on a public street with a crowd looking on. But he had died without recognizing Cord, without remembering Diana, without understanding the reason for his downfall. Somehow it didn't matter anymore.

Joseph Wharton moved to join the men. "If you like, I will make the necessary arrangements." As he spoke, he did not bother to look at his fallen friend. "It's the least I can do for Miss Calloway."

"The sheriff will have to be called."

It was the first time Lucky had spoken since he walked up with Jess and Cord.

"There were ample witnesses to the fact that you shot protecting the women," Wharton said. "I myself will testify to the circumstances."

Lucky shrugged and looked down at Jess.

"Thank you," Cord said to Wharton. "Kate will appreciate what you can do."

Wharton cleared his throat. "I realize it is a poor time to say this, but I offer you my congratulations on your impending wedding."

Cord shook his offered hand, and, when Kate stood, he went over to take her in his arms. She looked up at him, her cheeks stained with tears, her eyes dry.

"I don't know where to go or what to do," she said. "You'll have to tell me."

"My darling, you don't know how glad I am to hear you say that. Trust me. I'll take care of you."

When Jess rose to her feet, she went over to Lucky and held out her hand. He took it and they stood looking at one another. Kate looked at Cord questioningly, but all he could do was return her look of puzzlement. What was going to happen to those two was nothing he could guess. One idea occurred, but it was too wild to consider seriously.

Besides, he needed to comfort Kate. And if the truth were known, he needed a little comforting himself.

Chapter Thirty-four

Answering the sheriff's many questions took an hour. The crowd, satisfied there were nothing else to see, had long since dispersed. As Wharton had predicted, there was no shortage of witnesses to the fact that Lucky had fired to save the Calloway women.

Jess and Lucky left to inform Caprice ·of what had happened, and to spend the night in the Calloway house. For Kate, Cord chose what he hoped was a discreet hotel at the edge of town. He arranged for two rooms, but as they walked up the stairs, she informed him that she was given to restlessness and preferred not sleeping alone.

Cord quickly acquiesced.

The room was warm from a crackling fire in the fireplace, the bed high and soft, the counterpane trimmed with lace. A fine wool rug covered much of the polished wooden floor, and lace curtains hung from the lone window. He had got the best that he could. For the rest of her life, Kate deserved the best.

She seemed not to notice, not even the warmth. Hugging herself, she looked out the window onto the street.

"The sheriff seemed satisfied," she said.

Cord held himself away from her. "He was."

She thought a minute. "The pastor seemed surprised at what happened. T. J. didn't go to church very often, but when he was there he gave every indication of being pious."

"The pastor understood, Kate. He'll do a fine job with the service tomorrow."

She turned to look at him. "Did I do right arranging it so soon? A private service and burial seem, I don't know, somehow inadequate."

"Today was public enough. Your family needs time to mourn without the world watching."

"It's not much of a family. Two women. Two orphans. That has a strange feeling to it, Cord."

"I know," he said, and could not resist adding, "I've been an orphan since I was fifteen. I had felt like one for years before that."

She reached out to take his hand. "I'm sorry. Here I am thinking only about myself."

He wanted to take her in his arms and make her forget the past hour, and if he could, her past life. But she let him go and returned to staring out the window, although twilight had already settled on the town and there was little to see.

"You ran away, didn't you? So did Papa. I guess it's all right to call him that now. He was born in Tennessee, but he ran to Alabama. That's where he met Mama. After her death, I found a letter—"

Her voice broke.

"You don't have to tell me anything, Kate."

"I want to. I've never told anyone, not even Jess. My grandfather, my mother's father, was a Methodist minister in a small country church. By the time she met Papa, he already had a law degree. When she married him, her father disowned her for taking as her husband a godless man. That's how he viewed Papa. A shyster, he said. Or so Mama wrote. The letter was addressed to me. I guess she wanted me to know about her family, about where she came from."

She turned to smile at him. "It's important to know family, Cord. When our children are old enough, we need to tell them what we know of ours. Most of it, at least."

"We won't have pretty stories to tell."

"I imagine most families don't. Especially the ones that have come to Texas. I don't know if you've noticed, but there are lots of rough people here. And smooth ones who act rough when they think no one is watching."

"Thieves," he said. "Shysters."

"And good people, too. The best." The look she sent him left little doubt about whom she meant.

At last she studied the room. "Nice," she said, and then she spotted something he hadn't seen, a small valise beside the door. She looked inside. There were toiletries for them both, a black shirt for Cord, and for her additional items: a nightgown, a blue dress, and a petticoat. At the bottom of the valise she found a pair of sheer stockings and a pair of slippers, too.

A note was enclosed: *Condolences and congratulations*. It was signed *Rebecca*.

Staring at it all, laid out on the bed, Kate shook her head.

"I can't figure that girl," she said.

"I can't figure women."

She looked at him. "What do you want to know?"

"Everything."

She started to speak, but he couldn't let her get started. There was no guessing how long she might speak or what demonstrations she had in mind. Before she began, he wanted to be sure there were no lingering questions between them.

"I never slept with Diana," he said. "I was very noble and very proud. I pledged marriage, but I wouldn't allow myself to bed her before I could afford to take care of her. But that did not keep me from kissing her. I kissed her a great deal."

Kate held up her hands. "You don't have to tell me the details."

"In frustration, she looked elsewhere for satisfaction. Too, she wanted to make me jealous."

"She turned to T. J."

"It was not a wise choice." Cord could have said more, but he knew Kate understood.

But he was not done.

"When I returned, I planned to ruin him. The fact that I had not done so earlier ate at me until I knew no peace. My first idea was to squeeze him out of the ranch. That was why I bought so much land—not to build a home, but to create a vise that would catch him and break him. The investigation through the lawyer was arranged on a whim."

"But he left running the ranch up to me. If your original plan had worked, he was not the one who would have been broken."

"That was one of the many things I found out. The first was how much I became interested in creating my own place. Texas felt right to me; the ranch felt right. I thought about building an empire. It sounds foolish to say it, but that was the way I began to feel. When I was honest with myself. Which wasn't very often. Especially when it came to you."

"So you fell in love with me, did you?"

"You like to hear me say it."

"That's one of the main things you need to know about women. We like to hear our men say how they feel."

"I did not fall in love with you at first. Not even after you gave yourself to me. But oh, how I wanted you. It was wrong. I wanted revenge, and you were always there, from the beginning, getting in the way."

"If you're trying to make me feel better, you're doing a very poor job. For a while you were doing all right, but you've strayed from the good talk."

"It's the streak of honor in me. I want you to understand. I fought against loving you and wanting you. It was not in my plan. But you were the most wonderful thing that had ever happened to me. It took almost losing you to get that very obvious fact through my thick head."

"I'm beginning to feel a little better. Go on."

"Here is where I begin to get physical."

Kate sighed, but when he stepped close to her, she held up a warning hand.

"Not just yet. It's my turn for confession. When you came storming into my house at the ranch, the night you proposed, I let you believe I was expecting your child. I wasn't. And as far as I know, I'm still not. So you don't have to marry me. I'm so easy, there's no reason to put a ring on my finger. Or swear to any vows."

"If you're not with child, we'll have to start working at changing your condition."

Kate grinned. He grinned right back at her.

"That's the first time I've ever seen you really smile," she said.

"Love will do that to a man."

She lowered her gaze to the definite swelling in his trousers.

"That's not all it will do."

When she looked back up into his eyes, the grin was gone.

"I had thought about playing games with you, about teasing and driving you insane."

Her voice was small, tremulous, and there was a return of the haunted look in her eyes, the one he had seen as she closed her father's eyes.

"You were doing a splendid imitation of teasing, and the insanity part is close to complete."

"I tried, but it won't work, not tonight. Not after all that has happened. Just hold me tight and tell me you love me, and assure me everything will be all right."

It was the easiest request she had ever made of him.

They cleared the bed, she put on the gown, and he pulled her under the covers against his naked body. He held her for a long time while she talked through her sorrow, and when at last she looked up at him, it was with unfettered love.

"You promised to get physical. I think that's the way you put it."

"I am a man of honor. If that's what I promised, it's exactly what I have to do."

For the rest of the night he kept his promise, and a few more that she elicited from time to time. When dawn came, he knew two things more than ever: first, he loved Kate, and second, he would never truly understand her, not even after they had lived together fifty years.

Epilogue

Kate and Cord were married in San Antonio a
month later on a crisp, cold Sunday afternoon.
Kate would have preferred a ceremony at the
Lone Star, but Cord's family had traveled a long
way for the event. Along with Jess and Lucky,
there was not room to accommodate everyone.

The Calloway house in town provided beds
for most of them. Having been given her freedom, Caprice insisted on remaining to help.
Jess and Lucky stayed elsewhere. Kate did not
know the location, nor the sleeping arrangements, and she did not ask.

She and Cord chose the hotel where they had
stayed after her father's death. Cord insisted on
separate rooms this time, and she was not in-
clined to argue, especially since he was kissing
her while he was doing the insisting.

They were married in a small chapel near the

Alamo. Kate wore a dress made by her sister, white linen decorated with white embroidery around the skirt and blue trim around the neck, to match her eyes. She wore her hair down because Cord wanted it that way, but she pulled a swatch of curls to the top of her head, secured by a circle of white linen flowers Jess had made to match the dress.

In his morning coat and straight black trousers, Cord was the handsomest man she had ever seen. For the first time he wore a white shirt. It looked incredibly wonderful against his olive skin.

Lucky gave her away, and Jess was her only attendant. Cord's best man was his brother, Cal. Most of the women cried, except, of course, for Jess, and the men did a great deal of smiling. Except, of course, for Lucky.

Cord had rented a hall next to the chapel for a reception. Kate's new sister-in-law, Ellie, walked her over when the nuptials were done.

"Cord will have you around the rest of his life," Ellie said as she linked her arm in Kate's. "If he's fortunate, that is, and behaves himself. The Hardin boys are not easy to live with."

"They're hard to live without, too," Kate said.

Ellie kissed her on the cheek. "I knew I was going to love you. And I do."

As they walked inside the hall, Ellie pulled her aside from the throng of well-wishers, especially her watchful-eyed husband, who had got there first.

"I know you two had a difficult time for a while. And then there was the trouble with your father. It may not be smart of me to mention it now, but I want to get it out of the way. Cal and I didn't have what you would call a peaceful courtship. And there was trouble, bad trouble, before he finally came around to realizing he loved me."

"It must be a family trait," Kate said.

"I wanted you to know that once he finally understood how he felt, he's been the best husband a woman could have. We have three children, a beautiful ranch, and more love than I knew existed in the world."

"Cord told me a little about the troubles."

"He was involved. And he was very brave."

Before Kate could respond, a long-legged boy dashed by her, and after him, a flurry of petticoats in hot pursuit.

"Henry Houston Hardin," Ellie barked in a most unladylike manner, "stop that running this instant. And stop teasing your sister."

At the sound of his mother's voice, the boy came to an immediate halt and turned with a sheepish look on his face.

"Margaret started it," he said. "Besides, she was chasing me."

Behind him, the guilty party grinned a very girlish grin. The boy was dark like his father, the girl fair like her mother; both had the blue Hardin eyes.

"He was looking at a girl, Mama," Margaret said. "All I did was point out that if he wanted to know her, all he had to do was ask me to tell her and I would. That's when he pulled my pigtail and I went after him."

Cal Hardin walked up carrying a third child, another girl, this one dark, also blue-eyed. A three-year-old toddler, she was squirming to be put down.

Her father complied, and she made for the table where the food had been laid out.

"You spoil Abbie," her mother said.

Cal grinned. "I spoil you, too, but I don't hear you complain."

All her in-laws began to talk at once, and Kate eased away from them. There was one more member of her new family she wanted to talk to, Cord's half-sister Madeleine, who had come all the way from New Orleans. She and Cord hadn't seen each other in fifteen years, just about all of Maddie's life.

She found Maddie tapping her foot and listening to the small band that had begun to play at the far end of the hall. The music was Mexican, played primarily on three guitars and a trumpet. The featured soloist was the concertina player from the inn where Jess had lived for two years. His brother was tending the bar.

"You like the music?" Kate asked as she came to a halt beside her.

"I love it."

The girl didn't smile, just nodded in a friendly manner. Unlike her brothers, she was fair, but she had the obligatory blue eyes. Tall for her age, she was slender and she was pretty, but like her brothers she was quiet and had a private nature that would take some breaking through.

Kate figured that if she had broken through Cord's armor of self-restraint, she could get through Maddie's, too.

"I'm sorry your mother couldn't make the trip," she said.

"She wanted very much to be here, but she was too ill."

"That's what Cord said. I hope it's nothing serious."

Kate could tell from the look on the girl's face that, unfortunately, it was something from which her mother would probably not recover. But she didn't ask for details. There were some confidences that could not readily be shared. If anyone knew that, it certainly ought to be her.

She felt more than saw Cord sidle up to her. He nuzzled her neck. "How about a dance, Mrs. Hardin?"

She looked up at him in surprise. "Why, Mr. Hardin, I didn't know you knew how."

"Let's find out."

He held her in the traditional way, and Kate took heart. When he whirled her to a clearing on the floor, she knew her husband understood far more than the basic moves of dancing. She grew dizzy from all the turns, but he was in control and she could do nothing but drop back her head and laugh.

When the music stopped, she leaned against him to let her head clear.

Again, he nuzzled her. "You can do that forever."

"What?" she mumbled against his white shirt.

"Lean on me."

Her heart filled with warmth. "I'll need to, Cord. I most certainly will need to."

Then Cal claimed her for a dance, holding

her apart, talking about the Lone Star, which he had toured two days before.

"My brother has made a fine start," he said. "It's none of my business, but are you going to combine it with your land? If so, you'll just about equal what I have. Can't let Cord get ahead of me. I'll have to expand, too."

"Do you two have an empire challenge going on?"

Cal chuckled. "Maybe. Now that you mention it."

Kate grew solemn. "We haven't talked much about the Calloway. I'd like to give it all to Jess. The town house will go to pay my father's legal debts, but the ranch is free and clear."

"No wonder my brother fell in love with you. You're as generous of heart as Ellie is. And as blunt-spoken, too."

"It's what you Hardins need."

The dancing ended, and she spied Joseph Wharton on the floor with Rebecca Netherby. She couldn't hear what the girl was saying, but she was certainly dithering on about something while her dance partner was solemnly watching and listening.

Oh, dear, she thought. Did the poor man need rescuing? He had confessed to being terrified by women. Rebecca might decide to take advantage, especially where a man of means was concerned.

Just as she was about to go over, he looked past Rebecca, saw Kate, and winked. It was fast and subtle, but it was definitely a wink. She smiled at him and winked back. He could take care of himself.

Not so she. When Cord claimed her again, she held on to him firmly. "Don't leave me again. I need you."

"Don't worry. Family is wonderful, but there are times a man wants to be alone."

"You want to be alone?"

"A man and woman want to be alone. Is that better?"

"It's perfect."

And so they danced and they laughed and they hugged, and on more than one occasion, they stole hungry kisses. They would be spending their wedding night back at the hotel, but in the morning they would return to their real home, the Lone Star, where they would begin their life.

Everyone was bidding them good night when Jess and Lucky walked up.

"This is good-bye, Captain," he said. "We'll be leaving early in the morning."

"We?" Kate asked.

"Jess and I."

Jess smiled at her sister. "We've been thinking about it for a few weeks."

"You've known each other for only a few weeks," Kate said.

"Some things you understand right away," Jess said.

Kate looked at her husband. "We've got to stop them. They can't leave. They're family."

He gave her that skeptical look that said perhaps she needed to think over what she had said.

Kate looked back at Jess. "What about the ranch?"

"I don't want it. And neither does Lucky."

"It'll just tie us down," Lucky said. And then to Cord, "We're heading west, maybe all the way to California. Texas is getting too crowded for us."

Kate started to argue, but then she saw the way Jess and Lucky looked at one another, and she felt in her heart the rightness of the situation. Both considered themselves outcasts, but they had been fortunate enough to find one another.

Lucky was indeed well named.

After a few tears and a hundred hugs, the bride and groom found themselves alone back at the hotel.

They shed their clothes, with a great sense of naturalness, and stared at each other across the high feather bed.

"Everybody's leaving, Cord. We're alone."

Her husband looked her over. "Right now, that's a pretty good thing." He began to fold down the top cover. "So you're not with child?"

"No. I had proof last week."

"And you want a family."

"Very much."

"Then I suggest you get in the bed and let me have a try at changing your condition. It could be that since we made our relationship legal, our unconceived child will decide it's time to begin his presence in the world."

"I'll do my part. If we have to make love for a month, it won't be too great a sacrifice."

"Sacrifice?" He threw a pillow at her and

came across the bed. She laughed. He laughed in return. As he pulled her into his arms and started his stroking and kissing, she decided his laugh was the most beautiful sound in the world.

EVELYN ROGERS

TEXAS EMPIRES: Crown of Glory

It is nothing but a dog-run cabin and five thousand acres of prime grassland when Eleanor Chase first set eyes on it. But someone killed her father to get the deed to the place, and Ellie swears she will not leave Texas until she has her revenge and her ranch. There is just one man standing in her way—a blue-eyed devil named Cal Hardin. Is he the scoundrel who has stolen her birthright, or the lover whose oh-so-right touch can steal her very breath away?

___4403-X $5.99 US/$6.99 CAN

BETRAYAL *Evelyn Rogers*

By the Bestselling Author of
The Forever Bride

If there is anything that gets Conn O'Brien's Irish up, it is a lady in trouble–especially one he has fallen in love with at first sight. So after the Texas horseman saves Crystal Braden from an overly amorous lout, he doesn't waste a second declaring his intentions to make an honest woman of her. But they have barely been declared man and wife before Conn learns that his new bride is hiding a devastating secret that can destroy him.

The plan is simple: To ensure the safety of her mother and young brother, Crystal agrees to play the damsel in distress. The innocent beauty has no idea how dangerously charming the virile stranger can be–nor how much she longs to surrender to the tender passion in his kiss. And when Conn discovers her ruse, she vows to blaze a trail of desire that will convince him that her deception has been an error of the heart and not a ruthless betrayal.

___4262-2 $5.99 US/$6.99 CAN

WESTON'S BOBBI
Lady SMITH

There are Cowboys and Indians, trick riding, thrills and excitement for everyone. And if Liberty Jones has anything to say about it, she will be a part of the Wild West show, too. She has demonstrated her expertise with a gun by shooting a card out of Reed Weston's hand at thirty paces, but the arrogant owner of the Stampede won't even give her a chance. Disguising herself as a boy, Libby wangles herself a job with the show, and before she knows it Reed is firing at her—in front of an audience. It seems an emotional showdown is inevitable whenever they come together, but Libby has set her sights on Reed's heart and she vows she will prove her love is every bit as true as her aim.

___4512-5 $5.99 US/$6.99 CAN

THE LADY'S HAND
BOBBI SMITH
Author of *Lady Deception*

Cool-headed and ravishingly beautiful, Brandy O'Neal knows how to hold her own with the riverboat gamblers on *The Pride of New Orleans*. But she meets her match in Rafe Morgan when she bets everything she has on three queens and discovers that the wealthy plantation owner has a far from gentlemanly notion of how she shall make good on her wager.

Disillusioned with romance, Rafe wants a child of his own to care for, without the complications of a woman to break his heart. Now a full house has given him just the opportunity he is looking for—he will force the lovely cardsharp to marry him and give him a child before he sets her free. But a firecracker-hot wedding night and a glimpse into Brandy's tender heart soon make Rafe realize he's luckier than he ever imagined when he wins the lady's hand.

_4116-2 $5.99 US/$6.99 CAN

Dorchester Publishing Co., Inc.
P.O. Box 6640
Wayne, PA 19087-8640

Please add $1.75 for shipping and handling for the first book and $.50 for each book thereafter. NY, NYC, and PA residents, please add appropriate sales tax. No cash, stamps, or C.O.D.s. All orders shipped within 6 weeks via postal service book rate. Canadian orders require $2.00 extra postage and must be paid in U.S. dollars through a U.S. banking facility.

Name_____
Address_____
City_____ State_____ Zip_____
I have enclosed $_____ in payment for the checked book(s).
Payment <u>must</u> accompany all orders. ☐ Please send a free catalog.

TEXAS PROUD
CONSTANCE O'BANYON

Rachel Rutledge has her gun trained on Noble Vincente. With one shot, she will have her revenge on the man who killed her father. So what is stopping her from pulling the trigger? Perhaps it is the memory of Noble's teasing voice, his soft smile, or the way one glance from his dark Spanish eyes once stirred her foolish heart to longing. Yes, she loved him then . . . as much as she hates him now. One way or another, she will wound him to the heart—if not with bullets, then with her own feminine wiles. But as Rachel discovers, sometimes the line between love and hate is too thinly drawn.

___4492-7 $5.99 US/$6.99 CAN

COUGAR'S WOMAN
Ronda Thompson

On the journey to meet her fiancé in Santa Fe, Melissa Sheffield is captured by Apaches and given to a man known as Cougar. At first, she is relieved to learn that she's been given to a white man, but with one kiss he proves himself more dangerous than the whole tribe. Terrified of her savage captor, she pledges to escape at any price. But while there might be an escape from the Apaches, is there any escape from her heart? Clay Brodie—known as Cougar to the Apaches—is given the fiery Melissa by his chief. He is then ordered to turn the beauty into an obedient slave—or destroy her. But how can he slay a woman who evokes an emotion deeper than he's ever known? And when the time comes to fight, will it be for his tribe or for his woman?

___4524-9 $4.99 US/$5.99 CAN

Dorchester Publishing Co., Inc.
P.O. Box 6640
Wayne, PA 19087-8640

AMBER FIRE

ELAINE BARBIERI

Melanie Morganfield has grown from a precocious child to a beautiful woman in Asa Parker's lavish home. Melanie is grateful to Asa for all he has done for her, and in her devotion, she longs to make happy the final years of the man who has cared for her in every way that he could. But when she meets Stephen Hull, his dark and youthful sensuality heats her blood in a way which she can neither ignore or deny. She knows instinctively that she must not ever see Stephen again, or she will be fanning the flames which are destined to lead to amber fire.

___52290-X $5.50 US/$6.50 CAN

Dorchester Publishing Co., Inc.
P.O. Box 6640
Wayne, PA 19087-8640

Please add $1.75 for shipping and handling for the first book and $.50 for each book thereafter. NY, NYC, and PA residents, please add appropriate sales tax. No cash, stamps, or C.O.D.s. All orders shipped within 6 weeks via postal service book rate. Canadian orders require $2.00 extra postage and must be paid in U.S. dollars through a U.S. banking facility.

Name_____
Address_____
City_____State_____Zip_____
I have enclosed $_____ in payment for the checked book(s).
Payment <u>must</u> accompany all orders. ❑ Please send a free catalog.

RECKLESS HEART

MADELINE BAKER

They play together as children—the Indian lad and little Hannah Kincaid. Then Shadow and his people go away, and when he returns, it is as a handsome young Cheyenne brave. Hannah, now a beautiful young woman, has never forgotten her childhood friend—but the man who sweeps her into his powerful arms is no longer a child. He awakens in her a wild, erotic passion she has never known. But war is about to erupt in the Dakota Territory, a war that will pit the settlers against the Indians. Both Hannah and Shadow know that the time is coming when they will have to choose between happiness and hatred, between passion and duty, in a conflict that will test to the limit the steadfastness of their love. . . .

___4527-3 $5.99 US/$6.99 CAN

Dorchester Publishing Co., Inc.
P.O. Box 6640
Wayne, PA 19087-8640

Please add $1.75 for shipping and handling for the first book and $.50 for each book thereafter. NY, NYC, and PA residents, please add appropriate sales tax. No cash, stamps, or C.O.D.s. All orders shipped within 6 weeks via postal service book rate. Canadian orders require $2.00 extra postage and must be paid in U.S. dollars through a U.S. banking facility.

Name_____
Address_____
City_____State_____Zip_____
I have enclosed $_____ in payment for the checked book(s).
Payment <u>must</u> accompany all orders. ❏ Please send a free catalog.
    CHECK OUT OUR WEBSITE! www.dorchesterpub.com